Bow-Wow Rescue

Second Edition

Bow-Wow Rescue

Second Edition

Mike Faricy

Library of Congress Control Number: 2023915501
paperback ISBN: 978-1-962080-35-4
e-book ISBN: 978-1-962080-36-1

MJF Publishing books may be purchased for education, Business, or promotional use. For information on bulk purchases,
please contact the author directly at mikefaricyauthor@gmail.com

Published by

MJF Publishing
https://www.mikefaricybooks.com

Acknowledgments

I would like to thank the following people for their help and support:
Special thanks to my editors, Kitty, Donna and Rhonda for their hard work, cheerful patience and positive feedback.

I would like to thank Ann and Julie for their creative talent and not slitting their wrists or jumping off the high bridge when dealing with my Neanderthal computer capabilities.

Special thanks to Ann for her patience.

Last, I would like to thank family and friends for their encouragement and unqualified support. Special thanks to Maggie, Jed, Schatz, Pat, Av, Emily and Pat for not rolling their eyes, at least when I was there, and most of all, to my wife Teresa whose belief, support and inspiration has from day one, never waned.

Prologue

Seymour Smeelie filled the crystal glass with a half-inch of rum and handed it to the small man seated across from him. He was seated in the wingback chair, his feet almost but not quite touching the oriental rug on which the chair sat. "Thank you, Seymour," the small man said without smiling.

"Thank you, sir. So very kind of you. Havana Club Anejo Especial, one of my favorite rums, and next to impossible to get here in the states. I was fortunate to obtain a bottle in Florida, but it cost a pretty penny, and though I've sipped it sparingly, it's almost gone. However did you know? Oh, and umm, your driver?" Seymour said, indicating the large man quietly standing in front of the office door with his hands clasped in front of him.

The man had a large, shaved head with a number of scars and almost no neck, just that large head resting on massive shoulders. His nose had a peculiar bump, suggesting that on more than one occasion, he had been rather difficult to deal with. He wore a black suit and a starched, open-collar white shirt. "Would he care for a glass?"

"No, Bumpy's driving, Seymour. Besides, one is too many, and that entire bottle would never be enough for him." He set his glass on the edge of the end table as Seymour poured rum into his own glass and settled into the wingback chair opposite the small man. He waited a moment before he said, "It would appear there's a problem, Seymour."

Seymour took a hearty gulp of rum, liquid courage, although it didn't seem to be working at the moment. "I can promise you, sir. This is simply a temporary setback. A modest, temporary setback."

"Modest? This will be the third month I've not received payment. That's no longer modest, nor temporary, Seymour. It's an absolute disaster!" The small man shouted those last four words, causing Seymour to flinch. Rum spilled from his glass onto his suit coat and across his silk tie.

"I can assure you, sir, it's only a matter of time before—"

"I can assure you that your time is up." He nodded at the large man stationed at the door. "The contract," he said.

The giant stepped forward, reaching into the inside pocket of his suit coat. Seymour actually recoiled, expecting to see a gun emerge in the giant's massive hand. He exhaled once he realized it was merely a multi-page document.

"I'll need your signature, Seymour. Initial the three areas marked in yellow and then sign on the bottom of the second page. No need to date it."

Seymour blinked, attempting to focus on the document. At the moment, the stress of the situation seemed to be making it hard for him to breathe.

"Relax," the small man said, handing Seymour a pen. "Initial and sign. This is simply a backup. Should things not work out, I gain control, and everything reverts to me until we get them back in the profitable column, whereupon you regain control. I want both of us to be successful. The contract is valid until one of us passes away, and then everything reverts to the other. I'm a good twenty years your senior, so things definitely lean in your favor."

"But I'd like to have my attorney take a look and—" Seymour swallowed, or tried to, without much success. He felt his nose running, coughed, and shuddered from a quick spasm.

"Initial, Seymour. Yes, right, good, good. Now the next page, sign at the bottom. Excellent. Here, a toast to success," the small man said, raising his glass.

Seymour reached for his glass, almost knocking it off the table before he grabbed hold.

"Drink up, my friend, my partner," the small man said as Seymour attempted to do just that. He poured the liquid into his mouth and was vaguely aware of it running down his chin. As the first seizure struck him, he convulsed, falling from the chair and dropping to the floor.

"Get the contract," the small man said, pouring his glass over Seymour's face while he convulsed on the rug.

Bumpy pulled on a latex glove, picked up the contract, quickly stepped back, and handed the contract to the small man.

"Excellent. Now, if all goes well, this shouldn't be more than ten minutes." Five minutes later, he said, "Check for a pulse." Blood was running from Seymour's nose and mixing with the yellowish discharge oozing from his mouth.

The large man placed his gloved hand on Seymour's neck for the better part of a minute, searching for a pulse, then looked up and shook his head.

"Wonderful, check his pocket for keys."

Bumpy rifled through Seymore's pockets. He pulled out a set of keys and a wallet. He handed the keys to the little man, opened the wallet, and pulled out three twenty-dollar bills.

"Well done. Put one of those twenties back in the wallet, leave the bottle, Bumpy, and get my glass and the pen. Oh, and grab that other bottle out of his cabinet. We'll point the finger at the woman," the small man said. A minute later, they cautiously peeked out into an empty hallway and hurried to the elevator.

One

Taffy stuck her chest and bottom lip out at the same time, just to emphasize the point and asked, "Oh, come on, Dev! Why do you always have to be such a party pooper?"

It was Thursday night, and we were sitting out on her friend's deck. They'd just hurried into the house after inviting us up to their lake place tomorrow. Based on the reaction Taffy gave me, I knew I was in a losing battle before it even began, but I had to try. "I would love a weekend away with you, Taffy. Honestly, nothing would be better. It's just that going up to Kevin and Stacy's lake place is not my idea of a relaxing weekend."

"Oh, right, I forgot it would be more fun for me to sit on the couch and watch you play video games."

"First of all, I don't play video games. And second—"

"Mmm-mmm, sorry, I forgot. I meant throw a football back and forth for six or seven hours while Stacy and I run around getting dinner ready and making sure that, at all times, you have a cold beer within easy reach."

"Where is this coming from? Why am I getting accused of stuff I don't do?"

"Well, if you don't like my friends, you can just say so. You don't have to beat around the bush."

"Taffy, I'm not knocking your friends. It's just that, whenever someone invites me up to their lake place, it never really works out. I know you aren't going to like it up there. Were you listening? They described the place as rustic. Now we can—"

"That's not fair. I like the lake. I like laying in the sun. I like listening to birds chirp, the sound of the waves, the whole back to nature thing, and I'd like to go for a ride on their pontoon boat. You could go fishing off the dock. Sleep in. I bet they've got a private guest room. Very private," she said, raising her eyebrows and thrusting her chest out again.

It was obvious I didn't have a snowballs chance. "Okay, if it means that much to you, yeah sure, we'll go. You like back to nature, okay, your call."

"Mmm-mmm, you're gonna love it," she said then kissed me on the cheek and whispered, "We can be really naughty, and no one will hear."

"Okay, you guys, dinner is served," Stacy called as she stepped onto the deck. She carried a platter with a half-dozen hotdogs in buns. Her husband Kevin was right behind her with a bowl of potato salad and thankfully, a pitcher of beer. Stacy set the hot dog platter on the picnic table, swatted the flies away, and sat down. "So, what'd you guys decide."

"We'll be up tomorrow," Taffy said, which caused both women to scream as they reached across the table and grabbed one another's hands.

"Oh, this is going to be so much fun," Stacy said.

"We're heading up bright and early tomorrow morning," Kevin said as he slathered mustard up and down a hotdog bun. "You guys come on up whenever you can."

Stacy got a concerned look on her face and said, "Taffy and I were thinking they could just ride up with us."

Kevin crammed almost half a hot dog into his mouth, chewed two or three times, and said, "Oh, yeah. I suppose we could do that. Mmm-mmm, we were planning on leaving around ten."

"Well, actually," I said just as Taffy slid her hand beneath the picnic table, reached over between my legs, and pinched my inner thigh. "Awe, umm, that would be great. Yeah, we can be here a little after nine."

Taffy smiled.

I reached for a hot dog.

"Thanks for saying you'd go up to their lake," Taffy said and stroked my arm. We were on the way home, and I'd just turned onto her street.

"Well, you made it pretty clear you really wanted to go, and then when you mentioned the very private guest room, you know," I said and gave her a look.

"Well, I'm maybe presuming that a little, but they probably do."

"What? I was hoping to have some, you know, *special* private time together. Just you and me."

"God, is that all you ever think about?"

"Yeah, probably. But that's because you're so good," I said, pulling to the curb in front of her condo. I turned off the car and started to climb out from behind the wheel.

"Don't, Dev. I'll just let myself in."

"Huh?"

"Besides, I have to pack tonight and get about a thousand things ready. Just relax. You'll get taken care of tomorrow night. Thanks," she said and leaned over to give me a peck on the cheek before she hurried out of the car.

I watched as she input her security code at the door, stepped inside, and disappeared behind the door. If this was the way the weekend was going to go, it was shaping up to be a long two days at the lake, and we hadn't even left town.

TWO

I was up before my alarm went off the next morning. I tossed a pair of shorts, two t-shirts, my swimsuit, socks, and a baseball cap in a brown paper grocery bag and hurried downstairs. I put the coffee on, fired up the computer, filled Morton's food and water dish, and went online. I heard Morton hop off the bed and do his morning stretch about a half-hour later. He came downstairs, walked into the kitchen, stretched once more, and walked over to me for his morning heavy-duty scratch behind the ears.

I let him out and went back on the computer. I emailed Louie, my office partner, asking him to watch Morton for the weekend while Taffy and I headed up to the lake. No sooner did I send that email than I received an email from an old flame, Brianna Di Salvo, asking for an appointment today. Actually, the email read, *'Hi Baby, Need to see you today. The earlier, the better. Strictly business, unless...'*

It had been at least four years since I'd seen her. She'd dumped me two or three times before I finally got the message. Over the course of the next year, I'd learned I hadn't been the only guy in her life.

I replied, saying, *Long time no hear, Brianna. I can meet you at 8:15 this morning or anytime Monday.*

She called about ninety seconds later.

"Haskell Investigations."

"God, no other business sounds as sexy when they answer the phone."

"Brianna?"

"I knew you couldn't forget, Dev. Wonderful to hear your voice. Just confirming I'll be at your office at eight-fifteen. Are you still in the same place?"

"Yeah, Randolph Avenue, just kitty-corner from The Spot Bar."

"Oh," she said, not hiding her disappointment. "Well, anyway, I'll see you then," she said and hung up.

That was just an hour away. I let Morton in. Once he emptied his food dish, I tossed the dish in a bag with his dog food, and we headed down to the office.

Louie wasn't in yet, and I knew he had something at the courthouse scheduled for ten. He was one of the go-to guys in town if you were charged with a DUI, Driving Under the Influence. In the past four years, his client list had grown exponentially. He'd left the coffee pot on overnight, and there was about a quarter of an inch in the pot that had been going for the last twenty-four hours. I dumped it in the sink then checked to see if the coffee had damaged the porcelain. Fortunately, it hadn't.

I brewed a fresh pot, rinsed out Louie's mug, and sat at my desk sipping coffee and looking out the window for Brianna Di Salvo to show up. I was scanning the apartment building across the street with my binoculars, but unfortunately, the only shades that weren't pulled was a unit with a fat guy in boxer shorts. Not what I really needed to see first thing in the morning, let alone any time.

After about twenty minutes, a dark blue Mercedes pulled to the curb behind my 2014 ugly, pea soup green Dodge Dart. The door opened, and gorgeous Brianna stepped out of the car. She gave my Dart a quick look and shook her head as she crossed the street. A moment later, I heard the stairs begin to creak as she made her way up to the second floor.

I had my cellphone up to my ear and started a fake conversation as the door opened. "No, you'll be much better off if you wait until this evening." Brianna struck a pose in the doorway for a moment. She was wearing black hose, an extremely short designer skirt, and what looked like a five-hundred-dollar low-cut top. A diamond about the size of my eyeball rested on top of her massive cleavage. I waved her in and pointed to a client chair. As she approached, I continued my conversation, and a wonderful perfume drifted across my desk. "Knock on the door about seven tonight. He'll answer. Make sure you have the backdoor covered, and you can make your arrest. He doesn't own a gun but be careful. Yeah, okay, glad to help, detective," I said and set the phone on my desk. Brianna and I studied one another for a long moment.

"Brianna, it's been a long time, what three, maybe four years? It's nice to see you," I said as I rose out of my desk chair.

She extended her hand across the desk, nodded, and smiled, suggesting everyone always said it was nice to see her. When I took hold of her hand, she grabbed on with both hands and stroked the back of my hand.

"It's all my fault, and it's been way too long. Do you know I actually dream about you, Dev Haskell? I dream about you all the time. What was I ever thinking? You, well, you umm, look the same," she said, taking in my camouflage shorts and the navy-blue t-shirt that said, 'The Spot Bar.' "You haven't changed a bit. You're just the same as I remember," she said and shook her head. I wasn't sure she meant that as a compliment.

There were a number of ways I could have replied. Instead, I said, "Your email sounded somewhat urgent. What's up?"

"Well, would it be fair to say that, based on our history, we can be honest with one another?"

I wanted to say, based on our history, it would be the first time for you. Instead, I replied, "Absolutely, Brianna."

"And you're a private investigator. So, I'm guessing that covers a variety of, shall we say, circumstances you have been involved in over the past few years."

"Well, I investigate a number of different situations, everything from work history to extramarital affairs. On occasion, I've provided security for people. Usually, some individual arriving from out of town for a meeting or, in one or two instances, a court case."

"I have an individual I would like you to investigate."

"An individual? Just who would this be?" I asked.

"An individual who was, umm, an acquaintance. He's scammed me out of at least ten thousand dollars. His name is Seymour Smeelie. Now, I call him Seymour Smelly."

"Scammed you? How did that happen? A bad investment? Were you not paid for work or services?"

"Well, yes and no. We vacationed down in Florida this past winter. Seymour told me he was involved in purchasing stock options, and his accounts were tied up. Of course, I was only too happy to help. He told me I'd receive fifteen percent of the multi-million dollar deal he was involved in. But once the snow was gone and we returned up here to the world's biggest small town," she wrinkled her nose, "I haven't been able to contact him."

"Does this guy travel? Is he busy? I mean, surely you can—"

"Were you listening, darling? I said I haven't been able to contact him. He's blocked my email, Instagram, Facebook, Snapchat, Twitter, and he's blocked my phone number. Now, as of yesterday, he's filed a restraining order on me," she said as she reached into her designer purse and tossed the restraining order across my desk.

"Someone served you yesterday?"

"Yes, some fat, smelly creature with dirty fingernails. Oh," she said and shuddered.

"Wow, sounds serious," I said, hoping she couldn't
tell how much I was enjoying her little problem.

"I'll say. Fifteen percent of a ten million dollar deal
is one point five million I'm owed."

"I don't suppose this Seymour gave you a contract,
a signed agreement, or anything along those lines?"

"That's beside the point. I do have a file full of receipts for everything from three months' rent in Florida
to food, liquor, fishing rentals, massages, waxings—"

"He got a waxing?"

"Well, no. Actually, I did but at Seymour's request."

"So, what did you want me to investigate? It sounds
like you might be better served by a lawyer, rather than
me, but I gotta be honest, Brianna. Without a contract or
a written agreement of some sort, I'm not sure you have
much of a leg to stand on."

"Interesting you put it that way because that's exactly where you come in."

"What?"

"If you could provide some little incentive, you
know, maybe break his leg. Or, better yet, break both his
legs. That would work as an encouragement for him to
make good on his promise."

I slowly shook my head and said, "Brianna, I'm
sorry, but I don't really do that kind of work."

"Dev, honey, did I happen to mention you would get
a very nice percentage as well? Say, ten percent. Let me

do the math for you and just think of it. A hundred and fifty thousand dollars and all you have to do is get him to pay me. I don't care how you do it. I don't even have to know. By the way, there would most definitely be a very personal bonus thrown in. The type of bonus I happen to know you would really, really, enjoy." She took her time crossing her legs, revealing the top of her hosiery and the black garter belt.

"So, tell me more about this guy." I said, leaning forward and staring at her upper thigh.

She grinned, pulled a sheet of paper from her designer purse, and handed it to me. "I knew that personal bonus would get you. His name is Seymour, Seymour Smeelie, but like I said, now I'm calling him Smelly. I know what you're thinking, how inappropriate. Now, here is his address, both office and condo. His phone number, email account, usernames for Instagram, Snapchat, and Twitter, as well as his Facebook page and the security code to his condo."

I unfolded the paper and read through the information. I recognized the condo address as some pretty pricey real estate. "Brianna, I wish I could help you out here, but I just don't do that. Check with an attorney and see what they tell you, but my sense is you might be screwed unless you have a signed document or evidence of some kind that proves you were promised fifteen percent."

She took a deep breath and exhaled, then shook her head and gave me a look that brought back a lot of memories, all unpleasant. "I should have known better. When will I learn? I bare my soul to you, and all you can do is throw up your hands. I offer to provide every perversion and pay you more money than you'll ever see in your entire life, and this is the thanks I get."

She glanced around the office at Louie's picnic table desk and Morton lying in his bed, chewing on a toy. "This is what I get for trying to help you," she said as she stood. "Oh, by the way, the dreams I had of you, not to worry, they were really nightmares. I'll just deal with this myself." With that, she picked up her list, turned and strutted toward the door, putting an extra effort into her backside. When she opened the door, she glanced over her shoulder, cocked a hip, and said, "Enjoy the view, that's all you're going to get." She closed the door behind her and headed down the stairs.

I watched out the window as she crossed the street and climbed into her Mercedes. She lowered the driver's window, stuck her hand out, and gave me the finger before she headed up the street. I was in the process of writing Louie a note when he hurried into the office.

"Hi, Dev. Sorry, can't stop to talk. I have to grab a file and head over to the courthouse." He stopped and sniffed. "You wearing some kind of perfume?"

I shook my head no and said, "Long story. Louie, I have to go with Taffy up to the lake. You okay to watch Morton? I got his food and water dishes along with his dog food. I can pick him up at your place on Sunday. I'll buy you dinner."

Louie was rifling through a stack of files, found the one he was looking for, and tossed it in his briefcase. "Yeah sure, whatever. I gotta run. See you," he said and hurried out the door.

I wasn't sure what I said had even registered with him, so I finished the note and left it on the picnic table. I gave Morton a rub and headed out the door.

Three

I made it over to Taffy's in record time. I pulled in front of her building then pressed her number on the security phone.

"Dev?" was how she answered a moment later.

"Yeah, Taffy. You all set?"

"Come on up. I've got one or two more things to pack." The security door suddenly buzzed. I pulled it open and took the elevator up to her third-floor unit. I stepped out of the elevator and headed down the hall. She opened the door to her unit when I was just halfway down the hall, gave a look at my camouflage shorts and t-shirt, and said, "That's what you're wearing?"

"Yeah, Taffy, good morning to you, too. Believe me. No one cares what I'm wearing. I could wear this every day, and no one would even notice."

"Well, I notice. Of course, too late now, I guess I'm stuck with it. Here, you can take these out to the car," she said and wheeled two suitcases out from behind the door. "I'll grab the rest of this and be right behind you."

"Honey, we're only going to be there for two nights, and most of the time, you'll be in a bikini. What's all this stuff?"

"Oh yeah, perfect. That'll work, fashion advice from you," she said, pointing and indicating my outfit.

I knew better than to respond. I dragged her suitcases down the hallway, stepped onto the elevator, and turned to hold the door. She was nowhere in sight. I held the door open for a minute or two until it began buzzing, then let it close and dragged her suitcases out to my car. I tossed the suitcases in the back and then leaned against the side of the car, waiting for ten minutes until she appeared. She was carrying a small pink case that I happen to know held about a thousand dollars' worth of makeup, and she had a yellow and blue computer bag slung across her shoulder.

She handed me the makeup case, and I set it next to her suitcases. As she pulled the computer bag off her shoulder, she said, "Careful, my laptop is in there."

"You think they'll even have internet access?"

"Dev. Really? Come on. Let's get going."

I closed the door once she climbed in and hurried around to the driver's side. The car started on the second try.

"Thanks for not driving us up there in this thing, Dev. It's liable to die in the middle of the woods, and no one would find us until next spring."

"We could have taken your car," I said as we turned onto Dale Street and headed toward Stacy and Kevin's.

"No. I think they're in some remote location on the lake, and you have to get there on a gravel road."

"Yeah, so?"

"Hello, I'm not driving my car on a gravel road." That was the last of our conversation until we pulled in front of Stacey and Kevin's house.

They lived in a story and a half cottage style home built in the 1930s in a nice corner of town. All the homes in the neighborhood were similar and built before the Second World War. Stacey and Kevin's was painted light green with white trim. It had a front porch with four large supports and an oak front door centered exactly in the middle of the house. Their car, a white Jeep Compass, was parked in front with the rear and both back-doors open. Kevin was loading the back of the car with grocery bags, two toolboxes, shovels, and a suitcase. I noted the single suitcase for the two of them but thought it might be wise to keep my mouth shut.

"Hi Kevin," we both called as we climbed out of my car. Taffy gave Kevin a hug and headed into the house. I began to haul out Taffy's luggage and then my grocery bag, lining it all up on the boulevard as Kevin pushed and crammed things into the back of the Jeep.

Once he filled the back area, he looked at Taffy's suitcases, the makeup case, and her computer bag and said, "I'm afraid that stuff is going to have to go in the backseat, between you two."

I shook my head and said, "Not a problem. Let's get it in there before the girls come out and make us rearrange everything."

Twenty minutes later, we were on our way, Kevin and Stacey in the front seats. Taffy and I in the back with her two suitcases and the computer bag stacked up between us. Her makeup case was on the floor with her feet resting on it. My grocery bag with the clean t-shirts, swimsuit, baseball cap, and socks, was on the floor next to my feet.

"Oh, we're going to have a great time. I can't wait until you see our place," Stacy said as we took off down the street.

Four

We drove two and a half hours up to Duluth and stopped for lunch. I offered to pay for lunch, and unfortunately, they took me up on it. We climbed back in the car and drove along the Lake Superior shore for another hour, and through the town of Two Harbors.

"Oh, you guys are so lucky," Taffy said. "I've just loved Lake Superior ever since I was a little girl and my folks would bring us up here. This brings back all sorts of wonderful memories."

Five miles later, Kevin made a left turn onto County Road 3, and we headed west, leaving Lake Superior and Taffy's memories behind us. We drove through the wilderness for another hour before Kevin turned off on a gravel road. According to the sign, we were headed toward Butt Lake.

"Oh. My. God. I don't believe it. Who would want to live there? Butt Lake, can you believe it?" Taffy laughed.

"Actually," Stacy said, turning around to look at Taffy, "that's our lake."

"No, come on," Taffy said, not quite catching on. With the suitcases stacked between us, it was impossible to elbow her.

"Yeah, that's where our place is," Kevin said. "Thankfully, because of the lake name, we could afford the property. Forty feet of lakeshore and once you get past the reeds and cattails, it's a great view."

"Oh, umm, good thing you found it," Taffy said in a failed attempt to recover.

Kevin turned on another gravel road and slowed. This road was in a lot rougher condition than the previous, and as slow as we were going, the gravel was still bouncing off the undercarriage and sides of the car. The lake occasionally came into view through the birch trees on the left-hand side. We passed three mailboxes and dilapidated structures that appeared to be lived in. At the fourth mailbox, Kevin slowed and turned onto a rutted trail that wound through the woods and over a slight rise. As we drove over the rise, I could hear the bottom of the car scrape the ground.

"You and I are going to level that out later today, Dev. It's the reason I brought the shovels," Kevin said. We cleared the rise and rolled down to little more than a shack with patches of different colored shingles on the roof.

"Here we are, our second home," Stacy said as Kevin pulled to a stop.

The "cabin" was a one-story structure that looked more like a work shed than something fit for human habitation. Along with the random patching on the roof, what I assumed had been a window at one time was covered by a sheet of warped pressboard. The two wooden steps leading to the backdoor were warped. The gray cedar siding hadn't seen a coat of paint since the Nixon administration, and most of the paint on the white trim had peeled off, exposing weathered and rotted wood.

"Okay, everyone out and grab something," Kevin said as he and Stacey opened their respective doors and hurried out.

Taffy looked at me with wide eyes, and her lower lip started to tremble.

"Come on. Let's get this stuff out of the car," I said, opening my door. I climbed out and reached back in, pulling out both of Taffy's suitcases. Two steps later, the mosquitos found us. I stopped twice and slapped a number of them on my arms and neck. Stacy and Kevin had run ahead to the door and unlocked it.

Taffy shot past me, slapping the air and mumbling, "Awe, icky, God, get away. Oh Jesus."

Kevin opened the door. Stacy hurried inside and stomped her feet a number of times. Kevin followed her in and did the same thing. Taffy was right behind them. She hurried inside and said, "What's that sound?"

Stacey ignored the question. As I stepped in, she pointed to the flowered sofa with the worn arms and the stuffing hanging out on the corners. "Dev, that's the

Hide-a-bed. Go ahead and pull that out for you and Taffy. Kevin, I'll do the counters if you'll bring the suitcase into the bedroom."

I wheeled Taffy's suitcases over to the Hide-a-bed. She was still standing just inside the door with wide eyes and her mouth hanging open. I pulled the cushions off the Hide-a-bed, revealing mouse droppings, lots of mouse droppings. I quickly unfolded the metal frame with the mattress— more mouse deposits, lots more. I thought I saw something scurry out from beneath the couch and under a chair. Taffy was still standing at the door, awestruck. Her mouth hung open, and she was slowly shaking her head from side to side.

"Taffy, maybe you could give Stacey a hand while I get the rest of your luggage out of the car. Taffy? Hey, Taffy?"

"What?" she said, shaking her head and coming back to reality.

"Give Stacey a hand while I get the rest of your luggage," I said and headed out the door.

I half-ran to the car, slapped a couple more mosquitos on the way, and grabbed Taffy's makeup case and the grocery bag with my clothes. On the way back to the 'Cabin,' I noticed an outhouse about thirty feet away with a path leading to it. Taffy was going to go crazy.

Five

Christine Abner gave hugs to her three girlfriends, and they all promised to meet for lunch again next month. Now all retired, Christine and Mary Jane widowed, and all four fleeing the midwestern winter in different directions from January until April or May, there never seemed to be enough time to catch up. Updates on grandchildren, high school classmates, God forbid someone passing, who is doing what to whom, and suddenly the two-hour lunch was over.

They split the bill four ways, each leaving a two-dollar tip, pushed back their chairs, and stood. Christine made a show of draping her shoulder bag across her chest then raised her eyebrows as her three friends focused on the classic Saint Laurent monogram.

"Well just look at you. Tell me that isn't some knock-off you got at the state fair," Sandie said.

"What can I say? The perfect birthday gift from the perfect son-in-law."

"Your son-in-law gave you that? I don't believe it," Kate said.

"Yes, he did, and my daughter Debbie is very jealous. I think he might just be buying another for her birthday."

"God, you are something. That's a long way from teaching kindergarten for forty years."

"Forty-three years. Our monthly mortgage payment was less than this cost. I'm only carrying it in nice weather, not far from home, and never, ever out of my sight.

All four of them stepped out of the restaurant and onto the street. Sunglasses immediately came out of purses, and one more round of hugs before they were off in different directions. The other three were driving, but Christine only lived two blocks away, so she walked. She gave a final wave and headed up the street. She stopped at the corner and waved the car on. The young man behind the wheel smiled and waved a thank you. She crossed the street and strolled past Fitz's and then the Red Cow, two popular restaurants. She passed the parking lot for the senior residence and smiled a 'hello' to the two women sitting on the bench in front. She crossed the next side street and walked halfway up the block then climbed the half-dozen stairs up to her building, input the security code, and opened the door.

"Oh, please, allow me," the young man said from behind and pushed the heavy glass door open so she could step in.

"Thank you," she said and smiled, thinking, isn't it nice some people are still raised to have manners. She pulled her keys out from her purse to open the inner door.

"I'll take that," he said.

"What?"

"Your purse, give it to me."

"Who are—"

"I'm not kidding, lady," he said and jammed a pistol into her ribs. "Now, give me the damn purse before things get a whole lot worse." He looked around anxiously, although no one else was in the small entry.

"But, this is—"

He jammed the pistol into her ribs again, this time a lot harder, and she groaned and winced. "Uff, please don't. It means so much—"

He tore the handbag from her shoulder, shoved her against the wall, and ran out the door. She was too frightened to move.

Six

It was after nine. A half-moon was rising over the lake. Taffy was seated in the upholstered chair the mouse had run under when we'd arrived. "I don't want to stay here," Taffy whispered as a tear ran down her cheek.

"We're gonna have to for two nights. Remember?" I said.

Kevin and Stacey were busy cooking dinner on the two-burner stove. Hotdogs again. Kevin had been hoping to do steaks out on the fire-pit, but the mosquitos were so bad he could barely get the fire started, let alone stand out there and cook for fifteen or twenty minutes.

"I want to go home, Dev."

"We can't, Taffy. Remember, you wanted to ride up with Kevin and Stacey. So we could lie in the sun." I held my hands out, palms up, revealing the blisters from the four hours of shoveling Kevin and I did to even out the rise on the trail into this hellhole, and we were only halfway finished.

"But I thought it would be nice up here. I wanted to go out on their pontoon boat, and—"

"They don't have a pontoon boat, Taffy. As a matter of fact, they don't have a boat. But that's okay because they don't have a dock. As a matter of fact, that forty feet of shoreline is all swamp with cattails and reeds going twenty feet out before you actually get to the lake. Did you happen to see that rusted out Volkswagen Bug out in the water about twenty feet offshore? The thing looks like it's been out there for at least thirty years. If this is Butt lake, guess which part we're on."

"Please, I can't sleep here. Maybe we could get a hotel," she said, suddenly looking hopeful.

"Taffy, there aren't any hotels around here. We're in the middle of nowhere. Now, it's only for two nights. You can do that. We'll make the best of this situation, and let's just enjoy the fact that we have two people cooking us dinner."

"Cooking? Dev, I thought it was chocolate sprinkles from cookies all over the counter. You know what it was? It was mouse shit. Mouse shit, Dev. And there was so much it couldn't have come from just one mouse. It had to be from hundreds of mice. I'm telling you, there's a mouse herd in this dreadful place, Dev. Stacey just brushed it off the counter and into the wastebasket like it was no big deal. Then every once in a while, she would stomp her feet, and you could hear the little bastards running around inside the wall and behind the kitchen cabinet. It's not safe here, Dev. We're going to get eaten alive. I'm not kidding."

"Okay, you guys, dinner's ready. A repeat of last night, hope you don't mind," Stacey said.

"Are you kidding? No complaints, we didn't have to cook, so like my mom used to say, eat it or wear it," I said.

"Oh, that's so cute. Come on, you guys, and sit down," Stacey said and placed a platter of hotdogs onto a Formica topped table from the Eisenhower administration.

Kevin set three beer glasses stolen from bars and one greenish colored glass on the table. They all looked like they could hold sixteen ounces. The greenish glass was emblazoned with the Coca-Cola logo. He poured some red wine maybe a third of the way up, into all four glasses. I led Taffy over to the table, and she stomped her feet before settling into the rickety wooden chair. Once she was seated, she grabbed her glass and gulped down half of her red wine. Stacey and Kevin shot a quick glance at one another.

We finished the hot dogs in about fifteen minutes. I ate three and a half, the half coming from Taffy's plate. I ate her BBQ potato chips as well. Taffy was apparently on the liquid diet, and at this point, she was about two glasses of wine ahead of us.

Stacey told us to stay seated as she hauled the plates and hotdog platter over to the sink. Kevin hopped out of his folding lawn-chair, grabbed a bag of bite-sized Snickers bars from the cabinet, and tossed them on the table. I noticed something had nibbled through the side of the bag and eaten the better part of a Snickers bar.

"Aww, Jesus. Snickers, my favorites," Taffy said. She was a little too loud, and her words were somewhat slurred as she grabbed the bag and tore it open. She either ignored the nibbling or hadn't noticed. She turned the bag upside down, dumped the candy bars out onto the table, and dug in.

Kevin smiled, raised his eyebrows, and deftly swept what was left of the nibbled bar into his hand. Once the candy bars were gone, mostly consumed by the now very intoxicated Taffy, Kevin and Stacey begged off to bed.

"See you guys in the morning," Stacey said. "First one up turns on the coffee. Taffy, honey, I left the aspirin bottle out on the counter in case you might want two before you go to bed. Might make for a better morning."

"Oh, yeah. Well, you better close your door unless you want to watch. I'm gonna put Dev to work," Taffy slurred and drained her glass.

Stacey flashed a momentary smile and said, "Thanks for the warning."

Once they closed their bedroom door, Taffy got up, staggered to the kitchen counter, and grabbed the last remaining bottle of wine.

"Hey, we should probably just hit the sack. Things will be better tomorrow. Want me to get you a glass of water for the aspirin?"

She shot me a look that suggested I wasn't making any sense. She twisted the cap off the bottle, then poured half of the bottle into her glass and dropped the cap on the floor. I figured the best policy would be to say nothing.

We sat quietly for the next twenty minutes, Taffy working her way through the glass of wine, me thinking about Brianna's threat to have someone break Seymour Smeelie's legs. I finally broke the silence. "You about ready for bed, Taffy?"

She raised her head, brushed her auburn hair back with both hands, and attempted to look in my general direction. With her glassy blue eyes, I wasn't sure she could see me only four feet away.

"You know what I wanna do now?" she said as her head swayed back and forth like a plate spinning on a stick.

"I think maybe bed might just be the best thing. We can—"

"We'll be in bed," she gulped and let out a loud burp. "But don't you plan on going to sleep anytime soon, Mister. I'm in need of some special attention. Very special." With that, she took her glass, drained it, and attempted to get to her feet.

After a couple of tries, I took hold of her arm and half-lifted her out of the chair. She smiled and said, "Mmm, this is going to be a night to remember. I'm thinking maybe we should come up to the lake more."

"Good idea, Taffy. I'll remember that."

"Just you wait," she said then reached down and squeezed my thigh. "Oh, wow, you're ready."

I got undressed and pulled back the covers on the Hide-a-bed. Thankfully, there were no new deposits since I'd cleaned it off. Taffy attempted to perform a striptease in front of the window looking out on the cat-tails and swamp reeds but ended up falling into a chair. Fortunately, she landed on the cushion and giggled for a long moment. She was down to just her bra and thong and halfway fell onto the bed. I pulled her in, and as I lifted the covers over her, she started to snore. It couldn't have been more than ten minutes later when she bolted up in bed and headed for what she thought was the bathroom. Unfortunately, the only door led into Stacey and Kevin's bedroom.

I was up just as Stacey yelled, "What the hell!" I grabbed Taffy by the arm and directed her out the back-door. We almost made it to the outhouse before she threw up. Yeah, definitely a night to remember.

Seven

arbara Jenson pulled into the parking area behind her condo. She was coming home from a wonderful night down at the Ordway theatre. She'd been to the St. Paul Chamber Orchestra concert. The orchestra performed Mozart's 40th symphony, directed by that special Russian conductor with a name she could never remember.

Her building was in the Macalester Groveland area of the city. Lovely, classic homes from the early part of the last century. Still largely single-family and then, of course, her building housing six condos. Two fireplaces in every unit, ten-foot high ceilings, gorgeous original woodwork, oak floors, and a large picture window with a stained-glass panel above it. The picture window looked out onto the tree-lined street and in the afternoons she would sit in her second-floor unit with a cup of tea, watching school children from the nearby elementary school walking home. Oh, but the energy those little ones had.

She pulled into her parking place, they were numbered, and her spot was in the back of the parking lot. The lot was surrounded by a hedge of pink Japanese lilacs that produced wonderfully fragrant flowers every

June. Barbara had helped plant the shrubs six years ago and then had to take three days off to recover, but it was worth it. Children from all over the neighborhood came by to smell the flowers, and all the condo residents helped themselves to lovely bouquets every year during the first week of June.

She turned off her car, grabbed her purse with the Chamber Orchestra program, and climbed out. It was a lovely evening and not too hot for a change. As she walked toward the entrance to her building, she wondered if she might open the bedroom window a bit and maybe put the light blanket on the bed.

The three-story building had screen porches on the front, and Barbara had just walked up the sidewalk between the two porches on the first floor when she turned at the sound. A hand grabbed hold of her purse, tore it off her arm, and pushed her down. She fell into the bed of mums not yet ready to bloom and never really caught sight of the person now running down the street. She made it back up onto her feet and hurried to the front door. Fortunately, her keys were still in her hand. She quickly unlocked the security door, stepped inside, and pulled the door closed behind her, grateful to hear the lock snap into place.

Eight

Taffy groaned and said, "Please, just go away and leave me alone." She was kneeling in the outhouse, in the process of getting sick once again. She'd been in there for at least a half-hour. I'd gone back inside and pulled on my shorts and a t-shirt. Taffy was still in her red thong, but given the circumstances, there was nothing particularly appealing to see at the moment. There was a slight breeze, so the mosquitos weren't too bad.

"Can I get something for you?"

"I said, Leave. Me. Alone."

"Okay, okay. I'll see you inside whenever you decide to come back in. Don't forget to close the door behind you when you—"

"Dev!"

"I'm going. I'm going."

I was vaguely aware of her slipping into bed at some point. I thought it best not to wake her when I climbed out of bed around six in the morning. She still wore her red thong, and now her lips had a red wine cast to them. Her hair didn't look the best, and from what I could see of her shoulders, back, and legs, it looked like she had measles— mosquito bites and lots of them. Once I was dressed, I left a glass of water and the aspirin bottle next to the Hide-a-bed. I clicked on the coffee and drummed my fingers on the table, waiting for the ten cups to get made.

Kevin tiptoed out of the bedroom just as I was pouring my first cup. He stopped for a moment and gave Taffy a long look before he hurried over to me.

"Can I pour you a coffee?" I said.

He nodded and glanced back at Taffy. "I'm guessing things didn't exactly work out the way you'd hoped last night. Man, it would take the better part of the morning to count all those mosquito bites," he said and then gave a little laugh.

"Let's just say she became intimate with the outhouse last night."

"Oh, well, that explains the knees. I thought maybe you guys went outside because she was making too much noise."

"Yeah, well, believe me, nothing happened." I glanced over at Taffy's knees. They looked like she'd crawled out to the main road and back. "God, sorry she wasn't the best guest last night. No offense, but she was expecting something a little different. How long have you guys had this place?"

"Let's see, it's August, so I'd say maybe a hundred days. I know it's a little rough. Okay, that's an understatement. But we're looking at it as a twenty-year project. We upped the electric from one-ten to two-twenty, and that takes care of this summer's project. Next spring, we'll do a new roof, maybe get wi-fi in here. The year after that, hopefully, we'll be able to afford indoor plumbing. It all takes time and a whole lot of money."

Stacey strolled out of the bedroom, dressed in jeans and a t-shirt. She looked over at Taffy, lightly snoring on the Hide-a-bed, and shook her head. She gave Kevin a kiss then pulled a white coffee mug from the cabinet with the image of a cactus. The mug said, 'Don't be a prick,' on the side. I looked at the mug and smiled as she sat down.

"Yeah, I got this for Kevin."

"Yeah, but she's the one who really deserves it," Kevin said.

Stacey took a sip, looked over at Taffy, and said, "So how long was she out there last night? I just remember her bursting into the room at some point."

"Not that anything was happening in our bed," Kevin said.

Stacey raised her eyebrows, and he got the message.

"How long? I don't really know. I was with her for about a half-hour, came back in, pulled on some clothes, and went back out. She just yelled at me to leave her alone. I'm not sure when she finally came back in. I was thinking it looks like she's got the measles with all those mosquito bites on her."

"Oh, the poor thing, and add a wine hangover to that. Once she wakes up, we'll get her in the lake and cleaned up."

Taffy was going to love that, not. We chatted for another half-hour. Stacey fried up some eggs and sausage for breakfast. Once we finished eating, Kevin and I grabbed the shovels, and we headed up the trail to finish our work removing the rise. The work went a lot faster than yesterday, and we were back for lunch just before two.

Stacey had made sandwiches that were resting on a platter on the Formica table. Taffy was up, dressed, and sipping a glass of ginger ale. The mosquito bites were still apparent and slowly but surely fading.

"Oh, you're not having wine with lunch?" I asked.

Stacey and Kevin laughed, and Taffy shot me a look. "Don't even joke about that," she said and took a sip of ginger ale.

"I'm thinking steaks and roast potatoes tonight," Kevin said. "There's enough of a breeze to keep the bugs away. We can eat dinner around the fire."

"Sounds like a plan," Stacey said.

"Anything I can do to help?" I asked.

"No, I'm thinking nap time after lunch," Kevin said. "I'll get the logs set up in the pit once we finish these sandwiches, so all I have to do tonight is strike a match, and we'll be set."

That sounded like a plan to me. We finished the sandwiches. Taffy and I flaked out on the Hide-a-bed. Kevin set everything in place for the fire. At five that evening, Stacey poured three glasses of wine. Taffy stuck to her ginger ale, and just about the time Kevin was

ready to light the fire, we heard thunder, and it started to
rain.

Nine

It kept raining through the night and into the next morning, a continual rain. More than a drizzle, but not a complete downpour, just a steady, unrelenting rain. After waiting several hours, Stacey gave up and cooked the steaks in the frying pan on the two-burner stove. The potatoes were underdone, the broccoli was burnt, but we were all so hungry no one seemed to mind.

I woke up to a bat flying around the room sometime in the middle of the night. Taffy was asleep, and I decided it would be best for all involved to leave her that way. So, I just pulled the blanket over my head and hoped the thing didn't land on me. We had coffee and breakfast the following morning, and I thought it best not to mention the bat flying around.

Taffy seemed on the road to hangover recovery, and with the rain continuing, we loaded all our luggage in the car. I carried Taffy's unopened makeup case and suitcases to the car and was able to stack them in the back of the car since Kevin was leaving the shovels at the lake.

We headed down the trail to the gravel road and immediately got stuck in the mud where the rise used to be. Kevin and I walked back to the 'cabin' in the rain to get the shovels. It took the better part of two hours for us to push the car, shovel mud, push the car back, shovel more mud, push the car forward and shovel again while Stacey drove. Through it all, Taffy sat quietly in the backseat.

When we finally made it to the gravel road, Kevin and I were so mud-splattered we took off our clothes. Kevin changed clothes. Since I didn't bring a change of clothes, I rode home in my boxers and yesterday's t-shirt. Other than Stacey's suggestion that we not stop for lunch, no one really said anything during the entire four-hour drive home.

After shaking off a couple of pounds of mud, I pulled my shorts back on outside of Kevin and Stacey's house. I loaded Taffy's luggage into the backseat, and we headed over to her place. I had the great idea that maybe we could share a hot shower at her place, but once I pulled in front of her building and wheeled her luggage up to the entry, she said, "Thanks, I can get everything from here."

Actually, that was just fine with me. I'd had two days of an unhappy, hungover camper, and that was more than enough. When I leaned down to kiss her, Taffy turned her head and I got a cheek instead of lips. We gave one another a quick wave goodbye, and I drove over to Louie's house to pick up Morton.

Louie's car wasn't in the driveway where he usually left it. I rang the doorbell, pounded on the door, and never got an answer. So I called him on my cell.

"Hi, Dev," was how he answered. "You staying up there for another day?"

"You kidding? It was the weekend from hell. Rain, mud, an unhappy, hungover woman who probably did a good job of ruining her friendship with our hosts, and those were the good points. Did I mention the place was mouse infested, had a bat flying around in the middle of the night, and there was no indoor plumbing?"

"Gee, it sounds wonderful."

"Yeah, right. I'm standing out on your front steps, here to pick up Morton. Where are you guys? Don't tell me you're taking him for some exercise."

"No, nothing like that. Actually, it sounds like you were probably out of touch up north, but there have been a number of burglaries and purse snatchings in town, specifically in your neighborhood. I just thought it might be a good idea if my car was in the driveway and the lights were going off and on at your place."

"Really? You're right. I had no idea. Aren't you worried about your place?"

"No, I don't have anything there someone would want. Probably serve them right if someone did break in. They'd find out they were just wasting their time."

"Well, okay, I'll see you in about ten minutes, heading home now," I said, walking back to my car.

"Hey, on the way, you should probably stop and pick up a sack of dog food. You've got just enough left here for a small snack."

"You kidding? There should be the better half of a twenty-five-pound bag right by the backdoor."

"Yeah, there was, but Morton and his pals ate it all."

"He ate it all? You were just feeding him once a day, weren't you? Wait a minute. Did you just say his pals?"

"Yeah, he had all these dinner guests. You know those other dogs, three or four of them chasing one another around the yard. As a matter of fact, he's out back running around with them now."

"Other dogs? What are you talking about?"

"His pals, the other dogs, they've been here the last two days. You weren't aware of this?"

"No, I've never seen any other dogs in the yard. It's why I have a fence, so other people's dogs can't get in, and so Morton can't wander off."

"Well, I don't know what to tell you except your fence doesn't seem to be working. They've been here every morning, playing all day. It's kind of like some kid having sleepover friends. Anyway, you're out of dog food. Oh yeah, and you're out of Jameson, too."

Ten

I picked up a bag of dog food, two steaks, and a liter of Jameson. Since Louie's car was in the driveway, I parked on the street in front of my house. Louie opened the door as I climbed the steps to the porch. "What the hell happened to you?" he asked by way of a greeting.

"Their car got stuck in the mud about thirty feet from the rundown shack we stayed in, and Kevin and I had to push it out."

"So you fell in the mud?" he asked, looking up and down at me.

"No, this is all from the rear tires throwing it up as we pushed. I just wore my boxers on the way home then slipped this mess back on when we pulled into Stacey and Kevin's. Pushing the car out was pretty much the icing on the cake for the whole weekend. I wish them the best on the place, but they're going to be working up there 'til the day they die."

"It's not some trendy lake villa?"

"You kidding? The place is a rodent-infested dive. There's nothing but a swamp in front of their place, literally, with some wrecked Volkswagen Bug in the water that's been there for probably thirty years. No indoor plumbing. Taffy was begging to go up there and then wanted to check into a hotel once she saw the place."

"There's a hotel up there?"

"No, there's not. So she was anything but pleasant the entire weekend. Throwing up Friday night, hungover Saturday, not talking to anyone today. Here, take this," I said and handed him the twenty-five-pound sack of dog food. "You said Morton has his pals over?"

"Yeah, out back. You didn't know about this? They seem to get along fine, chasing each other around. They take an afternoon nap on the back porch and then run around some more. He had everyone over for dinner last night. They're all really nice."

"Maybe so, but where the hell did they come from? Do they have tags?"

Louie seemed to think about that for a moment then shrugged and headed for the kitchen. "You got me. I never even thought to check," he said over his shoulder. "No big deal, they all seem nice."

I set the steaks and the liter of Jameson on the counter. "You have time to stay for dinner?"

"Not only can I, but I will. Maybe you could grab a shower and toss those jeans and t-shirt in the trash bin. I'll fill the food dish out on the back porch."

"Let me grab a shower, and then I'll deal with Morton's pals. I wonder where they came from. I haven't seen them around before," I said. Morton suddenly dashed past the window with a bright orange tennis ball in his mouth. A black Lab and a Border Collie were in hot pursuit. Morton faked left and right and then disappeared back around the corner of the house with the other two in hot pursuit. They all looked like they were having a fun time. "I'll be back down in twenty minutes," I said.

"Maybe toss that mud-encrusted outfit into the laundry before you track it through the house," Louie said.

"God, Louie, who knew you'd make such a good wife."

"Yeah, well, don't get any ideas, my precious."

For the second time that day, I stripped down to my boxers and tossed the camouflage shorts and t-shirt into the washer. "I'll run the wash once I'm out of the shower. See you in twenty minutes.

It was more like a half-hour before I came back downstairs. I'd shaved and then stood under the shower, letting the hot water run over me. It dawned on me while in the shower that I never did learn if Stacey was able to talk Taffy into bathing in the lake. My sense was she probably just sponged off in the kitchen or out on the back stoop since Kevin and I were up the trail, taking down the rise, getting things ready to be turned into a giant mud puddle later that night.

I tossed some more clothes into the washer and turned it on. Louie had placed two crystal glasses on the kitchen counter, one on either side of the bottle of Jameson. Showing great restraint, the bottle remained unopened.

"You up for a wee dram before dinner? Or I could get you an orange juice or something," I said.

Louie looked at me like I was nuts. "I think I've been more than patient," he said.

I opened the bottle, poured a healthy amount in each glass, and raised my glass to Louie. "Hey, thanks for watching Morton, and thanks for the concern about the house. You said purse snatching and break-ins?"

Louie took a sip and seemed to savor it for a long moment then said, "Yeah, the purse snatchers seem to be targeting women over forty. Some in the evening and a couple late at night, but the majority are happening in broad daylight. A number have been at gunpoint."

"Gunpoint? A purse snatching?"

"Yeah, fortunately, no one has been shot thus far, but if it keeps up, it's only a matter of time."

"How many are we talking?"

"We're at eighteen or nineteen, right now."

"Eighteen?"

"Or nineteen."

"That's crazy, and at gunpoint? What are the cops doing?"

"They're understaffed. They're trying to respond as best they can, but this is happening on busy streets, at condos, outside of restaurants. Descriptions vary on the perpetrators, teens, late twenties, black, white, tall, short, everything across the board. But there is a definite pattern, middle-aged or older women. It's about a thirty-second interaction, if that, and the bad guy is gone. Oh yeah, and they've got a gun that they jam into the victim just to get her attention."

"Jesus Christ."

"Yeah and get this. The city, in its wisdom, has reduced the number of new officer hires from seven down to two, and they're going to use those funds to increase the outreach program. Folks are more than a little pissed off."

I shook my head and heard some barking out back. "God, Morton, I completely forgot," I said, set my glass on the counter, and hurried out the backdoor. I had to sidestep the food and water dishes and the two saucepans with dog food.

Morton and the Border Collie were chasing the black Lab around the yard. Now the Lab had the orange tennis ball in its mouth. There was a small, fuzzy white dog lying in the late afternoon sun and, next to him, a German Shepherd. The Shepherd raised his head and stared at me as I stepped onto the porch, but he didn't move. The Lab with the tennis ball shot past with Morton in hot pursuit.

"Morton. Oh, Morton," I called. He looked back and then stopped and hurried up onto the back porch. I bent down, gave him a rub and a good scratch behind the ears. "Morton, did you miss me? Have you been good for Louie? How are you, Morton? Been playing and running around? Introduce me to your friends," I said.

His tail wagged, and he licked my face. I scratched him some more around the ears and then looked up, but the other dogs had disappeared. I went down the back steps and around the corner of the house, but the yard was empty.

Eleven

Amazingly, after going around the block twice, Delores found a parking space just across the street from the restaurant. She let the car behind her pass then backed into the spot perfectly, as if she were twenty years old. She turned off the engine and pulled down the sun visor. She checked her makeup in the mirror on the back of the sun visor, dug into her purse, and pulled out the lip gloss. She gave her lips a quick coat and then smacked them together twice. Satisfied with the result, she checked the sideview mirror and waited for three cars to pass, then opened the door and climbed out from behind the wheel.

She clicked the button on her carfob to lock the doors and waited for two cars to pass in the far lane. Another car suddenly appeared down the street, and she took a step back to let it pass. The car pulled alongside her and stopped. The passenger window suddenly came down.

"Excuse me, ma'am. We're a bit lost," the polite young man said. "Could you tell me how we get to Lexington Avenue?"

Delores smiled and gave a little chuckle. "You're not that lost. Let's see four, no wait, five blocks ahead. The second set of stoplights up ahead is Lexington."

"Thank you, ma'am. Why don't you give me that purse so you won't have to carry it," he said, reaching out the window and taking hold of her purse.

The car accelerated down the street. Unfortunately, the strap on the purse was still wrapped around Delores's arm. She took a hop, followed by a jump, and then was dragged twenty-five feet while the young man repeatedly hit her on the side of the head in an effort to make her let go. Thankfully, the leather strap finally broke, and Delores bounced to the curb just before the car skidded around the corner and disappeared.

Twelve

I just shook my head. "I don't know, man. One minute they're running around the backyard, and the next minute they're gone. I was scratching Morton for ten or fifteen seconds, and I look up, and they've disappeared. Really strange."

"Well, maybe they heard what a jerk you are, and as much as they enjoy Morton, they figured they didn't want to deal with you," Louie said and sipped his drink.

We were out back. I was doing the steaks on the grill and had just turned them. They were seared to perfection. I figured maybe three or four minutes on this side, then I'd bring them inside, cover them with foil, and let them sit for a few minutes. I'd had a craving for steaks on the grill ever since Kevin said he was going to cook them over an open fire that never materialized. Louie was sitting on the back porch steps. I had the baked potatoes on the grill along with foil wraps of mushrooms, onions, and red peppers. It was the perfect summer evening to sit and chat with the grill going. Morton, exhausted after an afternoon of chasing around, was lying on the porch, no doubt hoping for some steak.

I loaded the foil wraps with the mushrooms, onions, and red peppers on a platter and handed it to Louie. "Take that inside and set it on the kitchen counter. I'll be right behind you." I turned off the grill, put the steaks on the platter, and Morton and I followed Louie inside.

"You want a top up?" Louie asked, pouring more Jameson into his glass.

"No, I'm good." I covered the steak platter with aluminum foil and checked the clock on the oven. I pulled two dinner plates from a cupboard and some silverware from the drawer and set two places at the kitchen counter. "You want some wine with dinner?" I asked Louie.

"No, I'm good with the Jameson."

I grabbed Morton's water dish from the back porch and filled it, then pulled a dog biscuit from the cookie jar and tossed it to him. He grabbed it in midair and hurried into a corner so he wouldn't have to share with Louie or me. I poured myself a glass of wine, distributed the mushrooms, onions, and peppers between the two plates, then uncovered the steaks and placed them on our respective plates. My stomach made a loud growl in response.

Louie took a sip of his whiskey and cut into his steak. He stabbed his fork into a piece, then held it up and examined the meat. Tender and red in the center, nicely done on the outside. He put the piece in his mouth, closed his eyes, and gave an orgasmic groan.

"You like it?"

"Oh, Dev, it's delicious. Mmm-mmm, the absolute best."

I cut a piece, topped it up with some onions, and took a bite. Yeah, it was really good. The best meal I'd had in two days. "So, tell me more about this pack of dogs that was in the yard," I said.

"Not an awful lot to tell," Louie said and shoveled another piece of steak into his mouth. "Mmm, pack might be a little too strong a description. There were just the four of them, same ones you saw." He cut another piece of steak and shoveled it in along with some onions and red peppers. They were here Saturday morning when we woke up. I let Morton out, and the next thing I know, they're all chasing around, having a good time. I had his food dish in here and when I called him in to eat, he pushed the food dish toward the backdoor like it was the natural thing to do. So I put the dish out there, and they were all eating from it, obviously not enough to feed all of them. I filled up a couple of saucepans so there was enough for everybody."

"No snapping at one another over the food? No growling?"

Louie shook his head and shoveled in more steak. "No, at least not that I could see. They all got along so well I just figured it was an everyday occurrence. You've never seen them here before?"

I shook my head. "No, never. They seem nice. I'm thinking the lab, the German Shepherd, and the Border Collie could probably hop the fence, but I don't know how that little fuzzy white thing got in here. I did a quick check of the fence line thinking maybe they dug a hole to climb through, but I didn't see anything."

"I wonder who they belong to? With the leash laws in this town you don't see a lot of stray dogs, in fact almost never," Louie said and cut another piece of steak.

"A dog getting loose, that maybe happens occasionally. But four of them showing up, that's really strange. No collars on them, I guess they could all be strays, but that's highly unusual. At least they seem to be nice."

When we finished dinner, the plates were so clean I told Louie I wouldn't have to wash them. I filled two dishes with sea salt caramel frozen yogurt. Louie topped up his glass up, again. I sipped my wine. We headed out to the front room and chatted some more. I was ready for bed around eleven, and Louie had been over-served.

"Hey, Louie, why don't you spend the night here? I don't want you getting pulled over on the way home."

He seemed to think about that for a brief moment and said, "Yeah, probably a good idea."

"You can grab the guest room upstairs."

"Not to worry, the couch is just fine. I've slept here the last two nights. One more isn't gonna make a difference."

"You sleep in those clothes?"

"Yeah, so like I said, one more night isn't gonna make a difference."

"Okay, well, I'm heading up to bed. Catch you in the morning and thanks again for watching Morton."

"My pleasure, I can tell him all sorts of secrets, and I know he won't pass anything on," he said and then topped up his whiskey glass.

"Okay, catch you in the morning. Morton, come up to bed." Morton looked from Louie to me then back to Louie and settled onto the floor alongside the couch.

"He's been down here with me the last two nights, Dev. Relax, we'll be fine."

"Okay, as long as you're cool with it."

"Not a problem, see you in the morning," Louie said and took another sip from his glass.

I left the two of them to their own devices and headed upstairs to bed. I debated sending Taffy a text message and decided against it.

Thirteen

Unbeknownst to me, sometime in the middle of the night, Morton had climbed in my bed. Just now, he was pushing his paws into the back of my head. As I opened my eyes, I heard my cellphone signaling an incoming call. I glanced at the number but didn't recognize it. I did notice the time, five-ten in the morning.

"Hello?" As I answered, I heard Morton take a deep breath and drift back to sleep.

"Dev, it's Brianna. Please don't hang up."

"Brianna, it's just after five in the morning. Is everything all right?"

"No, it's absolutely awful," she said and sounded like she was about to cry.

"Where are you?"

"I'm in jail, is where I am."

"Jail? What did—"

"I didn't do anything. It's all crazy. Abuse is what it is, and I'm going to be suing the police, and the city, and—"

"Why are you in jail?"

"Oh, that's the craziest part. Murder. That bastard, Seymour Smeelie, went out and got himself killed, and now they think I'm the one who did it. Not that I wouldn't have liked to."

"Okay, first of all, Brianna, are you calling from the police station?"

"Yeah, what the hell? Were you even listening?"

"Okay, please, do not say another word. You need to button your lip and keep quiet."

"That's all I've been doing since they pounded on my door in the middle of the night. I haven't said a damn thing. I need you to find me a good lawyer and get me the hell out of here before I lose what's left of my mind."

"Okay, okay. Now just calm down. I just happen to know the right guy for this," I said. I didn't mention he was asleep downstairs on my couch in the same clothes he'd worn for the past three days, he hadn't shaved, and no doubt hadn't taken a shower. "I'll give him a call, and we'll be down there just as soon as we can. Do not say another word. They'll probably put you in a cell and—"

"What is it with you? You're just as bad as these stupid cops. I said I didn't kill him. Not that it hasn't crossed my mind, and believe me, I'd love to right about now, but somebody beat me to it. I outta pay whoever it was."

"Brianna, you need to stop saying that. All you're doing right now is helping to build a case against you. Now, this is serious business. So it would be best if you refrained—"

"Dev, the guy scammed me out of ten thousand dollars, and now, I'll never get it back. All I can say is I'm glad he's dead, the miserable bastard."

"Okay, Brianna, here's the deal. If you want my help, you need to shut the hell up now! Do not make one more comment. I'm not kidding."

"But—"

"Stop. I'm not kidding. One more comment and I'm hanging up." I waited for a long moment. Fortunately, she kept her mouth shut. "Okay, thank you. Now, it's early in the morning. I'm going to call that attorney. We'll be down there as soon as possible. You are not to say anything to anyone. Now answer with a simple yes and do not say another word."

"Okay, I heard you the first time, yes. There, happy?"

Typical. "Thank you. We'll be down there just as soon as we can. I want you to do two simple things until we get there. Be quiet and behave. Now, I'm going to hang up. What two simple things are you going to do?"

"Be quiet and behave… While I think of ways to sue the police department and the city. Because even though I wanted to—"

"Good-bye, Brianna," I said and disconnected. It was five-fifteen. Morton was back asleep. Louie was no doubt still sound asleep, and there was no point in waking him up. I was too upset to go back to sleep, so I grabbed a shower instead.

I heard Louie coughing and groaning a couple of hours later. Ten minutes after that, I heard him making his way upstairs to the bathroom. I put the eggs and sausage on. I had sliced tomatoes, red peppers, black olives, a little feta cheese, and some basil mixed in with the eggs. I set two places on the kitchen counter and filled Morton's food and water dishes. Louie wandered into the kitchen five minutes later.

"Good morning, Louie. Can I get you a coffee?"

"Humf," he half-groaned, sat down at the counter, and rubbed both hands back and forth over his face. I set the coffee mug in front of him and stepped over to the stove to turn the sausages. After a couple of sips of coffee, he said, "Mmm, whatever that is, it smells good."

"Eggs and sausage, I know you like that for breakfast. How's the head?"

"It's beginning to come around. How long you been up?"

"I've been up for a while. A phone call came in around five and woke me."

"A phone call? At five? Is everything okay? It sounds like someone's in trouble."

"No, everything is not okay, and yeah, someone's in trouble. You remember a gal I used to date named Brianna Di Salvo?"

"Oh yeah, who could forget? Great looking and really impressed with herself. Didn't she dump you a couple of times?"

"Three to be exact."

"She the one who called you from California and told you she never wanted to see you again? You found out later she was out in Hollywood with a supposed producer, only he was really some guy just running errands for folks on the set of some reality show?"

"Yeah. The show was called Fatties. Overweight folks who couldn't lose weight. I think it was cut after three or four episodes. It was bad, really bad," I said then loaded up a plate full of scrambled eggs and a half-dozen sausages and set it down in front of Louie. As he took a bite, I refilled his coffee mug. "Yeah, she ended up waiting tables at some diner hoping to be discovered. When that didn't work, after a couple of months, she came back here. I think she's been looking for a sugar daddy for the last couple of years."

"So what did she want at that hour of the morning, or did she just dial a wrong number?"

"No, actually, she's been arrested. She's in jail at the moment."

"Here in town? You're kidding. What's she been charged with?" Louie asked and slurped more coffee.

"She's been charged with murder. Some guy she claims scammed her out of ten grand was murdered, and the cops picked her up last night."

"Why her?"

"Actually, she didn't say. Based on the way she was ranting, they picked her up for no reason. I'm finding that a little hard to believe. She came to my office last

Friday and wanted me to break the guy's legs and tell him he had to pay her ten grand."

"What?"

"Long story, background history now."

"So she called you because…"

"Because she needs a lawyer first and foremost, and then she's gonna need someone to do some investigatory work and come up with an alternative besides herself as the prime suspect."

"Who you got in mind to do the legal work?" Louie said and stuffed the better part of an entire sausage into his mouth."

"I was thinking of you."

"Me?" Louie half-choked, coughed, and swallowed what he hadn't spit out. "Dev, I get people off or hopefully get them to plead down on drinking and driving offenses. Murder is a little out of my league."

"Come on, Louie. You were on the prosecution side of the table on murder wraps when you worked for the city."

"Yeah, but that was different. I—"

"Come on. It wasn't different. Look, I know this woman. She's capable of doing a lot of stupid things, and she can be a major pain in the ass, but killing some schmuck is not in her job description. She's her own worst enemy here, telling the cops she's glad the guy is dead, but she didn't do it. Then threatening to sue them along with the city. She needs someone like you to get her out of this mess before she digs herself in so deep she can't get out."

"I don't know, man."

"Do it, Louie. I'm thinking, once you get her off, that's going to serve as some great advertising for all the folks who end up getting arrested every night for driving under the influence. You couldn't buy advertising like this for a million bucks."

Louie gave a long sigh. "And she's been arrested? She didn't just go down there for an interview?"

"She said she was arrested. I hope she hasn't agreed to an interview. The problem is she's no doubt uncooperative, bitchy, and can't keep her mouth shut. I'm not kidding. If she doesn't get out of there soon, they're liable to lock her up and throw away the key."

Louie chuckled for a bit. "She's lucky they even let her make the phone call."

"That's why she needs you to get her the hell out of there before she does any more damage to her case."

"Okay, Let me finish this breakfast. Then I'll head home and get cleaned up. Great eggs, by the way," he said and shoveled another heaping forkful into his mouth.

Fourteen

It was almost noon before Louie pulled into the parking lot across from the police station. I'd been waiting for him for the better part of forty-five minutes. The parking lot sat on an old factory site that had been vacant for the last forty years. The factory had been a limestone building originally built in the late 1880s and torn down a hundred years later. Now it was a gravel parking lot with potholes large enough to swallow a vehicle. I watched as Louie drove in and hit two of the larger potholes before he pulled his rusty Honda Accord into a parking place.

I climbed out and headed over to his car. "Thanks for doing this, Louie. I was beginning to worry you may have changed your mind."

"I was thinking about it, to tell you the truth, but at the end of the day, the woman deserves decent legal representation. So here I am," he said, then reached in behind his seat and pulled out a brown leather briefcase. "How do I look?"

At least there was only one stain on his suit coat, and it was relatively small. He'd shaved, which was a plus.

"Mmm, you might want to button that top button on your shirt and tighten your tie."

"Sorry, I tried, but no can do. The shirt must have shrunk in the wash. I grabbed it because it was the cleanest one I had."

"Let me straighten your tie for you, and hopefully, that'll do the trick." As I tightened the knot in Louie's tie, he raised his head toward the sky, stretching out his chins at least for the moment. I adjusted the knot and moved it up toward the open collar as best I could and said, "Okay, now you look a hundred percent."

Louie lowered his head, and his chins pretty much covered the tie knot along with the unbuttoned shirt collar, and in a generous comment way, he seemed to look a little better. We headed into the station and were ushered into an interview room in short order. The room was about ten steps above the interview rooms I'd been subjected to. It was a pleasant off-white color, with beige carpeting, a window and four comfortable cushioned chairs. Two detectives were in the room with Brianna. She wasn't handcuffed or in an orange jumpsuit. Everyone seemed to be behaving, and all three were drinking coffee from white paper cups. The two-way mirror was on the opposite wall from the table, and the cameras mounted in two opposite corners of the ceiling appeared to be recording based on the illuminated green light on each of them. I could only hope she hadn't said anything more about wanting to murder Seymour Smeelie.

"Gentlemen," one of the detectives said as they both stood.

If I'd met either one before, I couldn't recall, and their reaction suggested they didn't know either Louie or me. We all shook hands, and Louie said, "I wonder if I might have a few private minutes with my client."

Both detectives smiled, nodded, and then one of them said, "We'll just be waiting out in the hallway. Knock on the door when you're ready. The sooner we get going, the sooner, hopefully, Miss Di Salvo can return home."

As they headed for the door, Louie said, "Dev, would you mind joining them, please?"

"What? Oh, yeah, sure Louie. Just knock on the door—"

"Yeah, I know," he said and smiled. "We'll knock when we're ready. Shouldn't take more than a few minutes," Louie said.

I stepped out into the hallway with the two detectives. The one with the mustache looked at me and said, "Dev Haskell? Are you the private investigator?"

"Yeah."

"Our boss wanted to see you after this. If you can fit it in."

"Aaron LaZelle?"

"Yeah, he said it would only take a couple of minutes. Apparently, you two go back a ways."

"Yeah, we played hockey together as kids. He's been a good friend."

"Yeah, he's okay," the guy with the crew cut said. "Umm, word to the wise. Detective Manning is also aware you're here. Maybe approach with caution," he said and smiled.

"Thanks for the warning. I always try to tread lightly where Manning is involved."

"Don't we all," he said, and the three of us laughed.

Detective Sergeant Norris Manning has had it in for me almost since the day we met. Not if, but when Louie gets Brianna off, there's a good chance Manning will try to pin the Smeelie murder on me.

About ten minutes later, Louie knocked on the door, and we went back in. One of the detectives offered to get me a chair, but I declined and decided to lean against the wall.

Once we were situated, Louie cleared his throat and said, "Detectives, I understand the need to look at all sorts of different options regarding the unfortunate circumstances leading to Mr. Smeelie's death. But certainly, the arrest and incarceration of Miss Di Salvo is a step in the wrong direction. My client is one of dozens of individuals who have had interactions with Mr. Smeelie and certainly not the most recent. It would seem to me that investigatory time could be better spent if you—"

"Actually, Mr. Laufen," one of the detectives said as his partner slid a manila file folder over to him. "Your client, Miss Di Salvo, has become our top suspect.

We've motive, the lack of payment on an apparent verbal promise regarding money spent in Florida. We've means, the poison in the bottle of rum. Havana Club Anejo Especial, as a matter of fact. This was the same rum your client admitted to purchasing for Mr. Smeelie in Florida. And opportunity, your client had confirmed an appointment with Mr. Smeelie for yesterday evening. Over the course of the past few hours, we've come into possession of four items. Here is a copy of the back and forth emails establishing the appointment," he said and slid a sheet of paper across to Louie.

Louie shot me a quick glance. Apparently the email and appointment were news to him. He didn't look happy.

"Additionally, we have these three, handwritten threats. Each one suggesting your client planned to kill Mr. Smeelie. Miss Di Salvo was kind enough to leave one at his home, one on the windshield of his car, and finally, this third one was attached to his office door, where his body was found. It would appear she was quite successful in carrying out her threat," the detective said.

He smiled as he slid copies of three threatening notes from Brianna across the table to Louie. "We have the originals here if you'd care to compare," he said and held up three pieces of paper, each enclosed in plastic.

They all looked like they had been written with a sharpie. Comparing them, there seemed to be a visibly increasing anger issue based on the exclamation points and the size of the words, '**KILL YOU!!!!**' at the bottom of each note.

"I just wanted to make sure that bastard saw those after he stood me up. I wouldn't go—"

"That's enough," Louie said.

"But he really pissed me off. I—"

"I said, be quiet. Now, not another word," Louie said in a raised voice.

Brianna flashed her eyes, but at least she shut up.

"Gentlemen, I still believe you're making a mistake, and I believe an investigation by our private investigator, Mr. Haskell, will help point you in the right direction. We'll leave things as they are for the time being. But I can assure you, my client is innocent. If you would allow me a few more minutes to consult in private with my client, it would be much appreciated," Louie said.

Both detectives smiled and stood, gathered up their files, and headed for the door.

"Dev, why don't you take a seat. It will be a short discussion," Louie said. I knew him well enough to know he was working very hard to keep himself in check. He looked like he wanted to strangle Brianna, and if he didn't want to, I certainly did.

Fifteen

As the detectives closed the door behind them, I took a seat across the table from Brianna and Louie.

"So, how soon do I get out of here? I've got a hair appointment scheduled for this afternoon and dinner at—"

"Stop," Louie said. He took a deep breath, exhaled slowly, then leaned in close to Brianna. "First of all, I want you to shut the hell up. The cameras are still on, so everything you say is probably being taped. Next, the fact that you didn't mention the email confirming a Saturday evening appointment. Oh, and by the way, your little love letters." He held up the copies of the three notices she'd apparently left at Smeelie's home, office, and on the windshield of his car.

"That doesn't—"

"Please do not say a word, not one word. Let me explain something to you. Right now, you are your own worst enemy. You had better learn to keep that mouth of yours shut, or you can find yourself another lawyer, and when you do, I'm going to tell him he doesn't have a chance at winning because you won't shut up."

"Brianna," I said, "Louie is absolutely right. You do not know how things work here. No one is going to give you a break because you're gorgeous. That just makes them think you're all the more guilty. If you don't learn to be quiet, there is nothing anyone can do to help you. You're sinking your own ship. These notes you left on the door, why didn't you tell us? Oh, and don't answer, because it's too late. They've got the originals. The bottle of Rum? Just for the record, what did that cost, by the way?"

"Can I answer, or do I have to keep quiet?" Brianna snapped at Louie.

Louie shook his head and said, "I'm sorry, but this isn't going to work. Brianna, I wish you the very best, but you had better get control of yourself, or you're going to end up doing some serious time. Right now, you are your own worst enemy. Dev, I'll see you out in the hallway."

Louie stood, put the copies of the emails, and the threatening notes from the detectives in his briefcase and, without another word, headed toward the door.

"I don't believe it. He's really dumping me? No one dumps me."

"Looks like he already has, and I can't say that I blame him. When you realize maybe we know more than you about what's going down, give me a call. Until then, taking direction from the person who knows the least, namely you, is not the way to win. I'll tell the detectives, and they can take you to your cell."

"My cell? You gotta be kidding. I'm not spending another minute here. You can't just leave me here. Are you even listening to me? I've got a hair appointment I'm going to miss and get charged for. Dev, get your ass back here, damn it. Dev, did you hear me?"

"Brianna, you put yourself in this position, and you refuse to listen to the people who know what's happening here. So listen to me. You are in deep shit, lady. Now you had better get hold of yourself because we're not going to be wasting any more of our time."

"Dev? Dev?" She tried the tears routine as I knocked on the door.

The detective with the mustache opened the door. "All set?"

"She's all yours. Thanks, fellas."

"Don't forget LaZelle wanted to see you when you're finished," the crew cut said. They both headed back into the room.

"Let's get out of here before they bring her out," I said to Louie. We headed down the hall and around the corner to the bank of elevators. No sooner did I press the down button, than the doors opened, and we stepped in.

"Talk about being your own worst enemy," Louie said. "Did she think the cops wouldn't see the email? Not to worry, just in case they didn't see it, she went around and put up threatening notes. But why bother to mention that? Then she tells them she wanted to kill the guy. I mean, what the hell?"

"So, you're off the case?"

Louie looked at me for a long moment. "Against my better judgment, hell no. Just for starters, I'm convinced she didn't kill this guy. I want you to find out everything you can about this Seymour Smeelie creep. I don't know this, but if he's anything like Brianna suggests in her sane moments, the list may end up being fairly long with people who would be happy to see him dead."

"Thanks for hanging in there," I said.

He looked at me and shook his head.

Sixteen

ouie had left to do some case research. Probably a lot of research based on the way our meeting with the detectives had gone. I was now up in Aaron LaZelle's office, sitting across the desk from him.

"Dev, relax, I know you had a relationship with her. Hell, you've had a relationship with almost half the women in town. Fortunately, most of them were happy enough to finally tell you to stay away. This Brianna, it's starting to look like things are set in stone. The threats, the appointment, the emails. She admitted she bought that bottle of rum that you're not even supposed to be able to get here in the US. It's not much of a jump from buying the rum to lacing it with cyanide."

"Yeah, she bought a bottle of rum, but she didn't put cyanide in it. Come on, Aaron. Where is someone like Brianna going to get cyanide in the first place? The woman's lucky if she can put the right kind of gas in her car. And by the way, Smeelie could have purchased that bottle of rum, after all; he was in Florida for three months, too. Maybe someone who was trying to get on his good side gave it to him. It could have been someone who wanted to invest in one of his projects. Or, it could

have been someone who felt ripped off and wanted re-
venge."

"You mean someone like say, Miss Di Salvo? Dev,
if someone wanted to invest in one of his projects, I
doubt they would have put cyanide in the rum bottle.
From what we can tell, the guy was a major league scammer," Aaron said. "He had a number of business interests
stacked one on top of the other. He built a regular house
of cards, and it's all tumbled down more than once. The
list of people who were not happy with him is definitely
long. But no one left notes saying they wanted to kill
him. No one sent emails setting up an appointment yesterday. No one bought him a bottle of Cuban rum. The
same rum laced with cyanide. I'm sorry, but this looks
like a clear case of her getting to him first."

"I'm going to check into the guy. I'm not doubting
some of what you say, except for the conclusion. I just
don't see her doing it. On a different subject?"

"What's that?"

"I was out of town over the weekend, and when I
got home, all these purse snatchings had been going on.
Any idea who's doing it?"

Aaron shook his head. "No, unfortunately. The
things are happening so fast, literally in under a minute.
From what we're picking up in our interviews, it's two
people, males. Possibly the same two, although we can't
be sure at this point. One of them is waiting around the
corner in a getaway car. They dragged a woman down

Grand Avenue the other night. She's in the hospital, recovering, fortunately. Thus far, that's been the most vicious attack. Otherwise, it's usually been bumps and bruises from a fall."

"Anything like a similar description? Maybe part of a license number?"

Aaron shook his head. "As far as a vehicle goes, we've got everything from red to blue, and Mercedes to Ford. As for a description of the perp, it's still all across the board, race, age, height, weight. Again, it's happening so fast. I said it happens in under a minute, but in all honesty, it's probably happening in under fifteen seconds. Definitely targeting older women, three were in mid-forties, but the majority have been fifty and above."

"Do they seem to be targeted, you know, watched for a couple of days, to get a feel for where they go, or—"

"No, it appears to be opportunistic, and given the circumstances, there are plenty of opportunities."

"Anything I can do to help?"

"Yeah, don't carry a purse."

Seventeen

Jackie Thomas was heading into Hanley's Steak House. She was meeting three other women she worked with. They all taught at the same elementary school, and they all loved line dancing. Tuesday nights, the Bucking Broncos played from nine until midnight, three full hours of line dancing and God forbid, maybe a glass or two of wine.

She pulled into the parking lot and slowly drove through four rows of cars before she found a parking place in the back row. No surprise, it was like this every Tuesday, and she was arriving a half-hour later than her usual time. She locked the car once she climbed out, did a quick look around, and waited for a car to pass. She knew she was lucky to get one of the very last parking places. She slung her purse over her shoulder and cut through two rows of parked cars. Now she could actually hear the band starting up inside. They were playing "Boot Scootin' Boogie," one of Jackie's favorites, and she picked up her pace.

A couple was just hurrying in the front door. They were dressed in blue jeans, boots, and wearing white Stetson hats. Jackie had to turn sideways as she hurried through the narrow path between the last two cars. She had just cleared it when she was spun around, literally lifted off her feet, and slammed into the rear of a car. She caught her breath, shook her head slowly, and realized her side hurt. At first, she thought she'd been hit by a car, but no one had stopped, and she didn't see any taillights.

Had she slipped? It was summer and way too warm for ice. What in the hell happened? She slowly got up on all fours, looked around, then put a hand on the bumper, and raised herself up onto her feet. The elbow on her shirt sleeve was torn, and the right knee in her jeans was ripped. Now, where was her purse?

Eighteen

I was sitting at the kitchen counter eating cold pizza and drinking sparkling water while I googled Seymour Smeelie. I'd been reading up on him for the past half-hour. He seemed to have had a lot of good ideas that, for one reason or another, went bust, leaving a trail of extremely unhappy investors in their wake. What I took from the various articles, and there were hours more to read, was typical of people like Smeelie. It wasn't his intention to steal your money, so the fact that you got screwed out of your investment wasn't his problem; that was just an unfortunate happenstance.

The problem was that taking people's investment and ultimately providing little or nothing in return seemed to be a very common denominator in Smeelie's businesses. His most recent fiasco had been plans to purchase a number of vacant buildings along the lower riverfront and then tear them down with the idea of building a series of seven to ten-story loft apartments. The project was stopped when it was learned that the city code prohibited any structure over four stories along that area of the river front and prohibited residential structures in general due to the floodplain location. One would think investors would have checked those two items prior to the purchase of a number of properties, but apparently not. In fact, that seemed to be a repetitious trend in Smeelie's projects; some outside influence always hampered completion or continuation. Reading up on the guy, I began to think it might be intentional. The next step would be going through city and county records and seeing exactly who had been investors in Smeelie's past projects.

I let Morton out the backdoor before we went to bed, then looked online for articles on Smeelie's murder. Thus far, there really wasn't anything other than he had been found dead in his office, and the police were investigating the circumstances. That wasn't going to last for more than twelve hours, and then Brianna's name would be out there.

It suddenly dawned on me that I'd let Morton out about a half-hour ago, and he hadn't come back in. I looked out the back window but didn't see him. I stepped outside and was about to call him and then thought better of it. I went down the steps and peeked around the corner of the house. There was Morton, sitting with the four dogs from the other day. They looked like kids sitting around a campfire telling stories, only there wasn't a fire, and they weren't telling stories. I thought for a minute and then decided to leave him out there for a while longer.

I went back inside, through the house, and out the front door. I walked to the end of my front porch and peeked around the corner. All the pickets were in place. They must have all jumped the fence, which maybe wasn't that big a deal for three of them, but I couldn't figure out how that little fuzzy white dog had gotten in the yard. I made a mental note to check the fence again tomorrow morning for an area where he could crawl under and went back inside.

Louie phoned me about a half-hour later. "Am I interrupting anything?" was how he started.

"No, just reading up on your pal, Seymour Smellie," I said.

"Oh, damn it. I wanted to interrupt some passionate sexual interaction."

"Well, then you called the wrong number. What's up?"

"I've been chatting with some folks at the city. Everyone is aware of Seymour Smeelie down there. Currently, there are no less than three pending indictments. Obviously, they're not going anywhere now, but that begins to give you an idea of his business sense."

"Yeah, well, I've been reading local articles on the guy for the better part of the evening— that certainly fits the picture. His routine seems to be to find a bunch of investors and pitch them on a project that doesn't have a chance in hell, and then when it fails, they're out whatever they invested, and he moves onto the next group of folks he's going to screw. It always amazes me that guys like Smeelie can continue to find investors."

"Yeah, or women to pay three months' worth of their bills down in Florida," Louie said. "I've got a list of his investors on the last couple of projects. You think you might have time to talk to these folks and get a feel for them? I'm thinking there's a good chance somewhere in that group is the person or persons we're looking for."

"Yeah, I can do that."

"Good, I'll be in early tomorrow morning. I'll leave the list on your desk. I'm going to be doing research for the better part of the day over at the law library at the U, so if you need me, just call. Next thing, our client."

"Brianna?"

"Right, I'm going to start my day seeing her, get the worst part of the day out of the way. You might want to check on her after the noon hour. Right now, I'm think-ing the best place for her might be behind bars, give her a taste of what awaits her if she doesn't start keeping her mouth shut."

"Let me know how your visit goes. Morton and I should be in the office around nine."

"Let's talk tomorrow," Louie said and hung up.

I thought for a moment, then remembered Morton was still outside. I felt sorry for the other dogs, not a col-lar on any of them and no doubt strays. But I couldn't take them in. I could maybe try to find them a home or get them into a rescue shelter. Against my better judg-ment, I filled two saucepans with dog food and another with water and brought them out into the backyard. The moment I came around the corner, they all sat up, and everyone except Morton hurried to the far side of the house. The German Shepherd seemed to have a slight limp. I called to them and shook one of the saucepans with food, but they hurried to the fence. The Shepherd placed his nose between two pickets and pushed them apart. They all hopped through the opening, and by the time I put the pans down and hurried over to the fence, they were nowhere to be seen, and the pickets had been pushed back in place.

I looked at the pickets, and sure enough, the lower nails had rusted through, and the bottom portion of two pickets could move from side to side. How they ever found it out, I'd never know. Morton gave me a look like I'd ruined his evening.

"Let's go inside, Morton. They'll be back tomorrow. We'll leave breakfast out for them." I lined up the saucepans along the foundation wall and took Morton inside.

I turned off the lights, double-checked the locks, and we headed up to bed.

Nineteen

Mercifully, no one called at five the following morning. I woke up under my own power, showered, dressed, and headed downstairs. I turned on the coffee and filled Morton's food and water dishes. I thought about checking the saucepans out in the backyard but decided against it. If the stray dogs were out there, I didn't want to scare them off.

I was finishing my second cup of coffee and reading up on Seymour Smeelie when I heard Morton hop off the bed and stretch. A few minutes later, he came down the stairs and into the kitchen for his perfunctory morning head scratch. Once I'd finished, he hurried to the backdoor and glanced over his shoulder at me with a look that suggested, *'Come on. Let me out. I got things to do and other dogs to meet.'* I let him out, and he hurried down the steps and around the corner of the house.

I went back to reading up on Smeelie. Once I finished, the online article from the business section of the Star Tribune, I made myself a French Toast breakfast. After breakfast, I pulled five dog biscuits from the cookie jar and stepped out the backdoor. I quietly went down the porch steps. Sure enough, there they were, Morton and his guests.

I stepped around the corner, and the German Shepherd's head immediately popped up. I took a dog biscuit and tossed it at him. He sniffed it for a moment, then quickly snapped it up and eyed me cautiously. I took a step closer and tossed a biscuit to each of the dogs. I checked the saucepans. They were all empty. I picked them up and carried them back into the house. I filled all three with water, brought them back outside, and lined them up against the foundation wall.

I debated calling Morton inside and decided against it. I set his food and water dish on the back porch just outside the door and headed down to the office.

Louie was nowhere to be seen, but the coffee pot was on, and amazingly, there was still coffee in it. I poured a cup then settled in at my desk and went through the list of Seymour Smeelie's investors. With a few exceptions, they appeared to be local individuals. There were some funds listed, three with Florida addresses, one with a Texas address, and two with St. Paul addresses.

It was just after nine, so I decided to give Taffy a call. We'd had almost forty-eight hours to recover from the weekend at the lake, and I figured tonight might be the perfect time to get my, 'Thank you for being so patient' reward. After five rings, I was dumped into her voicemail.

"Hi Taffy, Dev calling. Wanted to check in and see if you've recovered from the weekend. The blisters on my hands from shoveling have just about healed up. I'm wondering if you'd have time for dinner tonight. You pick the place. Looking forward to seeing you. Enjoy the day."

I emptied what coffee was left in the pot and turned it off. I settled back at my desk and began calling Smeelie's investors. My first call was to a gentleman by the name of Thurlow Dempsey. He answered after a couple of rings with one word, "Dempsey." His voice was loud, and he didn't sound young.

"Good morning, Mr. Dempsey, my name is Dev Haskell, and I'm calling regarding an investment you made in a project called Mid-City Tenant."

"If this has anything to do with Seymour Smeelie, I'm not interested," he said and hung up

"Good morning, may I speak with Arthur Knight, please?"

"Who may I ask is calling?"

"My name is Devlin Haskell."

"And what is this about?"

"I'm calling regarding a defunct St. Paul construction project called Bayview. I have a couple of questions—"

"If this is regarding an investment with Seymour Smeelie, let me give you some quick advice. Run, don't walk, in the opposite damn direction. He'll take your money, and you will never see one red cent. Good day."

"Vivian Goldman, please."

"Speaking."

"Miss Goldman, my name is Devlin Haskell, and I'm calling to inquire about your investment in the City Living project back in two thousand-eighteen. Seymour Smeelie was—"

"Stop right there. Seymour Smeelie is the most crooked, dishonest bastard that ever walked the face of the earth. He took our money, and in return, gave my husband a heart attack. I just heard on the news this morning that he was murdered. All I can say is it's been a long time coming. Too long, in my estimation. They ought to give whoever did that a medal. Anything else I can help you with?"

"No ma'am, you've pretty much answered all my questions. Thank you for your time," I said, but she'd already hung up.

That pretty much described the calls as I went down the list until the third name from the bottom. Casper Worthington.

"Hello."

"Casper Worthington, please."

"Speaking."

"Mr. Worthington, my name is Devlin Haskell, and I—"

He chuckled, "I bet you're calling about Seymour Smeelie, aren't you?"

"Why, yes, I am."

"Yeah, got a pal warning me someone called this morning. How can I help you?"

I was so taken aback I wasn't sure how to respond.

"Hello, you still there?"

"Yes, I am. Sorry, it's just that everyone has been extremely short and very unhappy at the mention of Mr. Smeelie's name. So now, actually hearing a friendly voice just caught me off-guard."

"Yeah, well, in fairness, whoever you spoke with has every right to be upset. Smeelie was an absolute con-man, a criminal of the worst sort. He was allowed to continue for far too long as a dupe for an even more sinister organization. But that's just my opinion. What can I do for you?"

"I wonder if we might meet and chat. I'm attempting to get a better understanding of how he operated, and as you may have heard, apparently he was murdered sometime Saturday evening."

"Yeah, I heard that on the news this morning. I have to say, no loss there, and frankly, the inevitable outcome of his behavior over the years. Tell you what, nowadays I lunch at the Cherokee Tavern up on Smith Avenue. You familiar with it?"

"Yeah, I've even been there a time or two."

"Join me for lunch, 1:00. I have a table reserved. Just ask for me when you get there."

"That's very kind of you, thank you in advance."

"My pleasure, I look forward to meeting you. Tell me your name again."

"Haskell, Dev Haskell."

"I'll see you at 1:00, Mr. Haskell," he said and hung up.

Twenty

The Cherokee Tavern is located in the city of West St. Paul as opposed to St. Paul. A difference only locals would know. The Tavern first opened in 1933, changed its name to the Cherokee Sirloin Room around 1970 when sons purchased the business from their parents. It reverted back to the Cherokee Tavern in 2019 under new ownership. It had been a couple of years since I'd been in the place. As I drove across the High Bridge and up Smith Avenue, I wondered what in the hell I was going to ask Casper Worthington.

My guess was he got just as screwed as everyone else who made the mistake of investing with Seymour Smeelie. He just seemed to be handling it better. I parked across the street from the Cherokee Tavern. Since I was fifteen minutes early, I thought it would be a good idea to call Taffy. After five rings, I was dumped into her voicemail again. "Hi, Taffy. Dev, here. Calling to see if you'd be interested in dinner tonight. I can pick you up. You name the time and the place, and I'll be there. Looking forward to seeing you tonight. Have a great afternoon. Bye, bye."

It dawned on me as I hung up that the phone had rung five times before I went to voicemail. That suggested that she'd answered other phone calls and was not answering mine— food for thought.

I crossed the street and went into the Cherokee Tavern. Maybe it had been more than two years since I'd been in the place. Antique light fixtures, wooden floors, linen tablecloths. The place looked completely different. "Good afternoon, just yourself?" the girl behind the reception area asked. She looked to be in her mid-twenties, blonde and wearing a wedding ring.

"Actually, I'm meeting with a man named Casper Worthington. He said he has a reservation."

"Oh, sure, follow me. He's not here yet, but he should arrive at any moment. He's in here every day for lunch." She showed me to a corner table with a reserved sign sitting on it. I took a chair with my back to the wall so I'd see him when he came in, maybe. Since I'd never met the guy, I had no idea what he looked like. I did notice a number of glances from folks at other tables and one or two whispers. Maybe they weren't used to people from outside the neighborhood.

A few minutes later, a lean, dapper, white-haired guy walked in the door, gave a friendly wave to the blonde at the reception area, and apparently told her a joke because they both laughed. She said something back. He nodded and headed my way. It wasn't far, but it took him a while because he stopped at every second table and talked to people.

He wore a trendy brown leather jacket, navy blue trousers, and a starched blue shirt with a button-down collar. I pegged him at maybe seventy. When he finally arrived at the table, he thrust his hand out and said, "Nice to meet you, Dev. I'm Casper Worthington."

I stood as we shook hands and said, "Very nice to meet you, Mr. Worthington. Thank you for making time to talk with me."

"My pleasure, not a problem, and please, do me a favor and dispense with the Mr. Everyone calls me Casper, at least to my face. God only knows what they say when I can't hear them. Did you order anything?" he asked as he pulled out a chair and sat down.

"No, sir, I didn't order. Whatever you want, and by the way, I got the tab here."

"Thanks, that's very kind, but I always pay my own way. I'll pick up the tab. I usually have a glass of red wine, just the bar pour."

"Make it two," I said just as a waitress walked over to the table.

"How are you today, Casper?"

"Marie, if I was any better, there'd be two of me. Two glasses of red, I'll have my usual and better get a menu for my friend here."

"I'll be back with that wine right away."

He watched her as she made her way to the bar then shook his head. "Nice hard-working girl," he said. I figured she was mid-forties. "Has a lovely daughter, special needs I guess it's called these days. Poor Marie works so hard," he said and shook his head. "So, you said you wanted to discuss Seymour Smeelie."

"Yes, I've spoken, or actually attempted to speak with a number of individuals who have invested in a variety of his opportunities over the years," I emphasized the word opportunities to suggest anything but. Marie returned with two glasses of wine, in my estimation filled way more than what would be normal. She set a menu down in front of me.

"To be honest, Casper. You're the only person who agreed to speak with me. Some people hung up as soon as I mentioned Smeelie's name. A number said they were glad he got what was coming to him. One woman told me Smeelie gave her husband a heart attack, and whoever killed him should be given a medal."

Casper laughed at that last line and raised his glass in a toast. "May the bastard roast in hell," he said, smiled, and took a sip. I did the same.

"Do you recommend anything in particular?" I asked, looking at the open menu but not really reading it.

"I'm partial to the garlic pasta. A warning, they give me a triple dose of garlic. Good for the heart," he said and took another sip.

"I'll go for that. The triple dose sounds good."

"Are you meeting with anyone else this afternoon?"

"No, like I said, you were the only one who agreed to talk to me."

He smiled and said, "Okay, then the triple garlic will be okay, as long as you don't have anything scheduled. After lunch, I'll go back home and work. I have them tone down the garlic if I've got an afternoon meeting scheduled."

"What is it that you do?" I asked, expecting Casper to tell me he was retired

"What do I do," he said and got a faraway look in his eyes. He seemed to think for a long moment and then looked at me. "Let's just say I work on financial things."

"You're an accountant?"

He shook his head. "No, nothing like that. You give me too much credit. I came from a working-class family. The old man went off to the Second World War back in '43. My mom raised us for the next three years until my dad returned. He started taking night classes through the GI Bill, got a pretty decent job with a plumbing company that went on to grow into a commercial construction firm. I went to college for a semester, hated it, drafted in '58, did two years, came out, and started a little painting business. Did pretty well at it, too. I had eight employees, along with working myself and doing the books at night. We did a lot of work for the old man's firm along with some others. I was able to set money aside, and I was aware of Seymour Smeelie and his projects."

Actually, his first two or three projects were successful. You know that string of four three-story structures along West Seventh, buff-colored bricks with black trim?"

"River View Terrace or something like that?" I said.

"Yeah, that's the name. He did those, nice buildings, profitable. I think they were his first project. Did another one out in the Phalen Park area of town, again a decent profitable project. Another one after that on the Eastside, same thing, profitable. I've just described maybe ten or eleven years. Then in 1996, he's doing a project over in the Midway area. I begged him to let me invest. He didn't know me, but he'd heard of my old man and knew he had some influence. So, he let me in on the deal."

"How much we talking?" I asked.

"Fifty Grand. I had to remortgage our house to get the money, but it was such a sure thing I knew it was worth it. Of course, the rug got pulled out from underneath us a year later. The plan was to build all sorts of residential units along Energy Park Drive. The project was called Central City something or other."

"But Energy Park Drive is all industrial," I said.

"Exactly. Which is why the project ultimately fell through. Smeelie gets taken to court by the investors and says he'd love to pay us back, but the money supposedly went to cash upfront expenses, and as much as we lost, he lost a hundred times that and since it was an LLC, he wasn't liable anyway."

"So, you lost fifty grand?"

"In a manner of speaking. I go to the guy, make up a line that he'll never do another project again in the state, and throw around my old man's name. Low and behold, I get his attention. He tells me he can't pay back the fifty grand. I make a couple of other suggestions we don't really need to go into, and he finally agrees to give me twenty cents on the dollar in a private agreement. I'm not happy, but I know it's all I'm going to get. He has his shyster attorney, a scrawny, crooked little bastard named Soapy McGriff, draw up the paperwork, and I walk out with ten grand cash."

I shook my head and said, "So you're still out forty grand. Why aren't you as pissed off as everyone else? Maybe even more so because I get the sense you know Smeelie is lying."

Casper smiled and said, "Call it one of life's little lessons. What's the old adage? Whenever one door closes, another door opens, Alexander Graham Bell, by the way. So I've got ten-grand cash. I know the wife is gonna kill me. I was fifty-nine years old, and I'm thinking, what the hell am I gonna do? I heard about a little company out on the west coast that's just about to go public, and their stock was priced at eighteen bucks a share. They had a profitable first year or maybe a couple of years; I can't remember now. Anyway, my back is up against the wall. I throw another five grand from my retirement account on top of the ten and invest fifteen grand in the company. Literally, about all the money I had. In fact, that five grand was set aside to pay for our daughter's wedding. So it was one hell of a big gamble. I got about eight hundred shares."

"So, you must have eventually made your money back."

"Yeah, something like that. It's worked out pretty well for us."

"What was the company?"

"You ever hear of Amazon?"

"You have eight hundred shares of Amazon?" I said, not meaning to say it so loud. Two guys at the next table glanced over at us.

"No, I've increased my shares every ninety days for the past almost twenty-five years."

"How many shares do you have now?"

He shook his head. "Let's just say the wife and I are in a very good position, all the grandkids have been to college, and we're happy. But my point is, if Seymour Smeelie had been successful with the Central City project, I would never have invested in Amazon. Never would have taken the chance. So, I can't complain."

Marie suddenly appeared with two bowls of pasta that reeked of garlic. She set Casper's down first and then mine. She stepped aside, and a young girl placed a basket of bread and a small bottle of olive oil on the table.

"Can I get you anything else, Casper?" Marie asked.

"Mmm-mmm," Casper said and swallowed. "Thanks, but this is perfect. Dev?"

"More than enough for me, thank you."

She smiled and disappeared. We ate in silence for a couple of minutes and then I asked Casper, "What was the attorney's name you mentioned? Soapy?"

He nodded and swallowed. "Yeah, Leon 'Soapy' McGriff. Little bastard, I'm not sure that he's even five feet tall. He's been the real brains behind Smeelie's operations. Keeps a very low profile. Has a muscle-bound numbskull that drives him around by the name of Bumpy. Scary looking bastard."

"What's your relationship with this McGriff character?"

"Relationship? There isn't one. Suffice it to say, I'm more than well-funded enough to have him blown out of the water should I so choose. He knows that and stays away, and I don't want anything to do with him, or by extension, his muscle man, Bumpy.

We chatted for another fifteen minutes, covering general things regarding Seymour Smeelie. Nothing new was really added to what I had already learned. Seymour was a bit player for this Leon 'Soapy' McGriff character. I'd have to do some serious digging. At some point, it was clear Casper had nothing more to say to me, and he smiled and said, "I've enjoyed meeting and talking with you, Dev. If I can be of any other help, please let me know. I wish you all success and hope, if your client is indeed innocent, that she is ultimately set free. If she is found guilty, know she has the indebted thanks of a number of people."

We shook hands, and I made my way out of the Cherokee Tavern. When I reached the door, I gave a quick glance back. Casper was on his feet, chatting with a couple at a nearby table. It looked like there were three other tables hoping to get his attention on his way out.

Twenty-one

I slid behind the wheel, pulled out my cell, and phoned Louie. "Hi Dev," was how he answered.

"Hey, Louie. You still over at the U?"

"Yeah, been here for a couple of hours going through case studies. You talk to Brianna yet?"

"No, that's my next stop. Did you see her this morning?"

"Yeah."

"And?"

"I don't know, man. There's an attitude there that is not going to help her when she makes an appearance before a judge. She's arrogant, not really interested in listening, and has absolutely no clue as to what she's facing. She remains her own worst enemy."

"Was she surprised to see you?"

"Funny thing. I got the distinct impression she viewed me as some idiot boyfriend who had come crawling back to beg forgiveness. Our meeting only lasted a few minutes. I do have an idea, however."

"What's that? I'm all ears."

"I've spoken to a couple of pals, and they're on board, so hopefully, you will be too."

"I guess that depends on what it is, exactly."

"I've got their names here, three of them. When you see her this afternoon, tell her I'm off the case. Give her the names of these three guys. She can call them, tell them her story, and try to hire them. They'll tell her no, and, after three rejections maybe, just maybe, she'll get back to you, and you can try to set her straight. Let her know she has to start listening to us and keep her damn mouth shut. Otherwise, she is going to do some real damage to herself."

"Is that even legal?"

"Right now, I'm of the opinion if she doesn't shut up so we can get her out of there, she's going to do nothing but create a team of witnesses who will eagerly testify she said she wanted to kill Seymour Smeelie. Like I said, she's her own worst enemy."

Unfortunately, I couldn't disagree. "Yeah, go ahead and give me the names, Louie," I said and pulled a pen from the console and began writing on the back of an envelope as Louie gave me the three names and phone numbers. They all sounded familiar, but I didn't think I'd ever met any of them.

Once Louie finished, he said, "Did you learn anything this morning?"

"Yes and no."

"Care to be a little more specific?"

"Two things. First, at no surprise, the laundry list of former investors in various Seymour Smeelie projects had no problems telling me they were glad he was dead.

One woman told me he gave her husband a heart attack and whoever killed him deserved a medal. A number of them hung up on me the moment I mentioned Smeelie's name. Not very happy people, that was for sure. I did talk to one guy— fella by the name of Casper Worthington. To make a long story short, twenty-some years ago, he got screwed by Smeelie on a project, just like everyone else. The difference is, it served as a warning to him and, suffice it to say, through another investment, luck, and incredible timing, I'd guess he's sitting on more money than he ever dreamed possible. More importantly, he told me that Smeelie was working as a pawn for some lowlife attorney named Leon McGriff. Ring any bells?"

"You mean Soapy McGriff? Yeah, it rings a bell, a warning bell."

"You know the guy?"

"Only by reputation, which is not good. I've seen him from a distance a couple times. Very short, can't be more than maybe five feet, at the most."

"Casper said he was under five feet."

"Yeah, quite possibly. He never seems to be out of sight of a muscular thug that follows him around. Actually, the guy serves as his driver, and I'm willing to bet, somewhat of an enforcer."

"That sounds like the guy Casper referred to as Bumpy. Big, muscular guy with a shaved head that has a number of scars."

"Yeah, that description fits. And Smeelie was involved with McGriff?"

"That's what Casper said. His exact description was that Smeelie worked as a pawn for McGriff."

"See what you can find out about that, but watch yourself. You're heading into the darker regions of the underworld."

"I might have a contact there."

"Don't tell me," Louie said.

"Yeah, Tubby Gustafson. I know you don't like him, hell, neither do I, but he's got a ton of information on the darker aspects of the city. It's just getting him to share it that makes things more difficult than they need to be."

"Well, watch yourself. And don't forget to share those names with Brianna. God, a classic case of someone who's attractive until you get to know her, and then you want to make tracks in the opposite direction."

Once Louie hung up, I debated calling Taffy. Ultimately, I decided I'd maybe just leave that alone. I had the sense another phone call from me would be like prodding a lion or in this case, a lioness. I turned the key in the ignition of the Dart a few times. It started on the third try. I was about to pull away from the curb when Casper Worthington stepped out of the Cherokee Tavern and headed up the street. He didn't have to walk very far. He stepped off the sidewalk and opened the driver's door on a white luxury sedan of some sort. Even parked at the curb, the thing looked like it was traveling at the speed of light. It had a streamlined front bumper, headlights angled for minimal wind resistance, sexy chrome rims.

Of course, there were about a dozen coats of wax on the thing. Casper backed up a few feet, and then suddenly he was in the street zipping past me. I watched in my sideview mirror as he shot down two blocks, made a left turn, and disappeared. I decided I needed to find out whatever the next Amazon was and invest in it.

Twenty-two

I pulled into the potholed parking lot across the street from the police station and surprisingly found a parking place. I headed into the main lobby. Fortunately, the Sergeant behind the desk was someone I knew.

"Hey, Gary, how's it going?" I said.

He looked up from a stack of files, and his frown turned into a grin. "Hi ya, Dev. You here to see Lieutenant LaZelle?"

"No, as a matter of fact, I'm not."

"Well, good, cause he ain't here. What can I do for you?"

"I'm actually here to see a woman by the name of Brianna Di Salvo. She's being held prior to her hearing regarding the murder of Seymour Smeelie."

He chuckled for a moment. "Funny, we've gotten two calls this morning from people wanting to contribute to her bail fund."

"She has a bail fund?"

"Not as far as we know. But these folks wanted to contribute. We told them we had no knowledge of anything like that. Hopefully, there isn't one set up. It would be bad press if there is and we didn't know about it."

"Well, I'm doing some investigating on Mr. Smeelie, and I recently spoke to the attorney representing her. Neither one of us knows anything about a bail fund. Sounds like some internet bullshit."

"You got me. So you want to speak with her?"

"Yeah. Just a couple of quick items. A visitation booth would work. I don't need an interview room."

"That'll make it easier. Why don't you take a seat, I'll get you lined up."

"Gary, can you help me here? I've got this list of three different attorneys I'd like to give to Miss Di Salvo. Can you see that she gets it?" I said and took the envelope with the lawyers' names out of my pocket.

"I'll give this to the appropriate staff, and they'll deal with it," he said, taking the envelope. I was seated on an uncomfortable plastic chair for the better part of a half-hour before an officer finally called my name. I hurried over to him. He was uniformed, black, about a foot taller than me, without an ounce of fat on him. "Mr. Haskell?" he asked as I approached.

"Yeah, that's me."

"Follow me, please," he said. I followed him down a short hallway to a booth that looked like one of the TSA scanning booths at the airport. "Empty your pockets please," he said and pointed to a gray plastic tray. I pulled out my car keys and my wallet. He placed the tray on a counter, and another officer put the tray on a shelf. "If you'd step inside, place your feet where indicated, and raise your arms."

I did that, and a moment later, the screen slid past, scanning me.

"Okay, step through to the other side," he said.

I did, and he led me to a door where he punched in a digital code. The door buzzed, the lock clicked, and he opened the door. I followed him down the hall. Another officer was standing by a door that required yet another digital code.

"This is Mr. Haskell to see Miss Di Salvo," my chaperone said.

The officer next to the door punched in a code. The door buzzed and unlocked. He opened the door for me and said, "Please take your seat, and Miss Di Salvo should be out momentarily."

"I can sit anywhere?"

"Position six, sir. When you're finished or your time expires, just press the buzzer next to the door. You have twenty minutes from the time she sits down," he said.

"Thank you," I said and headed to position six. The room was pretty much like you see in the movies— more or less private booths with what looked like a wall phone attached next to a glass panel. The glass appeared to be about two inches thick. The metal chair was bolted to the floor. When I sat down, the cold chair sent a shiver up my spine.

A minute or two later, Brianna was ushered in. I guessed she was probably the best-looking woman in an orange nylon jumpsuit in the place. That said, she did not look happy. The jumpsuit appeared to be a couple of sizes too big and disguised her gorgeous figure. There was a zipper down the front that was open, maybe just a couple of inches. A nine-digit number was stenciled in black over the left breast. I couldn't see Brianna's back from where I sat, but I knew the stencil on the back said, 'Property of Ramsey County Detention.'

A female officer pointed at the chair and said something like sit down, although I couldn't hear her. Brianna wasn't handcuffed, and once she sat down, she brushed her greasy hair back with both hands and picked up the phone from the wall.

I picked up the phone on my side and said, "How's it going, Brianna?"

"Dev," she said as her eyes began to water and a tear ran down each cheek. "Dev, get me the hell out of here. I just want to go home. Please. I can't stand it here. I'm scared to death. The food is dreadful. I'll need a long hot shower and a full day at the spa just to decontaminate. You can't believe the riffraff in this place, complete trash."

"I'm working on getting you out, Brianna. I left a note for you with one of the guards. Actually, it's on the back of an envelope."

"Directions for an escape?" she only half-joked and then had to bite her lower lip to stop from crying.

"No, sorry to say. It has the names and phone numbers of three attorneys. Give them a call and get one of them to take your case."

"Attorneys? Are you kidding me? So that fat guy really dumped me? He was here for just a minute this morning."

"You mean, Louie. I'm going to talk to him, but I gotta tell you, Brianna. No one needs the abuse. He—"

"Abuse? Look around, Dev. I'm the one who's locked up in this God-forsaken hell hole. I'm the one who's innocent here. I didn't do anything, and they've still locked me up in here. God only knows what disease I'll contract from this ridiculous outfit they've forced me to wear." She pulled at the collar, sniffed at a sleeve, and actually shuddered.

"I tell you, if I could get my hands on Seymour—"

"Stop right there, Brianna. Don't say it."

"But, Dev—"

"Damn it, will you just listen for once? I got news for you. No one cares how beautiful you are. You're in the damn jail now, and the reason you're here is because you won't shut the hell up. Yesterday you damn near told the cops you were guilty."

She looked like she was about to say something, but I held up my left hand to stop her. "No, I don't want to hear it— the one guy who can get you out of here. The one guy who could have had you home yesterday was Louie Laufen. But you didn't want to listen. You wanted to bitch and complain and in so many words tell him that you knew all about it and he, the attorney trying his damnedest to represent you, didn't know shit. Take a look around. How is that working out?"

"But I shouldn't be in here."

"That's right. But you are in here because you didn't listen to the guy who knows how to work this, and you left him with no choice but to throw up his hands and walk away. Call those other attorneys on the list and then get in touch with me to let me know which one is taking your case. I'll have information for them."

"Information? What kind of information?"

I shook my head no.

"Dev, come on. What have you found out?"

"Only that your Florida boyfriend screwed a lot of people. I'm still working on it. When I have something solid, I'll let your attorney know. In the meantime, I want you to repeat a thousand times that the only way you're going to get out of here is to keep your mouth shut. Understand?"

"Dev, I just want to go home," she said, and a tear ran down her right cheek.

I really felt sorry for her, but she had to shut the hell up. "Just remember, do not talk to anyone in here, and that includes the other women locked up. And then call me with the name of your new attorney. Now, don't say a thing, and just nod that you understand."

She bit her lower lip, nodded, and another tear ran down her cheek.

"Call me later today," I said and stood up from the chair.

She looked like she wanted to say something but thankfully didn't. I walked over to the door and pressed the buzzer. There were two uniformed officers at either end of the room, and they both watched me until the door opened, and I stepped into the hallway. I glanced over my shoulder, and Brianna was being escorted out by the female officer. The tall black officer was standing in the hallway.

"Hope you didn't have to wait too long," I said.

He didn't give a reaction and said, "Please follow me." We stopped at the counter where I picked up my car keys and wallet, and he led me out to the central lobby. He opened the security door, and I stepped into the lobby.

He gave me a perfunctory nod and quickly closed the security door behind him.

I walked over to the counter where Gary was still working his way through the stack of files. From what I could tell, he hadn't made any progress, but maybe someone had just piled more files on his desk. "Good to see you again, Gary. Stay safe."

He looked up and smiled. "I passed your note on to the powers that be. Miss Di Salvo should be getting it shortly. I'll catch you at The Spot sometime for pay-ment."

"Thanks, much appreciated. I owe you a cold one."

Twenty-three

I pulled out of the police station parking lot, dodging a number of potholes. Then, against my better judgment, I headed toward Tubby Gustafson's house. Tubby is our local crime lord, and for some strange reason I can't understand, he took an interest in me some years back. I can't say it's been a positive experience, actually far from it. But on one or two rare occasions, things seemed to work to my benefit. I was hoping for another rare occasion to happen this afternoon. Nonetheless, I took the long route to Tubby's. I arrived a lot sooner than I expected and still hadn't the faintest idea of what I was going to say.

Tubby's mansion is surrounded by an eight-foot-high brick wall. The entrance gate is wrought iron with security cameras focused not only on the gate, but the circular drive leading up to the mansion and the grounds as well. As far as I knew, some thug was watching all the screens twenty-four hours a day, seven days a week.

I pulled my car up to the gate, got out, and pressed the button on the speaker.

"Yeah," was the grouchy response I got, and whoever it was, that was probably their positive side.

"Hi, my name is Dev Haskell. I'm here to hopefully see Mr. Gustafson. I do not have an appointment," I said then smiled into the camera.

"Let me check."

Some minutes later, a familiar crabby voice boomed out of the speaker. "I should have known, Haskell. The day was going wonderfully up until a moment ago. I'm right in the middle of something. What do you want?"

"Hi, Tub— err, Mr. Gustafson. I was hoping you could provide me with some background information on a local lawyer who seems to be involved in a lot of, umm, different investment opportunities."

There was a long pause before Tubby said, "Thinking of trying to make something of yourself? Looking to upgrade your bottom of the barrel status?"

"No, sir, nothing like that. It's actually regarding a client of mine. She's been arrested for a murder. She claims she's innocent, and—"

"Haskell, everyone claims they're innocent. Don't tell me you believe her. Let me guess, did she murder her husband?"

"No, sir, actually a guy she had a relationship with. He owed her some money, ten grand to be exact. The thing is, the more I find out about this guy, the longer the list grows of people who are delighted to have him dead. I just don't think she did it."

"So, what makes you think I can help?"

"The guy did a number of real estate projects that always seemed to have the rug pulled out from under them, and the investors were always left high and dry."

"Please tell me you're not referring to a gentleman by the name of Seymour Smeelie."

"Actually, sir, that's exactly who I'm referring to. Well, him and then an attorney by the name of—"

"Soapy McGriff," Tubby interrupted, finishing my sentence for me.

"Yes, sir, exactly."

"Lord knows I'm going to regret this. Why do I even bother? All right, come in, God help me," Tubby said, sounding very disappointed. The iron gate suddenly began to slide open.

I hopped back in my car and drove up the large circular drive. The gate closed about fifteen seconds after it opened. There was actually a parking area for a half-dozen cars up by Tubby's mansion. There was only one open spot. I pulled in between a black Dodge Charger and a red Chevy Camaro SS. Both vehicles appeared absolutely spotless. As I parked between them, my pea-soup green Dodge Dart looked even worse than normal.

There was no point in locking my car. Certainly no one here would lower themselves to steal it. I headed towards the two thugs leaning against the wall on either side of the front door. They were both laughing, and one of them made a comment I didn't quite hear, which brought on more laughter. As I drew closer, one of them said, "Nice set of wheels, Haskell. Who did you piss off that's making you drive that thing?" That brought on another round of laughter.

"Mr. Gustafson is expecting me inside."

"Yeah, so we heard. He's in the library. You carrying?"

"No," I said as I shook my head. I stopped in front of them, stretched my arms out, and waited.

The guy who made the comment about my car waved a wand over me, checking for any metal object. He set the wand down on the windowsill then scrunched down and did a hand pat of my ankles and legs. "Good to go, Teddy," he said to his partner, who opened the door for me.

I stepped inside, and a bearded guy working a crossword puzzle in the newspaper gave me a look like I was interrupting and said, "You Haskell?"

"Yeah, Mr. Gustafson is expecting me."

He stood, tossed the paper on the chair, and said, "Follow me." We headed across the large formal entry, past the staircase and the framed painting of Tubby looking somewhat respectable in front of a fireplace, holding a number of documents. A fictional painting, if ever there was one.

We walked down a hallway to the third door, and the guy knocked on it. I'd been here a number of times and happened to know the room was the library and served as Tubby's office, although a good deal of the activity in the room had nothing to do with business.

As soon as he knocked, Tubby shouted, "Enter."

The guy opened the door, and as he nodded at me to enter, he said, "Here's Haskell, sir." As soon as I stepped into the room, he closed the door behind me.

Tubby was stretched out on a brown leather recliner. He was barefoot and clad in his silk paisley robe that he was just cinching closed. Two rather attractive Asian women were attending to him. One was seated at the base of the recliner, carefully filing his toenails. The other sat off to the side, applying a coat of clear polish to the nails on his right hand. Both women wore white lab coats, and from the little I could determine, nothing else.

Tubby had a white linen towel of some sort draped over his eyes. He didn't bother to remove the towel. Instead, he said, "All right, Haskell, tell me what you know about Soapy McGriff."

"To be honest, sir, at this stage, not much. I know he's an attorney, has a rather large driver by the name of Bumpy, who seems to be within just a few feet of Mr. McGriff at all times. The thing that got my attention is I was hearing rumors that Seymour Smeelie was nothing more than a front person or a pawn for McGriff. Logically, I wondered, with your knowledge of the business world in this town, if you might be able to shed any light on the subject."

Neither woman reacted. Tubby kept the towel covering his eyes. He gave a sigh and shook his head slightly. "Haskell, any fool knows that Soapy McGriff is the brains behind the various investment schemes that Smeelie has presented over the past twenty or so years.

Far from being failures, they were works of genius, huge returns for a limited amount of work, and all perfectly legal. Clearly, he has contacts within the city administration. Things were working wonderfully until Smeelie decided he didn't need Soapy's input any longer. Wrong guy to tangle with, and Smeelie quickly found himself in over his head. I have it on good authority that Smeelie signed everything on his current project over to Soapy and that shortly after that, someone killed Smeelie. You beginning to see any kind of pattern here?"

"It sounds to me like your accusing Soapy McGriff of murdering Seymour Smeelie."

Tubby kept the cloth over his eyes and slowly clapped his hands together. "Brilliant, absolutely brilliant," he said. When he had finished clapping, the woman sitting at his side took hold of his right hand and quickly ran a brush over each fingernail.

"Do you know any of the details in the project Smeelie signed over to Soapy McGriff, sir?"

"Not specifically, I've always done my utmost to stay a good distance from the two of them. At the end of the day, they were bound to do one of two things, get caught or screw the pooch. Either way, I thought it best not to be associated with them. This latest project, Environmentally Friendly Homes, or EFH as it's known, had upwards of six hundred investors. They promised returns of nine percent by 2018. To date, no one has been paid a nickel, and they never will be."

"So what does Soapy McGriff get by gaining control of the EFH headache?"

"Soapy gets a clean slate, along with acres and acres of property on the old Cummins factory site. In short, millions, and all the debt remains with Seymour or, in this instance, Seymour's estate. No, it was a good move on Soapy's part. Seymour got overly greedy, and Soapy played him to the hilt."

"Do you think Soapy killed him?"

Tubby pulled the towel from his eyes. "What is it with you, Haskell? Should I get some coloring crayons and draw you a simple picture? I would say anyone with any knowledge would have Soapy at the front of the line. But then, luckily for Soapy, there's someone who apparently is doing just about everything in her power to be accused of the crime."

"That would be my client."

"Yes, of course, at no surprise, Miss Di Salvo."

I nodded.

"Word to the wise, Haskell. Drop her like a hot potato. From what my sources tell me she's her own worst enemy."

I nodded and said, "Well, I want to thank you for your time and, of course, the information, sir. I guess I'll be heading out and—"

"Just hold on there a minute, Haskell. Not so fast. Nothing in life is free. I could use a little favor from you."

"A favor, sir. From me?"

Tubby smiled. "Not to worry. It's just a small favor."

Common sense told me there was no such thing as a small favor where Tubby Gustafson was concerned. "Um, happy to help, sir. What exactly did you have in mind?"

"That's the spirit. When you talk with Soapy McGriff, and I know you will, Haskell. It would be nice if you could get a copy of the EFH contract that he had Smeelie sign, turning over all the rights and none of the debt, to Soapy."

"I think there's an awfully good chance that's going to be privileged information, sir. I would have to think that would be almost impossible to—"

"Please don't attempt to think. It never seems to work out where you're concerned. That's exactly why I was asking you, Haskell. Asking you nicely, I hasten to add. But silly me, that never seems to work when you're involved, so I'll just tell you. If you approach this as if your life depended on it, I've no doubt you'll be successful." He paused to let that sink in. "I think you're done here. You've taken up way more of my time than I expected. I'd say that it's been a pleasure, but then we both know better than that. Now, if you'll excuse me, I have to get back to the business at hand." With that, he nodded at the towel resting on his chest. The woman working on his right hand smiled, refolded the towel, and carefully draped it over Tubby's eyes. As she stood, her lab coat failed to cover appropriately. She strutted to the other side of the chair and began to gently file the fingernails on Tubby's left hand.

"You may go now, Haskell, and quickly," Tubby said from beneath the cloth over his eyes.

"Just one more quick little question, sir, I—"

"Silencio!" Tubby shouted. "Get the hell out of my sight, now!"

"Thank you, sir," I said, seeing no point in pointing out he had the towel covering his eyes. I hurried out of the room before my life became any more complicated.

"All finished?" the guy with the crossword puzzle asked. He tossed the newspaper on the chair as he stood. A quick glance at the paper suggested he hadn't made any progress on the crossword puzzle since the last time I saw him.

Twenty-four

arla Quinn couldn't find a parking place in the lot and drove back out onto the street. By the time she found a parking place, she was two blocks away from W.A. Frost's, the trendy St. Paul restaurant. No doubt she'd be the last one in, and her three girlfriends would just love to give her the needle. They'd met in high school, now more than thirty years ago. They still got together two or three times a year, although Carla was the last one still living in the city. The other three fled with their families to the suburbs. Not that Carla could blame them, between the rising crime rate, property taxes increasing five to ten percent every year, streets not plowed properly, she could go on and on, but there was no point.

She locked the car, slung her purse over her shoulder, and hurried up the street to Frost's. It was turning into a windy evening, and a threat of rain later tonight was in the forecast. She walked with her head down, and her eyes focused on the sidewalk in front of her.

Suddenly, there was another pair of feet. Black Adidas, would be all she could remember. That and the little dog.

She was punched on the side of her face, hard. The black eye would arrive in less than thirty minutes. She fell to her knees, and whoever it was scooped up her purse and was about to head down the street when the barking began.

It was a little dog, fuzzy and white. It barked and growled, and suddenly a male voice shouted, "Shut the hell up," and kicked the dog. There was a high-pitched squeal, but by the time Carla regained her senses, neither the little dog nor her purse were anywhere to be seen.

All she could tell the police was that the person who stole her purse was male, wearing black Adidas and that a little white dog had been barking and he kicked the dog before he ran away. Her friends all piled into Mary Anne's car and took her down to the ER. They waited for two and a half hours to be told nothing was broken, and when she arrived home, she should take two Ibuprofen. They all ended up in Carla's living room, ordering take-out, calling friends and drinking four bottles of wine over the course of the next three hours, after which her friends fled back to the suburbs.

Twenty-five

Louie and I compared notes later that evening. I told him about Smeelie's last fiasco, EFH, and the promise of a nine percent return by 2018 that never happened. Not only was Louie not surprised, his response was, "Typical. Smeelie has one failure after another for the past fifteen plus years, and there's a line of greedy fools waving their wallets and begging him to take their money. There's a vicious part of me that wants to scream, 'You got what you deserved. Namely, a big fat nothing.'"

"Yeah, but from the way Tubby told it, that was the plan from the get-go. Smeelie talked a good game, but he never, ever intended to pay anyone. That has always been the modus operandi, and with Smeelie dead, Soapy McGriff ends up with the property, and somehow none of the debt. There will probably not be anything built on that site in the next ten years, and at some point, Soapy will sell it for millions. Once again, the little guy, the taxpayer, gets screwed. I gotta tell you, Louie, this whole thing is starting to piss me off. Meanwhile, Brianna is locked up in an orange nylon jumpsuit. What the hell is wrong with the world?"

Louie scoffed and said, "How much time you got? We could discuss that point all day and never come up with an answer. May I suggest one thing?"

"Yeah, what's that?"

"You should see if you could talk to Soapy McGriff at his office. It's downtown in the American Bank Building."

"Why would I want to do that?"

"Just to get the measure of the man."

"I've got his measure. The guy is pure scum."

"Okay, just saying. You talked with Brianna?"

"Yeah, and I gave your list of attorney names to her. Actually, I gave them to a guy I know at the front desk, and he said he would get them to her. That's one very unhappy lady right now. She's in one of those orange nylon jumpsuits. Her hair needs washing. In a way, it was almost funny if it wasn't so sad."

"Well, hopefully, after making the calls and getting turned down by all three lawyers, she'll finally get the message to shut the hell up. She's got a two o'clock hearing tomorrow afternoon. With any luck, we'll post bail, and she'll sleep in her own bed tomorrow night. Alone," he added as an afterthought.

"You know who's on the bench tomorrow?" I asked, ignoring that last comment.

"No, I'll check it out tomorrow morning. Maybe we pay Brianna a visit later in the morning. All three will have rejected her by then. If she hasn't learned her lesson at that point, she's not going to."

"You'll represent her either way?"

"Yeah, I will, and as I said, with any luck, she'll be home tomorrow afternoon."

We hung up. I grabbed a handful of dog biscuits and stepped outside to check on Morton. He was out there with his four pals. They were lying in the far corner of the backyard, grabbing the last vestige of sun. I walked towards them, holding a dog biscuit in my hand. The Shepherd raised his head, but he didn't jump up. He watched me, or maybe he was just focused on the dog biscuit. I couldn't really tell. I walked up to about a ten-foot distance and tossed the biscuit to the Shepherd. I took a couple more steps and tossed one to the Border Collie, two more steps, and I tossed one to the Lab. I was now standing right next to them, and no one had made a move toward the fence. I dropped one in front of the fuzzy little white dog and then handed one to Morton. I stood there for a long moment. None of them seemed to mind, but I decided to head back to the house before I wore out my welcome. I picked up the three saucepans and took them inside. I refilled the one with water and placed it back outside. I refilled the other two pans with more food and set them on the kitchen counter for the morning.

Two hours later, I went out to call Morton in. He looked at me but didn't move. I debated walking over and dragging him back inside then decided against it. I'd give Morton a night with his pals and made a mental note to check with the rescue folks tomorrow. Obviously, they were strays. Maybe we could find four people willing to take them in.

It was a little after midnight when the thunder woke me. I was about to drift back to sleep when I remembered Morton was still outside. I slipped on my boxers and hurried downstairs as another blast of thunder rumbled through the house. I opened the backdoor, and Morton hurried in, followed by the Border Collie, who brushed me aside, and then the Shepherd who did the same. The fuzzy little white guy hurried in, followed by the black Lab. Morton headed into the far corner of the kitchen, and the others followed, each one stretching out on the floor. More thunder rumbled outside, and the rain started to pour down a moment later. I couldn't bring myself to kick them out. I placed the saucepans filled with dog food on top of the refrigerator, closed the door to the kitchen, and went back up to bed.

I was up early the next morning. I grabbed a shower and headed downstairs. I opened the kitchen door, and the Lab and Shepherd raised their heads but remained on the floor. I turned on the coffee pot and my computer and pretended to ignore them. After maybe two minutes, they seemed to doze off.

I studied the Shepherd. At first, I thought he might have brought a stick into the house, but on closer examination, it looked like he had a prosthesis on his leg. The thing appeared to be maybe four or five inches long. No stray dog has a prosthesis. A German Shepherd with an artificial limb? He almost had to be ex-military. Maybe trained in rescue or bomb detection. I wanted to get a closer look, but I didn't want to disturb him.

Forty-five minutes later, they began to wake up. The storm had passed, and it was a warm, sunny morning. I left the backdoor open, and over the course of the next ten minutes, they all made their way out into the backyard. Once they were outside, I quickly mopped the kitchen floor and carried the two saucepans of dog food into the backyard. I dumped the water pan, filled it with fresh water, and set it out next to the food. I went back inside and did some more research on Soapy McGriff.

Twenty-six

Leon 'Soapy' McGriff was fifty-seven years old and originally from the Chicago area. He graduated from Northwestern University, attended law school at the University of Minnesota, where he graduated fifty-fourth in his class. According to the online biography, he never joined a law firm. Instead, upon graduation, he started his own firm, servicing just one client, namely himself, Leon 'Soapy' McGriff. Almost immediately, he began acquiring properties and flipping them. Over the past thirty years, he had appeared no less than three different times in front of the Minnesota Bar Association, the defendant in disbarment procedures. He came away victorious all three times. His last appearance had been in 2011. From the laundry list of people he'd sued over the years, one would guess there were quite a few homes in town where he would not be welcome.

There was no mention of EFH, nor of Seymour Smeelie. His office, just as Louie had said, was listed as being in the American Bank Building. I decided to follow Louie's advice and pay him a visit.

I stepped outside and checked on Morton and his friends. The Lab and the fuzzy little white guy were at the food dishes. The Border Collie was pushing the orange tennis ball around the edge of the yard with his nose. Morton was playing the part of the perfect host, lying in the sun with the German Shepherd. I walked toward Morton, and the Shepherd's head was immediately up, but he didn't move. I gave Morton a rub behind the ears and told him to behave. I studied the prosthesis on the Shepherd for a long moment. He stared at me for a bit and then apparently decided that I was okay, or he simply didn't care. Either way, he lowered his head, took a deep breath, and closed his eyes. After a minute or two, I headed out to my car and downtown.

The American Bank building no longer houses a bank and hasn't for at least twenty years. I parked in a ramp across the street and down a block and walked back to the building. Today, the building consists of six floors of offices with a small coffee shop on the ground floor. Soapy McGriff's office was listed as, "Leon McGriff 515," on the framed roster hanging on the wall next to the elevators. No mention of him being an attorney or a scammer. I took the elevator up to the fifth floor.

I stepped off the elevator and into a nondescript pale-gray hall with gray floor tiles. There wasn't so much as a phone ringing or a voice coming from behind the doors up and down the hall. If you didn't know, you'd swear the entire floor was empty. The doors to the offices had the office numbers in black letters and nothing else. No company or firm names, no wall-mounted plastic holder with brochures, just the office number. 515 was halfway down the hall.

I stopped and stood for a long moment straining my ears. I didn't hear a thing, so I placed my ear against the entrance to McGriff's office. I still couldn't hear anything. Just as I pressed my ear a little more firmly against the door, it suddenly swung open, and a young woman about to step out half-screamed, "Oh my God." I stumbled a couple of steps toward her and into the office before I caught myself. She was blonde, nice looking, had sparkling white teeth, and a shocked look on her face.

It was a toss-up as to which one of us was more surprised. Fortunately, she had the common sense to step to the side and let the fool, namely me, bumble into the office. "Oh, man, I'm sorry. I wasn't sure there was anyone in here," I said. Just as a very large figure with a shaved head, no neck, and wearing a black suit stepped out of an office door looking ready to kill— Bumpy, in the flesh, muscle-bound and looking very unhappy.

"I, I was hoping I might be able to meet with Mr. McGriff," I said, keeping one eye on scary looking Bumpy. "Unfortunately, I don't have an appointment." She seemed too shocked to answer for a moment. "Is Mr. McGriff available?" I asked.

"Oh, sorry, you just surprised me. He is here, but I know he's very busy. What's this concerning?"

"It concerns a gentleman by the name of Seymour Smeelie."

"Oh, I see," she said, suddenly sounding a lot more guarded.

At the sound of Smeelie's name, the thug headed toward me. "What do you want?"

"Mr. McGriff?" I said and held my hand out to shake, even though I knew he wasn't McGriff.

He looked like he was going to slap my hand away but then changed his mind at the last second. His eyes were dark brown, and the bridge of his nose had a large bump that suggested he could perhaps be difficult at times, if not all the time. The black hair on his large head was no more than a thirty-second of an inch long and only served to accentuate a number of scars across his skull. Probably all from various differing opinions or possibly playing football without a helmet.

"Mr. McGriff ain't got time to see the likes of you today. Next time, call for a damn appointment. Now get—"

"That won't be necessary, Bumpy," a voice said from behind. Everyone turned, including me. I looked over and then down, and there he was, Soapy McGriff, in all his four foot eleven-inch glory.

He had dishwater blonde hair, close-cropped on the sides and no more than an inch long on top, with a razor-sharp part cut in on the left side. His eyes appeared to be a lifeless blue-gray, and his thin lips and skin were pale. He stepped around Bumpy, flashed a thin lipped smile, and held out his hand to shake. "Leon McGriff," he said. "And you are?"

"Pleased to meet you, Mr. McGriff. My name is Devlin Haskell," I said as we shook. At no surprise, his hand was small and soft, very soft, and very warm. A quick glance suggested he sported a manicure.

"I'm a private investigator, and I represent a client who was in a business relationship with a gentleman by the name of Seymour Smeelie."

"Ahh, yes, so sad, so very sad. Won't you step into my office, please?" he said, flashing a quick smile. He turned and headed back into his office. It was spacious with a thick, blue and red Persian rug on the floor. Dark oak wainscoting, maybe forty-eight inches high, offset all four walls. Wooden blinds drawn closed hung on all the windows. Heavy velvet drapes on either side of the windows were partially closed, placing the room in near-total darkness. Soapy stepped behind his desk, a heavily carved, antique piece of furniture with a gold embossed, black-leather top. He extended a hand toward a black leather client chair and said, "Please, take a seat."

Bumpy settled into a black leather couch in the back of the room and became lost in the shadows as if he'd entered a cave. A stained-glass lamp illuminated the desk, and I felt as though I was just outside the periphery of light. I began to take a seat and kept lowering myself further and further before my rear hit the actual seat. My shoulders appeared to be level with the top of the carved desk. Soapy settled into his desk chair then pressed a button that seemed to raise his chair four or five inches until he was looking down at me.

"So Seymour Smeelie and your client were in some kind of business relationship. Who, exactly, is your client?" Soapy asked.

"I'm afraid I'll have to claim client confidentiality."

"Not a problem, but I'm not too sure how I can help."

"My client feels she's owed some money by Mr. Smeelie and with his unfortunate passing she—"

"Would you happen to have a copy of her contractual arrangement with Mr. Smeelie?"

"I'm afraid I don't at this time."

"I see. Exactly which investment was she involved in?" Soapy asked. He forced his thin lips into a smile and suddenly leaned forward in what I could only describe as attack mode.

"Actually, it wasn't an investment per-say."

"Not an investment. No contractual agreement," he said, looking around and smiling. "I'm of the opinion there's really nothing further to discuss."

"My client has a number of receipts in her possession. All for items she purchased at the behest of Mr. Smeelie."

"And she has proof of this? Did Smeelie sign the receipts? Does she have a letter that states in some way, shape, or form he owes her this money? Because if she does, then she can get in line with the ever-growing list of individuals who feel they are owed some form of payment. Without the said document, my opinion is she has absolutely nothing to stand on. But then, let's be honest here, Mr. Hassle. I suspect you knew that before you came here. Why don't you level with me and tell me why you're really here?"

I thought about telling him I was just checking him out, wanted to see who Louie and I would be up against. But Soapy looked at me for a long moment, and then, just in case I had any doubts, he answered any questions I might have had. "Bumpy, would you please show Mr. Hassle that *shortcut* to the door."

"Actually, Mr. McGriff, I wanted to—" was all I got out before I was pulled up and out of the miniature chair by a massive paw on the back of my neck. Bumpy had a rock-solid clamp on my neck and moved me in the direction of the door. My feet didn't really touch the ground until he opened the door and shuttled me across the small lobby. As he opened the door, he kicked me so hard in the rear, he almost knocked the wind out of me, as the receptionist called, "Enjoy your day, sir."

Twenty-seven

My left butt cheek was throbbing as I rode the elevator down to the ground floor. Fortunately, I was the only one on the elevator so I could rub my rear in an effort to regain some circulation. I had no doubt Bumpy's size twelve shoe was going to leave one hell of a bruise. I got off the elevator and hurried into the coffee shop. I ordered an americano and asked nicely for a small plastic bag of ice. The woman behind the counter gave me a look, and I said. "I'm having a bout of sciatica, and I need to ice my lower back for a few minutes."

She nodded and said, "Oh, my husband has been dealing with that for the past ten years. Actually, his doctor recommends a heating pad and stretching exercises."

"That's what I intend to do as soon as I get home."

She nodded, filled a small plastic bag with ice cubes, and slid my coffee across the counter. I paid with a five-dollar bill and said, "Thanks, keep the change." She flashed an insincere smile, stuck the five in the cash drawer, and tossed fifteen cents into the tip jar.

I sat down in a chair near the front door with my back to the window. I slipped the bag of ice under my butt and took a sip of coffee. About five minutes later, the nice looking blonde receptionist from Soapy McGriff's office walked up to the counter and ordered a latte. I thought she hadn't noticed me, but as soon as the woman handed her the coffee, she turned and stepped over to my table.

"Would it be all right if I joined you?"

"Only if you promise not to tell Bumpy I'm down here."

She half-chuckled and said, "How's your ass?"

"I'm icing it as we speak if that tells you anything."

"Well, I've seen it get a lot worse."

"You seem reasonably sane, mind if I ask what you're doing there?"

"He's my uncle," she said and rolled her eyes. "So I work mornings five days a week and go to school in the afternoons."

"Your uncle is Bumpy?"

"No, thank God. Soapy, I mean Mr. McGriff."

"I think just about everyone in town calls him Soapy," I said. "I have to ask, what's it like working there?"

"Believe me, I'm painfully aware of my uncle's reputation. My mother, his sister, won't even talk to him. But, he basically pays my tuition. I'm finishing up a master's in education, and he and Bumpy serve as an added incentive for me to get that degree and a real job."

I held out my hand. "My name's Dev Haskell, by the way."

"Melinda Jensen," she said, and we shook. "Nice to meet you, actually interesting, I have to say," she said and laughed.

"Yeah, well, just a day in my life, I'm afraid."

"Sorry about that, but I think you're nice. Well, I should probably run. I'd better get back up there before Bumpy comes looking and sees me talking to you. Nice chatting," she said and stood.

"Hang on. You ever want to grab lunch, a dinner, or just a couple of drinks, give me a call," I said and pulled a business card from my wallet. I quickly checked the back of the card to make sure I hadn't written some woman's phone number on it and handed her the card. "Thanks for stopping, Melinda. Good luck with the rest of the morning."

She rolled her eyes, said, "Take care of that butt," and hurried out the door.

I watched her until she stepped onto the elevator and the door closed. I finished my coffee and headed out to my car, trying not to limp. Louie called before I got to my car.

"Where the hell are you?" Louie asked.

"I'm about to head to the office. I just finished paying Soapy McGriff a visit."

"How'd that go?"

"Literally, a pain in the ass."

"No surprise there. I'm on my way over to see Brianna. You want to meet me there?"

"Yeah, I can be there in about five minutes. You talk to her this morning?"

"No, I just called and set an appointment for ten-thirty. They'll have her in an interview room so we can get some privacy."

"Any word on the phone calls yesterday?"

"Oh, you mean for new representation? Yeah, I heard back from everyone. She was getting more desperate with each call. The last one she talked to, Ben Martinez, told me she was screaming and then crying into the phone. They all said they wouldn't have taken her case based on the brief introduction over the phone. If she does refuse my representation, she'll be assigned someone. I'm heading out the door now. I'll see you over there."

"I'll be waiting for you in the parking lot."

Twenty-eight

Amazingly, Louie pulled into the parking lot just after me. We climbed out of our respective vehicles and headed into the station to meet with Brianna.

Gary was seated at the front desk again, and he gave me a wave as we approached. "Hi, Dev, here to see Miss Di Salvo again?"

I nodded, and Louie said, "We are. I'm representing Miss Di Salvo, and we have an interview room set aside."

Gary looked at a clipboard hanging on the wall. "You're Mr. Laufen?"

Louie nodded and said, "Yes, and Mr. Haskell will be joining us."

"I'll give 'em the word," Gary said. "Why don't you grab a seat. Should only be a minute or two."

We headed over to a couple of plastic chairs and sat down. For the first time, I noticed Louie was wearing what looked like a pressed suit, no wrinkles, no food stains. The suit coat wasn't missing any buttons. "Louie, thanks for taking the price tags off that new suit coat."

"What?"

"A suit you haven't slept in. I just figured it had to be brand new."

"I thought it might be nice to dress appropriately if I was going to be representing my client in court this afternoon. Which reminds me, we're going to need an outfit for her to wear. Remember to see if you can get a key from her, so she's not standing there in front of the judge in that orange Ramsey County tracksuit."

"Yeah, okay. Did you ever find out who's on the bench this afternoon?"

"Mildred Collins. She's okay. I've appeared in front of her a couple of times. She's not big on drawn-out discussions. She'll have a full docket, so it'll be short and sweet. In our favor is that Brianna is an upstanding citizen, no criminal record, and if she'll just keep her mouth shut, we've got a pretty good chance of getting her out of here today.

"Mr. Laufen," a voice called from across the lobby. We both looked over as we stood. I recognized the large uniformed cop as the same guy who had escorted me the other day. He gave me a nod as we approached. We went through the same procedure as before. We were scanned and had the wand waved over us. I left my wallet and cellphone in the tray. Louie's briefcase was scanned and then opened and physically examined. We walked down the hall, past the door to the room with the visitation booths and past two more doors before we turned into a hallway. We stopped at a room with the number five on the door. The officer smiled and opened the door. "Miss Di Salvo should be along in just a minute or two."

The room was more like what I was used to. Cinder block walls painted a dark-grey halfway up and a lighter grey from there to the ceiling. There was a window that looked out into the hallway covered with white Venetian blinds. Although they looked closed, the blinds were adjusted ever so slightly, allowing someone from the hallway to peek in. Cameras were mounted on the ceiling, but the lights on them were red, so presumably, they were off. There was the standard two-way mirror on the wall across from the metal-topped table with a total of four chairs, two on either side of the table.

"I'm going to stress to Brianna that she states her name and that when asked if she is in agreement with bail and release terms, she replies with a yes and not another word." I winced as I sat down, and Louie said, "You okay?"

"Yeah, just a little earlier interaction with Soapy McGriff's thug, Bumpy. He kicked me in the ass when he was tossing me out of the office."

"He physically tossed you out of the office?"

"Yeah, pretty much. Not to worry, what goes around comes around."

"Did you learn anything?"

"Not really. I was only in Soapy's office for a minute or two before he told Bumpy to show me to the door. The guy pretty much picked me up out of the chair, tossed me out the door, and then kicked me in the ass for good measure. About all it did was confirm to me that Soapy is a self-absorbed sleaze bag. And if I find out he's the guy who poisoned Seymour Smeelie, I won't be surprised."

With that, the door opened, and Brianna was escorted into the room. She appeared tired. She wore no makeup and looked pale. She had bags under her eyes, and her usually perfectly styled hair hung loosely on either side. Her nylon jumper appeared to be the same one she'd worn yesterday.

"Gentlemen, I'll be out in the hall. You can either knock on the door or just press this button here when you're finished," the guard said, pointing to what looked like a doorbell. He waited half a second for a question, and when there wasn't one, he stepped out and closed the door behind him.

Brianna watched him leave then walked over to the table and settled into one of the chairs across from us. She did not look like the woman I knew. The woman who had dumped me three different times. The woman who turned heads wherever she went. The woman who—

"I just want to go home. Please," she said to Louie.

"Did you try to contact any of those attorney's?" Louie asked.

She half-scoffed and said, "Don't even ask. None of them were interested."

"I'll represent you if you want, or you can request a public defender, and one will be appointed."

"I just want to go home," she said and looked exhausted.

"Brianna, if I represent you, you're going to have to do what I tell you. No outbursts, no threats to sue, no foul language. You just sit quietly. Okay?"

She nodded.

"Okay. We've got a hearing this afternoon. Appearing before Judge Mildred Collins, with any luck, she'll set bail. You're going to have to wear an electronic monitoring device, an ankle bracelet. I know," Louie said when Brianna looked like she was about to protest, "but if you want to go home tonight and sleep in your own bed, you're going to be wearing an ankle bracelet. Relax, it's actually not that bad."

Brianna reluctantly nodded.

"You still living in the same place?" I asked.

"Yeah, why?"

"Is there someone who might have a spare key to your place? It would help if we could get a nice outfit for you to wear at your hearing, something better than that orange jumpsuit."

"My neighbor, Denise, has one. She lives next door in the house with all the rose bushes in front."

"You got something hanging in a closet, so I won't choose the wrong outfit? Something conservative, business-like."

She nodded. "There's a navy outfit with a skirt, jacket, and a white button-up. Have Denise show you. She was with me when I bought it for a funeral."

"Will she be home?"

"She should be. If she's not, there's an artificial rock next to the garage door that I keep a house key in. When you go inside, the alarm is set. The code is seven-eight-nine-one. 1987 backwards, that's the year I was born."

"Okay good, I think I can remember that."

Louie pulled a pen from his suit coat and said, "Dev, write down the code, just to play it safe. Maybe head over there now, see if you can get hold of this Denise. I've got some general stuff to go over with Brianna. We've got a two o'clock hearing, so we'll be at the court-house no later than one."

"Okay, I'll see you there," I said and wrote the security code on my hand.

"Thanks, Dev," Brianna called as I headed for the door. Surprisingly, she sounded like she really meant it.

Twenty-nine

Denise Strobel was probably in her mid-sixties and looked like she wouldn't take a lot of non-sense.

"Ms. Strobel," I said when she answered the door.

"Thanks, but I don't need any of whatever you're selling."

"Good because I'm not selling anything. I'm here on behalf of your neighbor, Brianna Di Salvo. I'd like—"

"It's probably something you should take up with her. Did you check to see if she's home?"

"I know she's not home. I just left her twenty minutes ago. She's been—"

"Just left her? I'm pretty sure she's out of town. What exactly are you trying to pull?"

"I'm not trying to pull anything. Brianna sent me to get an outfit out of her closet. Apparently, a navy outfit," I pulled the slip of paper from my pocket. "With a skirt, jacket, and a white button-up. I guess you were with her when she purchased it for a funeral."

"Oh yeah, that poor old bat, Agnes. Lived just across the street in that house with the green shutters, poor thing. She apparently had a heart attack and was there on the kitchen floor for two days before they found her. Such a shame. Now, how do you know Brianna, and exactly why are you here to get this outfit?"

"She's a bit tied up at the moment, but she needs it for a two o'clock meeting this afternoon. With any luck, she'll be home this evening, and I'm sure she'll want to answer all your questions."

"Mmm, it just doesn't sound right to me."

"She told me you have a spare key to her house and that you'd recognize the outfit hanging in the closet. If I have to pick it out by myself, there's a good chance I'll choose the wrong one."

"And you say she's not out of town."

"No, ma'am, she is not out of town. That I can assure you of."

"And just why did she choose you?"

I was running out of time and getting the third degree from this woman was quickly burning up what was left. "I tell you what, here's my card. I'm a private investigator," I said, handing her my card. "I'll just grab the key she has hidden and let myself in. Thanks for your time," I said, not meaning a word.

"This has a phone number and 'hot blonde' written on the back," she said, turning my card over.

"It's a joke."

She obviously didn't believe me, closed her door, and I heard the lock click in response.

God. And that was supposed to be the nice neighbor? Forget it. I walked up the driveway to the garage. The fake Styrofoam rock was alongside the garage. I'll give it this much, the thing looked real. I turned it over, and there was the brass key. I grabbed the key and hurried to the backdoor. I caught a lace curtain moving in the window next door. No doubt, Denise keeping an eye on me. I inserted the key, unlocked the lock, and opened the door. About five seconds later, the alarm system started chirping. Not loud, just the initial sound it made when you first opened the door. I figured I had a good thirty or forty-five seconds.

I opened the cover on the keypad next to the door, input 1987, and waited for the alarm to stop chirping—it didn't. I input the code again, and the alarm continued to chirp. I finally read the code I'd written on the palm of my hand. I quickly input 7891, and a moment later, the alarm stopped. I closed the door and looked around.

The place looked pretty much the same as I remembered it. The four kitchen stools were new, and the rack attached to the wall holding four copper pans had been added after my departure. But the black granite counters, the fridge, stove, and cabinets all matched my memory. I headed out of the kitchen and down the hall to Brianna's bedroom.

The bed was unmade, but then I remembered the cops had rousted her out of bed in the middle of the night. A white terrycloth bathrobe was on the floor next to the bed. The dresser was littered with makeup cases and brushes, and it would have been just like Brianna to take the better part of an hour to brush on makeup, eyeshadow, and lip gloss before being placed in the back of a squad car and driven downtown. Her walk-in closet had double-doors with a full-length mirror covering each door. I opened the closet doors, and a light automatically came on as I stepped inside. I stopped and just stared.

The place was the size of a small bedroom and had a leather ottoman footstool about five feet long in the middle of it. I guessed so Brianna could sit comfortably, while she tried on the two or three hundred pairs of shoes and boots on racks running the length of the closet. The shoes were arranged according to color. Two levels of dresses and blouses hung from steel rods. A built-in cabinet with glass doors had a dozen long formal gowns hanging inside. Two dozen little shelves each held a purse, no doubt each one more expensive than the next.

I thanked my lucky stars that the outfits were arranged according to color, and I started pulling the hangers on the blue outfits, looking for the navy outfit. I'd been going through outfits for a good five minutes and coming up empty-handed when a voice suddenly scared the living daylights out of me.

"Find the one you're looking for?" Denise said.

"God, I didn't hear you come in. You damn near gave me a heart attack. To be honest, I could have already passed it, and I wouldn't know," I said and took a deep breath to calm down.

"Here, hold this and let me look. You'll have everything messed up in no time," she said and handed me a claw hammer.

"What were you going to do with this?" I said.

"Make sure you weren't causing any trouble. Now step aside," she said and basically hip-checked me out of the way. Thirty seconds later, she said, "Here we go. This is it. Hold this." She handed me a hanger with a navy skirt and jacket hanging on it. She stepped over to the white blouse section of the closet and, in a matter of moments, handed me the white button-up. She waved me out of the closet then sat down on the ottoman footstool and began examining shoes. By the time I draped the outfit over the foot of the bed, Denise was coming out of the closet with a pair of navy-blue heels and a garment bag.

"Place that outfit and the top in this garment bag. There's a pocket on the backside of the bag to put the shoes in. I'll get her some sensible undergarments," she said, emphasizing the word sensible. I stuffed the shoes in the back pocket and zipped it closed. Then carefully laid the outfit and the top in the garment bag. Denise brought over the undergarments and arranged them in the bag, apparently so I wouldn't touch them. She picked up two or three of the makeup cases from the dresser and placed them in a glittery little silver purse with pink trim. "That should take care of things. Anything else she might need?"

"No, I think this should do it, Denise. Thanks for your help. I'm sure I would have messed it up, left to my own devices. I better take off and get these down to Brianna. Do you know the security code so you can turn the alarm back on?"

"Not to worry, you just get these things down to her and tell her I'll want a full report tonight when she gets home."

"Will do, nice to meet you," I said and hurried out the door. According to the clock in the kitchen, it was almost twelve-thirty. By the time I got downtown, parked, and found wherever Brianna was, it would be after one.

Thirty

Rather than waste thirty minutes driving around looking for a parking place on the street, I pulled into the parking ramp directly across the street from the St. Paul Courthouse. It was a real bargain, eight bucks for the first fifty-five minutes. I headed toward the courthouse with the garment bag in one hand and the sparkly purse with the pink trim in the other. I noticed a couple of guys behind the wheel, giving me a second look when they caught sight of the sparkly makeup box.

I entered through the revolving door, had to go through a security check, walk through a metal detector, have the garment bag scanned, and the sparkly makeup box searched. Once that was finished, I took the elevator up to the fourteenth floor and the secure holding area. Thankfully, Louie was in the waiting area. He rose to his feet as I came through the door.

"Oh, glad you made it. I was beginning to worry."

"It was like going through a department store with all the clothes she had hanging in the closet. Fortunately, Denise from next door helped me out, or I'd still be there looking for this stuff."

"Give it to me, and I'll run it back to her," Louie said, taking the garment bag and the little sparkly makeup box. He was back ten minutes later. The hearing was scheduled to begin in forty minutes.

"She gonna be ready in time?"

"She'll have to be," Louie said.

"How is she holding up?"

"I think she finally got religion on keeping her mouth shut. We went over what's going to happen in the hearing. With any luck, it'll be short and sweet and go our way. Let's head up to the courtroom. We're in number five. It's down on the tenth floor, room 1060," Louie said.

We took the elevator down to the tenth floor. The courthouse was built in 1932, and all the courtrooms were paneled and furnished in different exotic woods. The walls and furniture in room 1060 were paneled in American Black Walnut. The courtroom was small, with five wooden benches for seating and a large table standing before the judge's bench. The bench was raised maybe five feet. As we entered, an attorney was standing at a lectern in front of the judge's bench, and his client, attired in an orange jumpsuit, sat at the table staring off into space. We took a seat on one of the back benches. I had to sit leaning to one side to keep the weight off my rear-end, where idiot Bumpy had kicked me.

Today's court docket listed eighteen different initial appearances being presided over by Judge Mildred Collins. The attorney was currently in the process of explaining to the judge that his client was sorry for the assault he made on his girlfriend, who happened to be six months pregnant, and therefore, no bail need be required. Judge Collins was a slight woman with blonde hair and blue eyes. Just now, as she lowered her head to peer over her reading glasses, those blue eyes appeared to be flashing.

"Did I hear you correctly, Mr. Simpson? Bail should not be required?"

Simpson fidgeted briefly and then said, "Yes, your honor. My client's record—"

"Your client's record lists three assaults in the past eighteen months. Those are just the ones that were reported to the police. He's spent a month in the workhouse on each charge and had to pay medical bills. I hasten to add that Miss Alvarez had filed a restraining order on your client."

"It was merely a misunderstanding, and I can assure—"

"Save it for the trial, Mr. Simpson. Based on your client's history, I view him as a threat to society. Therefore, bail is denied. Your client will have time behind bars to ponder the exact meaning of a restraining order and the wisdom of assaulting anyone, let alone a pregnant woman." She slammed her gavel and said, "Next on the docket."

Two uniformed officers stepped over to escort Simpson's client back to the holding area. The man was handcuffed, wearing an orange jumpsuit, and stood maybe five and a half feet with dark black hair. The officers each took hold of an arm and headed toward a side door.

They'd only taken a step or two when he shook loose and shouted at the judge, "I ain't forgetting your name, bitch. We'll see how tough you are when you're dealing with me."

The judge slammed her gavel as the two officers took hold of his arms, and two more officers suddenly appeared. "That just cost you five hundred dollars. Anything else you'd like to add?" she asked and smiled.

"I'm going to kick your little ass, and when I'm done—"

She slammed the gavel again. "Another five hundred dollars and ninety days. Mr. Simpson, I suggest you get your client under control before I lock him away for good. Gentlemen," she said to the officers, "remove this individual from my courtroom." More than one person in the courtroom shook their head.

As the man was led from the courtroom, Louie leaned over and said, "Talk about being your own worst enemy. The word will be out on him, and when it comes to his sentencing, he's going to do some pretty serious time."

No surprise there. We waited through two more initial appearances before Brianna was brought in a half-hour later than her scheduled appearance. Louie walked through the swinging wooden gate and took his place at the table. Brianna was brought into the courtroom by the two guards. Fortunately, instead of wearing an orange jumpsuit, she was in the navy outfit and white top I'd brought. She looked like she had gotten at least a little makeup on her face, but it didn't hide the bags under her eyes and an overall exhausted appearance.

It was all over in about fifteen minutes. Bail had been set at fifty thousand dollars. Louie went back into the holding area with Brianna, and I left the courtroom to wait out in the hall for Louie. He came out maybe twenty minutes later.

"Can she make bail?" I asked when I didn't see Brianna.

"Yeah, setting up a bail bond now. It's going to take a little time. Why don't you go ahead and take off? I'll call you when we're getting out of here. I'm thinking I'll give her a lift home. She can get cleaned up, hopefully begin to dial down. Let's plan on all three of us getting together over dinner at her place. He reached into a pocket, pulled out his wallet, and handed me a couple of twenties. Maybe show up with a couple of pizza's, and we'll go over what we know so far and start making plans tonight."

"Give me a call, and I'll be there. You want anything with the pizza?"

"Yeah, some sanity. She behaved herself in the courtroom, and when I talked with her, she seemed to have gotten the message. Just in case, that idiot charged with assault they hauled out of here was the icing on the cake to what will happen if you open your mouth."

I hurried over to the parking ramp to get my car. It had been about two hours and twenty minutes. The parking attendant graciously rounded the time up to three hours. I paid the twenty-four-dollar fee with the two twenties Louie gave me and drove home.

Morton and his pals were all stretched out in the backyard, enjoying the sun. The food was gone but there was still plenty of water, so I didn't disturb them and went inside. I went upstairs to the bathroom, lowered my trousers, and checked my rear-end in the mirror. Sure enough, there was a bruise about the size of a salad plate on my left butt cheek, compliments of Bumpy. I took two gel packs out of the freezer and headed down to the office.

Thirty-one

I parked across the street from the office and hurried inside. I put one of the gel packs in the refrigerator, wrapped the other one in a plastic bag, and set it on my office chair. I turned on my computer and glanced out the window just in time to see Taffy pull in behind my car. She climbed out of her car, waited for a bus to pass, and then hurried across the street. I heard the stairs creak a moment later. I listened to her climb the stairs and then waited for her to open the office door, and I waited, and I waited. After a few minutes, which is an awfully long time to stand in the hallway, the office door opened, and she stepped in.

She was wearing a greenish-olive drab short play-suit with a V neck. The three-inch zipper on the V-neck top was pulled all the way down, hinting at some very nice cleavage. Her auburn hair appeared to have new blonde highlights. "Hi Dev," she said as she strutted toward my desk, acting as if we'd just met for lunch earlier in the day, and everything was great. "Just wanted to stop in and say hello. Am I interrupting anything?"

"No, it's nice to see you, Taffy. Did you get any of my phone messages? I've been worried about you."

"Yeah, I guess I just had a lot on my mind, and it took me some time to recover from our time at that dreadful lake," she said and rolled her eyes.

"Oh, okay. I thought since you enjoyed it so much, you maybe went back up there for the rest of the week and couldn't get any phone reception."

"Well, if that place didn't have phone reception, it wouldn't surprise me in the least. That had to be the absolute worst time I have ever spent at a lake. Then the rain, plus a dreadful hangover. God, if I'm ever up there again, it will be too soon."

"So, does this mean we're back talking to one another?"

She didn't respond for a moment then said, "I know, I know, it's just that you seemed to be okay with how very awful that place was, and I hated it."

"I wasn't okay with how it was, but then I wasn't the one who insisted we go up there. You insisted we ride up with Kevin and Stacey so we couldn't leave. I decided to make the best of a bad situation, and you decided to pout."

"Pout? God, the roof leaked; there were mice running around. I think I spent more time in that stinky outhouse than I did in the cabin. It was dreadful."

I had to chuckle at that. "Well, I offered to stay with you in the outhouse, and if you'll recall, you yelled at me and told me to please go away and leave you alone."

She wrinkled her nose and seemed to think for a moment. "Actually, I maybe don't remember that— exactly. I just remember waking up on my knees, and my head was hanging in the— Oh God, I don't even want to think about it. One of the absolute lowest points of my life."

"Well, at least you didn't get sick in their cabin."

"Oh please, I didn't find the wood tick until a day after we came home."

"A wood tick, where was it?"

"Let's just say a very private place and leave it at that. I'm sorry I made us go up there. It's just that Stacey has raved about the place all summer long, and I expected something completely different. That dreadful place didn't even pass the health code test. All that mouse poop, oh ick, and I could hear them running around in the walls. Probably making plans to crawl all over me. Yuck!"

"There was a bat flying around Saturday night, too."

"A bat?" Her eyes grew wide.

"Yeah, I told Kevin about it, and he casually mentioned that he'd looked for it from time to time, but he could never find where it was hiding in the cabin."

"Oh God, I should probably make a doctor's appointment and get checked out for a bunch of different viruses. What if the thing had landed on me and sucked blood?" She visibly shuddered at that thought.

"I think you're probably safe."

"Dreadful, absolutely dreadful. Well, thank you for putting up with me. Mouse poop and leaking roofs are just not my idea of a getaway weekend and now a bat. God!"

"Well, you survived."

"Barely. Thanks for not leaving me up there. Umm, do you think you might have time to come over for dinner tonight?"

"Oh, I would love to, honest, but I have to meet with a client and her attorney. She just got out of jail this afternoon, and we're going to be planning her defense."

"What did she do?"

"She didn't do anything, but she's accused of murdering a guy."

"It's not that cheater I read about in the paper, is it? That developer guy who ripped off just about everyone in town."

"If you're talking about Seymour Smeelie, yeah, that's the guy. But like I said, she's innocent. We just have to try and figure out who actually did it, and believe me, the list is long. I could maybe stop over later tonight for a little dessert if that would be okay."

She grinned, stood, and strutted around my desk. A wonderful scent of perfume drifted over me. She pushed my desk chair back a couple of feet until it rolled up against the wall. She leaned over and gave me a long, passionate kiss. "I think I might know just what you'd like for dessert. I'll see you later tonight. It might be a good idea to rest up," she said then strutted toward the door. She opened the door, looked over her shoulder, and blew me a kiss.

As the perfume faded, I watched out the window while she crossed the street and opened the driver's door on her BMW. She bent over and appeared to be adjusting something beneath the front seat. The view was great from where I sat, and I was tempted to grab my binoculars when she stood and slipped in behind the wheel. She buckled her seat belt, started the car, and pulled away without looking up at me, although I had the distinct impression she was very aware I had been watching her the entire time.

Thirty-two

I made a list of questions I wanted to ask Brianna about Seymour Smeelie. Leading the list was, where did he live and might she have a key to his place? I wanted to find out where Soapy McGriff lived, too. The more I thought about it, the more likely he became the guilty person in all of this. Louie phoned me about a half-hour later and said I could head over anytime. He had called me from Brianna's house. Apparently, she was still soaking in a hot tub, and Louie was in the kitchen.

I ordered two large-sized pizzas with everything except anchovies then drove over to the take-out place to pick them up. I had to wait about five minutes until they were ready and only then realized I'd paid my court-house parking fee with the cash Louie had given me. I went through the process of having two different credit cards rejected before the third one finally worked. The teenager ringing me up gave me a look that suggested, *'It never ends.'*

I pulled up in front of Brianna's house ten minutes later. Louie's car was sitting in the driveway. There was a small stain on the concrete from the oil dripping out of his engine. I decided tonight probably wasn't the best time to mention it. I grabbed the pizzas and hurried up to the front door. I didn't see any curtain movement from next door, which suggested Denise was probably on her phone, giving some poor soul directions, and I could sneak into Brianna's without her knowing.

I rang the doorbell, and a moment later, the door opened, and there stood Denise. "Oh, you," she said and didn't smile. She glanced down at the pizza boxes. "Mmm, I see you brought health food. Well, you might as well come in. Your friend is in the kitchen, Brianna's resting, and I've just put the coffee on." She took the pizzas from me, and I followed her into the kitchen.

Louie was seated at the kitchen counter with a number of files spread out. He was writing on a legal pad and said, "Hi, Dev," without looking up.

"How's it going?"

"We're getting there. Give me about twenty minutes, and I'll be finished."

I noticed Denise had removed the pizzas from the box, set them on two cookie sheets, and just now was placing them in the oven to warm. Louie working and Brianna resting left me with Denise. "Anything I can do to help?" I asked, hoping she'd just tell me to stay out of her way.

"As a matter of fact, come with me," she said and headed out the backdoor. "It's such a lovely evening. I think it would be nice if we ate out here." Automatically adding herself to the group. She walked to the corner of the house, pulled a push-broom off a rack, and handed it to me.

"If you could just sweep the leaves and the grass clippings off the patio, that would really help." She headed back in the house, and I looked around the patio. There were a couple of leaves and about four grass clippings. I could probably do the job faster if I just picked them up one by one. I was about to do just that when she came back out and handed me a dustpan and a red whisk broom. "You can just put everything in the recycle bin next to the garage," she said.

She held a plastic spray bottle of Windex glass cleaner and a roll of paper towels. She proceeded to spray Windex over the round, glass-topped table with the umbrella in the center. Then, using paper towels, she wiped off the table and repeated the process. When she was finished, you probably could have performed open-heart surgery on the table. I dutifully swept the patio and placed the three or four grass clippings and the couple of leaves in the recycling bin. I decided the safest place for me might be out here on the patio. I pulled out a lawn chair and cautiously sat down. My bruise felt as though it was beginning to heal; at least there wasn't the sharp pain I'd felt earlier in the day.

Louie joined me about ten minutes later, and Denise and Brianna, each carrying a pizza, came out a few minutes after. Denise hurried back inside and returned with plates, napkins, and silverware. She rushed back inside once more and returned with four mugs of steaming coffee.

"Don't worry. I made decaf," she said as she arranged a mug in front of everyone.

"Welcome home," I said to Brianna and raised a slice of pizza to her in a toast.

"Oh, it's just good to be home. I don't want to talk about it other than to say it was an absolutely horrible experience. Even with my new attire, I'm just glad to be back," she said then raised her leg and showed off her ankle bracelet. "What do you think?"

"I think it's good you're home, and that thing is no big deal," I said. I smiled and took a bite of my pizza. Denise cleared her throat, and when I glanced over, she nodded at the plate, the silverware and the napkin I hadn't bothered to place on my lap.

Brianna seemed to relax a little.

I did the only sensible thing I could think of. I took another bite of pizza, this time much bigger. A string of melted cheese fell onto my chin. I pulled the cheese using my tongue, faced her, and chewed with my mouth open. She shook her head and then cut a petit little piece, stabbed it with her fork, and placed it in her mouth. Brianna started to laugh, and then, so did Louie. Eventually, even Denise flashed a quick smile. I decided not to press my luck, grabbed my silverware, and used it for the remainder of the meal.

Once Denise cleared the table and loaded the dish-washer, she had the common sense to head over to her house so we could begin trying to plot a strategy. As the sun began to set, we headed into the house.

Thirty-three

Brianna pulled a bottle of red wine from the rack in the kitchen and said, "I don't know about you two, but I could use a glass of wine."

"I'm okay, but thanks," Louie said.

"None for me," I said as she twisted the cap off the bottle and filled her glass. She opened a lower cabinet and pulled out a box of chocolate-covered caramels. She took the lid off the box and placed it on the counter in front of us. Only one caramel was missing from the box. She raised her glass in a toast to the both of us, took a hearty sip, closed her eyes, and said, "God, it's good to be home. Thank you both for getting me out of that awful place."

"Thank you for staying calm and doing everything right," Louie said and took a caramel.

I pulled out a kitchen stool and apparently made a face as I sat down.

"You okay, Dev? You look like you're in pain," Brianna said.

"I was unceremoniously tossed out of Soapy McGriff's office this morning, and I'm still feeling the effects."

"Soapy McGriff? Was that awful, brainless monster with him? What's his name, Burpy?"

"Yeah, he was there. Actually, his name is Bumpy. And you're right. He is brainless, or if he has a brain, he doesn't know how to use it. He kicked me in the butt, hard. I've got a big bruise, and every time I sit down, I'm reminded about his little farewell message."

"Oh dear, you poor thing, would you feel more comfortable in the living room on the couch?"

"No, this is just fine, but thanks. How do you know Soapy McGriff and Bumpy? Talk about a couple of creeps. They're like something out of a movie."

"Yeah, a horror movie. Seymour and I had to go over to McGriff's house a couple of times. Let me tell you, not what you'd call an enjoyable evening. Then, when we were down in Florida on our ill-fated trip, they stopped in for an unannounced visit. I was told, in no uncertain terms, to go outside and lie in the sun. I could feel that dreadful Burpy person's eyes on me the entire time I was out there. He just stood inside in the air-conditioned comfort and stared out at me through the patio door. It was sunny, eighty-five degrees, and he actually gave me the shivers; he was so creepy. I literally had goosebumps." She suddenly shivered again, remembering the incident. She quickly took a large swallow of wine to aid in her recovery.

"What were they doing down in Florida?" Louie asked.

"I honestly don't know why they were there. I can tell you this, whatever it was, it wasn't very pleasant for Seymour. It was maybe a good hour before they left, and when he came out to tell me I could come back inside, he was a completely different individual. He didn't say anything for two days and the next morning we packed and flew back up here. The moment we landed, he wanted nothing to do with me. He told me he had to take care of something and that I had to take a taxi home. I'd paid for everything in Florida, ten thousand dollars, and he wouldn't even help me put my suitcases in the taxi."

"I didn't know what to think. At first, I wanted to just talk to him, make sure he was okay, you know, find out what had happened, but he wouldn't even answer my phone calls. I sent a bunch of text messages but never got a reply, and eventually, I just wanted to kill— Oh sorry, let's just say I wasn't very happy."

"And you never found out what set him off?"

She shook her head. "No, never. It had to be something the creepies did, Soapy and Burpy. But he never told me what it was. When I went to leave my ill-advised note on his office door, I saw the two of them coming out of the building. I was just about to get out of my car, and there they were."

"So, what did you do?" I asked.

"The only sensible thing I could think of. I ducked down in the driver's seat and waited a good five minutes just to make sure they were gone."

"And you said Seymour wasn't up in his office, right?"

"Yeah, which got me even madder. I had an appointment. I went up there and knocked on his door, and there was no answer. At first, I thought he might have changed his mind about meeting me and wasn't going to answer. In fact, I remember shouting something like, 'I know you're in there,' but then I figured Soapy and Burpy probably ran into the same thing, and when he didn't answer, they just left."

"What time was that?" Louie asked.

"Oh, gee, let me think. That was my last stop. I'd already been to his condo. I had a, umm, a meeting that night." She flashed a quick, insincere smile in my direction. "It must have been about four in the afternoon."

Louie took another caramel, popped it in his mouth, and opened his briefcase. He rummaged around in a stack of files and pulled out a document. I immediately recognized it as an autopsy report. He took another caramel, put it in his mouth, and chewed once or twice as he scanned the report. "Time of death is estimated to be between three-thirty and four-thirty." He set the document down and grabbed another caramel. "You're there around four. You're still sitting in your car when you see McGriff and his thug leave. You go up to Seymour's office, knock on the door, call his name, and leave when you don't get an answer. How long were you up there?"

"In the hallway?" She shook her head. "Couldn't have been more than two or three minutes. Like I said, I figured those two creatures had the same response, so I folded my note and left it wedged into the crack in the doorframe. Then in the elevator on the way down, I wondered if he might have been in there hiding, so I went down to the underground parking, and sure enough, there was his car. I placed a note under his windshield wiper. I thought about letting the air out of his tires but didn't. I figured his home, his office, and his car, there was no way he wouldn't know I expected to be paid."

Louie tossed the caramel in his mouth, licked his fingertips, and reached for another.

"So back up for a moment. You said you've been to McGriff's house. Where exactly does he live?" I asked.

"Soapy? He lives down on Summit Ave. He lives in a great big three-story place that must be about three hundred years old. It has a ten-foot hedge in front of it and a little circular drive, so we didn't have to park on the street."

"Do you remember the address?"

She shook her head. "No, I don't think I ever knew it. There's another mansion, well they're all mansions down there, but there's a big white mansion right across the street with massive white pillars. That place is right next door to a little park with a fountain. As far as I could tell, Soapy McGriff lived all alone in his mansion, well except for that Burpy creature. He probably has a cell that Soapy locks him up in every night. Oh, so creepy," she said and shuddered.

I knew the place, maybe. It was just a few blocks from my house, and I had to have walked past it a number of times. I certainly remembered the structure with the white pillars next to the park.

"What about Seymour's place? You wouldn't happen to know a way in there, would you?"

"Yeah sure, that's how I could leave the note on his door. He lives in a condo on a bluff overlooking the Mississippi. It's a really nice place, great view; in fact, that's the name of the place, The View. It has excellent security."

"And yet you managed to get inside and leave a note on his door. How did you get into the building?"

She gave me a funny look. "How? No big deal, I've got a set of keys."

"Is there a security system in his unit?"

She shook her head and said, "No, the place is so secure there's no need."

Louie took two caramels from the box and tossed both of them into his mouth.

"Do you still happen to have those keys?"

"Yeah, sure, I can give them to you, or I'd be happy to take you over there. Like I said, it's a lovely place. Despite him ending up being such an absolute jerk."

"I think it would be best if you didn't go anywhere near Mr. Smeelie's condo or office. In fact, let me be more specific. You are forbidden to go anywhere near either place, Smeelie's, or McGriff's, upon penalty of a twenty-year sentence. Do I make myself clear?" Louie said and grabbed two more caramels from the almost empty box.

"You've got the keys here?" I asked.

Brianna nodded and finished what little wine remained in her glass.

"Maybe if we moved to the living room and you left the keys on the kitchen counter while you refilled your glass, I could wander into the kitchen a minute later, take the keys, and you would never see me do that."

Brianna hopped off her stool and headed for her bedroom. Louie took the last two caramels, tossed them into his mouth, and we headed into the living room. Brianna came back down the hall and said, "I'm going to get a refill. You sure you two don't want anything to drink?"

"I'm okay," I said.

"I'd better have a whiskey, no ice," Louie said.

Brianna headed into the kitchen and returned a couple of minutes later with a Waterford glass full of whiskey for Louie and her glass of wine.

"Well, I hate to be a bore, but I should probably head out. Welcome home, Brianna. Louie, I'll see you in the morning."

"Thank you, Dev, and be careful," Brianna said.

"See you in the morning," Louie said and raised his glass.

"I'll just let myself out the back. Enjoy the rest of the evening," I said and headed out to the kitchen. Two brass keys were attached to a keyring with a red heart with an arrow through it. Beneath the keyring was the sheet of paper Brianna had shown me when she came to my office to ask if I'd break Seymour's legs. The list had his phone number, email account, usernames for Instagram, Snapchat, Twitter, and Facebook, along with all his passwords and the security code to his building. I picked up the keys and the list, placed them in a front pocket without missing a step, got in my car, and drove home.

Thirty-four

I planned to check on Morton and his pals, grab a quick shower, and head over to Taffy's. Unfortunately, Morton and the rest of the gang were nowhere to be found. Dusk was settling in, and I cruised around the neighborhood looking for them. I slowly drove up and down the streets and alleys but never saw a sign. There were two police cars about four blocks from my house, and I pulled over to see if Morton and his pals were there. The cops looked like they were interviewing two women. Fortunately, Morton and company weren't around.

It was after nine when I finally pulled into the driveway and headed inside. I gave a quick glance out the window, and there they were, all stretched out in the backyard. Morton was lying next to the German Shepherd. I was so glad to see them, I grabbed a fistful of dog biscuits and hurried out the door. Heads raised as I came around the corner, but no one made an effort to move.

"Oh, you guys had me really worried," I said, tossing biscuits to each of them. "Hey, I think I might have a hot, late-night date tonight. Morton, why don't you come inside with me, and you can join your pals tomorrow morning?"

Morton didn't move.

"Come on, Morton, inside. Let's go."

He just gave me a look, put his head down and pretended I wasn't there.

"Hey, Morton, come on. I'm running out of time here."

Still nothing. I debated pulling him in by the collar, but to be honest, that didn't really appeal to me. It didn't look like it was going to rain, but after the downpour the other night, I didn't want to take the chance. "Hey, okay, Morton, bring everyone inside. Come on, inside. Come on, everyone inside."

The Lab and the Border Collie raised their heads. Morton cautiously stood and shook. The German Shepherd raised his head and watched me. I signaled, moving my hands. "Come on, come on, you guys, everyone inside."

The Lab and the Border Collie were on their feet. The fuzzy little white guy joined them. The Shepherd was still watching, cautious.

"Come on, inside. Treat," I said. "Treat."

At the mention of a treat, even the Shepherd was on his feet following the other four and slowly limping toward the door. I let everyone in the backdoor, dispensed another dog biscuit to each one, dimmed the kitchen lights, and closed the door behind me. I phoned Taffy on my way up the stairs. She answered on the second ring.

"Please don't tell me you're not coming."

"No, just the opposite. I'm just out of that meeting, and I was going to grab a quick shower and come over. Should be there in about thirty minutes."

"You can take a shower over here, Dev."

"I'll just grab one here and—"

"Hello, are we listening?" She suddenly lowered her voice and spoke very softly. "Honey, after the long day you've had, why don't you come right over? I'll get the tub ready for a hot soak. We both could use it, and it will help us relax."

"I'll be right there. Can I bring anything? I could—"

"You've got everything I want. Now get your ass over here."

"On my way," I said.

I made the trip in almost ten minutes, and that was after waiting for an interminable stoplight. As I pulled up in front of her building, she waved at me from her balcony. She was wearing her short, red silk robe with white trim and called, "I'll buzz you in." She gave a quick glance around then opened her robe, exposing a lacy red one-piece. Some car driving down the street tooted it's horn a couple of times as I ran to the door. When I stepped inside, the buzzer for the security door was already buzzing. I took the elevator up to Taffy's. She opened the door as I hurried down the hall to her unit.

"Thank you for making the time," she said and grinned as she handed me a flute of what was either pink Champagne or Prosecco. I don't like either one, but under the circumstances, that didn't really matter. We clinked glasses and both took a sip.

"Join me. I just finished running the tub, so it's nice and hot."

She led me into her bedroom. There was a plaid flannel robe arranged on her bed. "You can slip into that and meet me in the tub," she said. We clinked glasses again and took a sip. She gave me a quick kiss and headed into her candle-lit bathroom. I tore off my clothes and slipped the robe on. It seemed to have a slight hint of aftershave, but at the moment, I didn't really care.

I headed into the bathroom. There were a half-dozen large, cream-colored candles lit and arranged across the double vanity. The flames from the candles reflected off the glazed white tiles on the walls. Taffy sat in the tub, sipping from her glass with soap bubbles up to her shoulders. The two-person white porcelain tub was fitted into a corner and more or less triangular in shape. I could hear the water jets running. Taffy's head rested on a black pad attached to the tub.

"Care to join me?" she said and flashed a gorgeous smile.

"I'd love to." I set my glass down on the shelf behind the tub, then turned around and pulled off the robe to hang on one of the chrome hooks on the wall.

"Oh my God, Dev," Taffy shrieked. "What in God's name happened to your butt?"

"Little misunderstanding with someone I'm in the process of investigating."

"Oh, it looks so awful. Come here, closer." She gently touched me. "Does that hurt? Can you even sit down?"

"Yeah, I think I can manage."

"Have you been to see the doctor? What did they say?"

"I don't need to see a doctor. It'll be a lot better in forty-eight hours."

"But how did that happen? Did someone try to run you over with their car?"

"No, this big dopey thug named Bumpy kicked me."

"Kicked? Are you kidding me?"

"I wouldn't lie to you, Taffy," I said and took a sip.

She gave me a look then held out a hand and said, "Let me hold your glass while you climb in and for God's sake, be careful, you poor thing."

Thirty-five

I was the recipient of a good deal of tender loving care. Taffy was sound asleep when I kissed her good-bye and tiptoed out at half-past five the following morning. Her red silk robe and lacy one-piece were still hanging in the bathroom. I headed home and stopped to pick up two coffees along the way. I drove past the house with the white pillars on Summit Avenue and pulled to the curb in front of Soapy McGriff's place. At this hour, I was only one of two cars on the street. I had definitely walked past the place a few thousand times, but I'd never been inside. With all the large homes up and down the street, I only knew maybe a half-dozen people.

The house sat on the bluff facing north, and the back windows would overlook the downtown area, the 35E interstate, and the Mississippi River Valley, although you wouldn't see the actual river. You would be able to see the northbound traffic on the interstate, but with the sound barrier walls, there would be very little, if any, noise.

The house was a three-story brick structure with a slate roof and cream-colored trim, and I thought back to the candles Taffy had arranged in her bathroom. Given the area and the size, I guessed it was built in the early 1900s. You had to climb six broad steps to reach the front door that was centered with four very large windows on either side. There was no stained glass that I could see, which surprised me in a way, but then it didn't really seem to fit with the design of the house. I knew there was a small street behind the property, more of an alley actually, although there were a few small houses facing it. The small circular drive Brianna had described was there behind the tall hedge. No vehicle was parked in the circular drive.

I drove around the block and then down to the small street along the back of the property. There was a double garage with a brick face that matched the house. The garage was built into the side of the bluff without any apparent entrance. That suggested it was accessed through some kind of short tunnel leading from the basement of the house to the garage. I made a note to check the county tax records on the property when I got home.

I drove up the hill that led me back to Summit Avenue, drove the few blocks to my house, and parked in the driveway. Once in the house, I tiptoed to the kitchen and quietly opened the door. Everyone was sprawled out across the floor, almost on top of one another, and still very sound asleep. The German Shepherd raised his head at the sound of the door opening, but once he saw it was me, he laid back down, took a deep breath, and went back to sleep. I took that as a positive sign.

I brought my computer out to the sitting room, turned it on, and began going through my emails. Most of the emails were either things I could delete or something I could answer later. Thankfully, nothing pressing had come across. I Googled the property tax records for the county and looked up McGriff's property. Thirty-two thousand dollars in property taxes annually, just for the pleasure of living in the place. Not to mention the fact that Summit Avenue was closed down about thirty days a year between marathons, walks for whatever political and social movement was popular at the moment, and various fundraisers for a variety of worthy causes. The house had an estimated value of two-point-four-million, and I couldn't come up with anyone I knew who would be able to afford that.

I checked the news stories online and landed on one regarding another purse snatching. Given the vague description of the location of the incident, it sounded like it could have very well been where I saw the two police cars last night talking to two women. The purse snatching had been thwarted not by the women or a good Samaritan stranger, but by what was described as a pack of four or five stray dogs.

The purse snatcher had suddenly appeared between two parked cars, pushed the woman with the purse to the ground, and then got in a tugging match with her as she held onto her purse. He began to shout something about shooting her but never finished when a small fuzzy white dog latched onto the calf of his leg. A number of larger dogs arrived barking and growling. The guy eventually shook off the little white dog, limped out to the street, and into a black SUV without the purse. The dogs watched the car disappear then headed down the street.

After reading the article twice, I was pretty sure the heroes might all be asleep in my kitchen. No name was given of the intended victim, but I sent myself a text message with the name of the reporter who wrote the article, Abigale Douglas. I made a mental note to try and reach her later in the day.

I heard movement out in the kitchen, so after a few minutes, I opened the door. Everyone was lined up, looking expectantly at the door leading outside. I unlocked the door and let them all out. I filled the saucepans with dog food, pretty much emptying the bag. I made another mental note to get more dog food, more biscuits, and maybe some bones for them to chew on as a reward for their crime fighting service last night.

I took out the food and water, checked the fence, then got in my car and drove over to the small park across the street from Soapy McGriff's mansion. I wore a baseball cap, settled onto one of the park benches facing the mansion, and waited. It took the better part of an hour and three different cars coming up the hill from the small street where Soapy's garage was, but finally, a black Mercedes pulled to the top of the hill. It waited for an opening in the rush hour traffic and then pulled onto the street and headed in the direction of downtown and the American Bank building. As the Mercedes drove past, I recognized Bumpy behind the wheel and Soapy sitting in the backseat. You could only see Soapy's head, not so much as a hint of his shoulders. He looked for all the world like a twelve-year-old whose mother had made him dress up in a suit and tie for school pictures.

I waited another five minutes, enjoying the morning sun, before I casually strolled across the street. I crossed the circular drive and stepped onto the narrow sidewalk that led to the back of the house.

Thirty-six

The first-floor windows in the back of the house looked out onto a large brick patio with three glass-topped tables, each with a folded umbrella in the center. Based on the grime on the tabletops, it seemed a pretty fair guess the tables hadn't been used in the last three and a half months. The patio was surrounded by a three-foot concrete railing with heavy concrete spindles made to simulate turned wooden spindles. Centered on the patio were three steps that led down to the backyard. The far end of the yard was fenced and on the other side of the fence was maybe a ten foot drop down to the small street. There was no garage entrance, which meant I'd been correct in my guess that it had to be accessed via the basement and a tunnel.

I walked up onto the patio and looked at the dozen windows running across the back of the house. They were all the same, with a single pane of glass in the lower sash and nine panes, three rows of three panes, in the upper sash. Each window had a brass crescent sash lock placed in the middle of the upper and lower sash, and every window was locked. I looked carefully but couldn't see any security alarm device on any of the windows. The screen door opened, but the storm door, which was wooden and appeared to be about two inches thick, was locked.

I tried the doorknob anyway, but it was definitely locked. I was about to leave when I saw it, at the far end of the patio, just sitting in a corner. What looked like the same Styrofoam rock that held the key to Brianna's house. Could it really be this easy? I hurried over, and sure enough, it was Styrofoam, and lo and behold, it held a brass key.

I inserted the key into the backdoor lock, turned it, and heard the lock click. The door appeared to relax from the frame by maybe a thirty-second of an inch. I opened the door, stepped inside, quickly closed it, and listened for any telltale alarm sound. There was nothing. I looked around the door frame but didn't see anything resembling an alarm. Then, staying in place, I cautiously scanned the room for anything resembling a motion detector or a camera. I didn't see anything. I took a few tentative steps, but nothing sounded. I listened for an alarm or maybe footsteps if there were servants or staff, but there was nothing.

I walked across the room and entered a hallway with four doors. The doors were all open. The first one led to what looked like a library and office, and I was reminded of Tubby Gustafson getting his nails manicured by the two scantily clad women in his so-called office. Another door led to a large dining room with an elegant table that seated twenty, nine on each side and two at either end. The table had a layer of dust across it, and I was tempted to write something vile or maybe just sign Bumpy's name, but then that would be a give-away, because I was sure he couldn't spell, let alone write.

Another door led to the kitchen and pantry, and the last door, in the front of the house, led to a smaller room. Small by the standards of this place. There were two couches, a fireplace, a game table with a built-in chess-board, and a cabinet with crystal glasses and two decant-ers. I took a pass on the liquor decanters and opened the cabinet doors. There was an impressive array of expen-sive whiskeys and bourbons and then, way in the back, surprise, surprise, three bottles of rum. Three bottles of Havana Club Anejo Especial, to be exact. One of which was nearly empty. I pulled my cellphone out and took a couple of pictures. I closed the cabinet door and hurried back to the library office.

All sorts of leather-bound books, many with gold lettering, lined the floor to ceiling shelves. There was a layer of dust on all the books, suggesting they hadn't been looked at in quite a while, maybe even years, if ever. A brass rail was attached to the top of the bookcase, and a ladder on wheels was connected to the rail, giving one access to the two upper shelves or, in Soapy's case, probably the upper four shelves.

I hurried over to the carved desk. Interestingly, the carving on the two front corners and in the center of the desk seemed to represent a satanic creature of some sort with horns, a beard, an evil look on the face, and bat wings. How perfect for someone like Soapy McGriff. I rifled through the desk drawers but didn't find anything that mentioned Seymour Smeelie. There was a cast-iron combination safe built into one of the bookcases behind Soapy's desk, but it was locked.

I'd been in the place for a good thirty minutes and felt like I was really pressing my luck. I gave everything a quick look around to make sure nothing appeared to be disturbed then left the way I'd come, out the backdoor, which I locked. I returned the key to the Styrofoam rock and placed it back in the corner of the patio then calmly walked back down the narrow sidewalk, out the circular drive, and across the street to the small park. I walked another block and a half to my car, checking a half-dozen times to make sure no one was following me, then climbed behind the wheel and headed down to my office.

Thirty-seven

I could smell the burnt coffee when I entered the office. Louie was at his picnic table desk with a half-dozen files scattered around him. He looked up as I walked in and said, "Sleeping in? Hey, where's Morton. Is everything okay?"

"No, and yes," I said, grabbing my coffee mug and pouring the remnants of the pot into the mug. It filled the mug about half-way, and I turned off the burner. "What time did you get in this morning? This stuff smells like it's been on the burner for about a week."

"I made it yesterday morning, or now that I think about it, maybe the day before," Louie said and opened another file.

I set the mug on the edge of my desk. "Hey, I got something for you," I said and pulled out my cellphone. I punched in Louie's number, loaded the two photos of the Havana Club Anejo Especial rum bottles, and sent them to him.

"If this is a picture of you without clothes on or a picture of your butt where Bumpy kicked you, I'm not interested."

"Unfortunately, neither one, but I think you'll be interested." I heard his cellphone beep, signaling a text message. He picked it up off the stack of files and turned it on.

A moment later, he said, "Where in the hell did you get these?"

"Soapy McGriff's liquor cabinet."

"You went to Soapy's house?"

"Maybe. Not really important, except that he's got three bottles of the stuff. One of which is almost empty, which matches what Brianna was saying."

"Help me out here. What was she saying?"

"She said that the bottle of rum she bought Smeelie down in Florida was almost empty. The bottle with the poison was full. It had been freshly opened. I know this doesn't prove conclusively that Soapy poisoned the guy, but it does give one pause to at least consider the possibility."

"I don't suppose you happened to come across any of the poison?"

"Not yet, but I'm working on it."

"Without getting into specifics, anything on Seymore Smeelie?"

"I'll be looking into Seymour this evening."

Louie held up his hand, signaling no more information. Which was fine with me. I dumped my mug of burnt coffee down the sink, went back to my desk, and phoned the newspaper.

"You have reached the St. Paul Pioneer Press. If you know the party's extension, you are calling, please dial it now. To list an item for sale…"

"God, but I hate recorded answering services. It'll be about thirty minutes before I get to the person I want to talk to," I said and hung up. I called my friend, Aaron LaZelle, in Homicide, next and ended up leaving him a message. At least his recording was about ten seconds long, in his voice, and at the end, I could say something he would eventually hear.

"Yeah, Aaron, it's Dev. I have a question for you. If you could call me back when you get a chance, that would be great. Not to worry, it's nothing regarding the Seymour Smeelie case. I just want contact information on the purse snatching's that have been going on. I might have some information for them on an incident last night a couple of blocks from my house where some dogs chased the guy off. Give me a yell when you have a chance."

I disconnected, and my phone rang almost immediately. I answered without looking at who was calling. "Haskell investigations."

"Dev?" Taffy cried into the phone.

"Hey, Taffy. What's wrong? Are you okay?"

"No, I'm not. I've got an intruder. Can you hurry over? Bring your gun."

"An intruder?" I said, suddenly up and out of my chair. I opened my desk drawer and stuffed my nine-millimeter into my belt. "Did you call the police? Did you call 911?"

Louie looked up wide-eyed as I hurried out the door.

"Are you safe? Where are you?"

"I'm up on the kitchen counter, and I— Ahh, get away from me, get away," she screamed.

"I'm hanging up and calling the cops right now," I said, hurrying down the stairs.

Taffy screamed once more and shouted, "It's a mouse, Dev. A mouse. It must have gotten into my suitcase up at Kevin and Stacey's lake. Oh, icky. I'm going to have to burn all those clothes."

"A mouse?" I said and stopped out on the sidewalk, not sure if I should laugh or cry. I went back inside the building and climbed the stairs to the office.

When I walked back in, Louie half-whispered, "Is she okay?"

I nodded at Louie as Taffy said, "Dev, this isn't funny. I don't know what to do."

"You just stay where you are, and I'll be right over. Don't worry. I'll deal with this."

"Oh God, I'm going to have to fumigate the whole unit, or maybe I should just set it on fire and close the door behind me on the way out. Can I please stay at your house tonight?"

"Don't set the place on fire. I'll be there in twenty minutes, and yes, you can stay at my place for as long as you want."

She sniffled into the phone and said a tearful, "Hurry, please," and then disconnected.

"Jesus Christ," Louie said. "Is she okay?"

"Yeah, she fine, crazy, but fine. The intruder was a mouse."

"What?"

"I know. I know. I'm going to pick up some traps and head over there. I'll be back later this afternoon. You going to see Brianna this afternoon?"

"I'll be talking to her, but I don't think I'll see her. Why?"

"I'm thinking, don't mention anything about those rum bottles. I don't want her telling anyone or making some comment and suddenly they're gone."

"Not to worry. Happy mouse hunting," Louie said and gave me a little wave as I headed out.

Thirty-eight

I left the office and swung by the Hardware store on Grand Avenue. I purchased four packages of Tomcat super hold glue traps. Each package held four cardboard panels of a high strength adhesive. If a mouse attempted to run across it, they'd be caught.

Taffy was waiting out on her balcony when I pulled up. Unfortunately, she wasn't wearing her red silk robe or the lacy red one-piece. She was dressed in jeans, a t-shirt, wearing knee-high black leather boots, and holding a tennis racket.

As I climbed out of my car, she shouted, "Hurry up, Dev. I'll buzz you in."

Just like last night, the buzzer on the security door was sounding off when I entered the lobby. Unfortunately, a passionate Taffy was not going to be waiting for me up in her unit.

When I stepped off the elevator, she was standing in the hallway, stomping her feet. "Oh, Dev, thank God you're here. Hurry, he's still in here somewhere."

As I drew closer, I could see that her face was tear-stained. Mascara was smeared for about a half-inch below each eye. "Are you okay?" I asked as she rushed into my arms, bouncing the tennis racket off my knee. I bit my tongue in an effort not to swear. "Okay, let's get this taken care of," I said and led her back into her unit.

"I don't want to go back in. I know he's in here somewhere, probably watching right now, planning to take a big bite out of me. You said I could go to your house. Please."

"We'll do that in a minute. First, let me set some traps for him. Show me where you saw him."

"I don't want to go in there. I'm scared."

"It's okay. I'll guard you. So, where did you see him?"

"He ran under the door into my pantry closet. There's probably a bunch of them in there just waiting to attack me the moment I open the door."

"Okay, come on in to the kitchen and—"

"No, I don't want to. What if he's in there? Oh, God, I can't believe this shit is happening to me."

"Come on into the kitchen with me. You can climb back up on the kitchen counter with your tennis racket."

"Oh, I don't know."

I gently pulled her toward the kitchen. When we were about to enter the room, she stomped her boots a number of times just to be sure, then half-flew onto a kitchen stool and from there hopped up onto the counter. She crossed her legs, held the tennis racket ready to swing, and glanced around like the enemy was about to attack from all sides.

I tossed the bag onto the counter and pulled out the glue traps. "What's that?"

"These are the best way to catch a mouse. We'll just set them all over the place. This guy won't have a chance. Don't worry, Taffy. We'll get him."

As I opened the closet pantry door, I could hear her draw in a breath, like she expected some giant thing to jump out and attack. I placed four of the adhesive sheets around the edge of the closet. Back in the far corner, I found a high protein low sugar nutrition bar on the floor. Something, presumably the mouse, had nibbled through the wrapper and had eaten a sizable corner of the bar.

"Well, look what I found. It looks like your mouse might be a health fanatic."

She looked at the bar in my hand and shook her head. "Oh, so gross. Get it away from me. Throw it in the wastebasket under the sink, please."

This was not the time to tease her or throw it on her lap. I did as instructed.

"Now wash your hands and use plenty of soap," she said.

When I was finished, I took the rest of the adhesive sheets and placed them in various areas around her unit. I placed three of them beneath her bed. "Okay, all done. Now, would you feel safer at my place?"

She just nodded, still really frightened.

"You stay here. I'm going to pack a little suitcase for you. I saw a suitcase in the closet. I'll pack enough for three days. Okay?"

"Yeah, but don't open the suitcase in here. Take it out onto the balcony just in case he somehow got back in there."

I went into the bedroom, pulled her suitcase out of the closet, and looked at it. There was no way in hell anything got inside the thing. "Taffy," I called, "the suitcase is closed. Nothing could get into—"

"Do not open it in my unit. Take it out onto the balcony, Dev," she shouted.

"Okay, okay, relax. I'm taking it onto the balcony." I walked past her, through the living room, and out onto the balcony. She slid halfway around on the kitchen counter to watch. As I was about to open the suitcase, she yelled, "Wait, Dev. Close the sliding door before you open it." I must have given her a look. She shouted, "Just do it, okay?"

I slid the door closed and opened the suitcase. At no surprise, there was nothing inside. I turned it upside down, shook it, then closed it and stepped back inside.

"Okay, mission accomplished. Let me pack a few things for you." I opened the suitcase and set it on her bed, then opened her dresser drawer and pulled out three thongs and three bras. I grabbed the lacy red one-piece and a black negligee from her closet and tossed them in the suitcase. I took her black leather skirt, the short one with the slits up the sides, off a hanger and put it in the suitcase. I reached between the mattresses and grabbed the battery-operated appliance, and tossed that in. She had two sexy tops in a dresser drawer, and I packed those.

"Put a pair of jeans in there, bottom drawer on the right," she called from the kitchen. I opened the drawer and noticed the black leather slacks folded beneath the jeans and decided those would be better. Added her make up kit, skin creams, hair conditioner, shampoo, electric toothbrush, hairdryer, a half-dozen other creams, and finally, I was finished.

"Okay, we're all set. Now, where are your keys?"

She pointed to the little rack hanging on the wall beneath a kitchen cabinet. I pulled the keys off the rack, picked up the suitcase, and set it outside in the hallway. I walked back to the kitchen counter, gave her a kiss, turned around, and said, "Hop on."

She hopped on my back, kissed the back of my head, and I carried her out into the hallway. She slid off, I locked the door, and we took the elevator down to the first floor.

"I'll drive over to your place," she said, already sounding a hundred percent happier. I gave her the keys, and she headed down to the underground parking while I carried her suitcase out to my car.

I was waiting for her on my front porch when she pulled into the driveway. Morton and friends were in the backyard, and I wanted to give her a little warning before she saw them. She climbed out of her BMW, grinned and hurried up to the front porch.

"Oh, thank you so much for doing this. I just can't believe it."

"I'm just glad you're here. Now, I'm going to have to go back to work, but I'll take this suitcase upstairs, and I need to tell you about Morton."

"Your dog? Is he okay?"

"Yeah, but he has some friends out back."

"What do you mean, friends?"

I went on to tell her about the strays. I might have embellished my suspicions regarding their involvement in foiling the purse snatching last night. "But the other thing I thought was, just in case that mouse followed us over from your place, I wanted them here to protect you."

"The mouse? Can they really follow you like that?"

"I don't know that they can't, so I thought it best to play it safe."

She seemed to think about that and finally nodded, suggesting it made sense. "How long are you going to be working?"

"Shouldn't be more than an hour or two."

"Can I get dinner ready for you?"

"I was thinking we'd just go across the street to LaGrolla. Great Italian food, we can have dinner there if that's okay with you."

She leaned up and gave me a kiss. "Thank you for being so kind."

"I'm just glad you're okay. Let me run this upstairs, and then I had better take off."

Thirty-nine

The View, where Seymour Smeelie had lived, was a six-story condo building on Shepard Road; a four-lane road running along the river bluff was out front. I parked a block away and walked back to the building. I crossed a small visitors parking lot, at the moment empty but for two cars, and entered through the rear door. I had the list Brianna had provided, and I punched in the security code on the keypad next to the door, heard the lock click, and stepped inside. I took the elevator up to the Sixth floor. Seymour's unit, number 606, was in the middle of the hall.

I noticed a two-inch length of yellow and black tape attached to the bottom of the trim around the door. No doubt it was police tape that said, 'POLICE LINE DO NOT CROSS.' The immediate question was, had it been removed by the police or one of the residents who didn't want it shedding a bad light on their unit? My guess was it had been a resident since the cops would have been more careful, always fearing a complaint. Whoever tore it off couldn't be bothered to reach down and just pull the bit of tape off the bottom of the frame.

It didn't matter. I slipped the key in the lock and opened the door, stepped inside, and quietly closed the door behind me. I entered a spacious living room with two leather couches arranged on either side of a gas fireplace. Two wingback chairs, a coffee table, and a lovely sideboard with a silver candlestick at either end made the room appear classy. At the far end of the room was an enclosed porch that overlooked the river. Unlike Soapy McGriff's place, you could actually see the traffic on the river. At the moment, a cabin cruiser was making its way downriver; two women and a man sat in the back and appeared to be drinking glasses of wine.

I opened the doors on either end of the sideboard. One end contained various liquor bottles, none of which held rum. The other end held a set of china dinner plates, salad plates, bowls, and two serving dishes. The kitchen and a bedroom were off to the left. The bedroom appeared to be a guest room with twin beds, a dresser with empty drawers, and a rocking chair. The walls were bare, and a door led to an attached bathroom with a shower tub combination, toilet, and a double vanity. Other than towels, soap, and toilet paper, the vanity was empty. I walked past the kitchen, across the living room, to the master bedroom.

A large king sized bed with an upholstered headboard was against one wall. The large dresser with nine drawers sat beneath a large mirror in a gold frame. The dresser drawers contained nothing but clothes, although two of the drawers contained women's clothing, and I wondered if maybe they belonged to Brianna.

The attached bathroom was basically a duplicate of the one in the guest room only larger. It struck me as strange that nowhere was there a semblance of anything resembling an office or a work from home area. Dishonest crook that Seymore was, he was still, essentially, his entire workforce. I knew a number of highly successful, self-employed individuals. Many had offices they traveled to daily, but all of them had an at-home office that they worked from in some way, shape, or form seven days a week. It appeared Seymour had nothing like that.

I looked between mattresses in both rooms, checked all the kitchen cabinets, looked beneath all the cushions on the couches and chairs, and found absolutely nothing. The place was almost too clean. The guest room closet contained two wool blankets, two empty suitcases, and about twenty empty hangers. I went through the closet in the master bedroom and found nothing out of the ordinary other than four blouses and a couple of skirts hanging at the far end, all of which seemed fairly normal.

I went back to the kitchen. There was an 'L' shaped granite counter with four padded kitchen stools along one side where the counter extended beyond the bottom cabinet. I opened the cabinet doors again and looked inside. The cabinet wasn't as deep as the outside dimension by a good foot. I pulled back the stools and looked for a door beneath the overhanging countertop, but there wasn't one.

I pulled out the pots and pans, plastic containers, and water pitcher from the cabinet and rapped my knuckles on the back of the cabinet. It gave a hollow echo. I checked the edges of the back of the cabinet. At the very top, I spotted what looked like the backs of two small brass hinges. I pulled out the center shelf, took hold of a small metal hook at the bottom, and pulled up. The back of the cabinet swung up, and as I moved my hand, the back of the cabinet, now perpendicular to the position it had been in, suddenly clicked into place against a magnet. In front of me, hidden in the hollow space of the cabinet, was a laptop and a number of files.

I pulled out the laptop and set it on the floor. I grabbed some of the files and placed them on the laptop. I grabbed another handful of files, stacked them on top of the others, reached in again, and pulled out a power cord and a computer mouse. I lowered the back of the cabinet into position, replaced the center shelf, and put all the pots and pans and things back in the cabinet.

I checked the other two cabinets beneath the counter, but they didn't have a secret storage area. The cabinet beneath the sink held the usual wastebasket, kitchen soap, and sponges. I checked the pantry closet— lots of canned goods, two packages of cookies, and a package of Hersey bars.

I hurried back to the guest room and grabbed the small suitcase. I placed the laptop and the files in the suitcase and, after giving it a moment's thought, tossed in both packages of cookies and the package of Hersey bars. I checked the kitchen and the other rooms to make sure everything appeared undisturbed.

I looked out the peephole in the front door and watched for the better part of a minute. Everything seemed quiet. I slowly opened the door and cautiously glanced up and down the hall. Mercifully, it was empty. I grabbed the suitcase, locked the door, and hurried down the hall to the elevator.

Forty

I tossed the suitcase into the backseat and sat behind the wheel for a moment, drumming my fingertips on the dash. I was wondering if I should take the computer and files to Louie to check out or turn them over to Tubby Gustafson and get him off my back.

I decided against both options, at least until I had some idea of exactly what Seymour thought was so important that he kept them hidden. Fortunately, I had a third option, someone who just might be able to do the research for me. I turned on the car and headed over to the Eastside.

The Leadbetter's lived in a small, 1920's white frame house in a neighborhood of similar structures. The computer-geek son, Preston, had been relegated to the basement. His mother kept the door leading to the basement locked at all times. Entrance and exit to Preston's basement abode was through the old coal cellar door. I didn't think she really needed to worry, because I doubted Preston, at close to four hundred pounds, could even make it up the stairs. If he did try, there was a reasonably good chance the basement stairs would collapse beneath his weight before he made it up to the locked door. I pitied the poor paramedics who would have to answer that call. They'd need a forklift to haul Preston out of the basement and a heavy-duty industrial truck to take him to the ER.

That said, Preston was nothing short of a computer genius, and he'd helped me out more than once, provided I got his attention away from the computer games that were his obsession.

I pulled in front of the house fifteen minutes later. Preston's mother was sitting out on the front porch in a rocking chair, reading a book. It was beastly hot; just about everyone who could was wearing t-shirts and shorts. Preston's mother was in a house dress with a gray wool sweater buttoned up over the dress. A steaming mug of what I guessed was coffee sat on top of the porch rail.

"Good afternoon, Mrs. Leadbetter," I called as I climbed the two concrete steps from the front sidewalk. She placed the book on her lap and looked up then smiled once she recognized me.

"Well, Devlin. How are you this afternoon?"

"Just fine, thank you. How are you? Enjoying the afternoon sunshine?"

"Yes, it's lovely sweater weather. Something for Preston?" she said, eyeing the suitcase.

"Yes, umm, my laptop and some files. I just need some things straightened out, and Preston is my go-to guy on computer problems."

She smiled and shook her head. "Hopefully, you'll be able to get his attention. Lord knows what sort of computer nonsense he's been involved in. Apparently, it's something international."

"Thank you for the update. I'll keep you posted."

"Good luck," she said then watched me as I headed around the side of the house toward the coal cellar doors that now served as the entrance to Preston's lair. I went down the stairs and tried the doorknob. Thankfully, it was unlocked. If Preston was involved in one of his games, he wouldn't hear me knocking, and if he did hear, I doubt he would answer.

I walked down the hallway, past both basement windows covered in tinfoil, past the futuristic posters and the life-sized cardboard cutout of Darth Vader. As I stepped into the main room, Preston was spinning 360 degrees in his desk chair with his arms raised and crying, "Victory. Victory." His computer screens, there were three very large ones in front of him, were all shooting fireworks.

"Hey, congratulations, Preston," I said, having no idea what he was celebrating.

He half-jumped, turned around wide-eyed, and then smiled when he saw me.

"Thank you, Dev. You are now looking at the new Intergalactic Grand Master Champion. I think I'll celebrate with another Red Bull." He was clad in his black silk bathrobe with the white lapels. He had bags under his eyes and at least a three-day growth on his face. The room smelled like a mix of stale pizza and a sweaty fat guy in need of a shower.

"Is the Red Bull in the fridge?" I asked.

"Yeah, help yourself."

"Thanks, but none for me," I said, opening the green door on the antique refrigerator. The fridge was pretty much empty except for mustard and ketchup containers, two pizza boxes, and what had once been a case of Red Bull, now down to about a half-dozen cans. I grabbed a can and handed it to Preston, reaching between two of the giant screens in front of him.

"Thanks." He popped the top on the Red Bull and gulped down half the can. He glanced at the suitcase. "You thinking of moving in? I got a cot if you want." He didn't sound like he was joking. He pointed at a cot beneath a pile of giant boxer shorts and t-shirts all in need of some serious attention.

"No, just loaded this up with a bunch of files and a laptop."

"Yours?"

"Mmm-mmm, not exactly. I'm working on a case. The owner is, well, he's recently deceased, and I'm trying to find out the status of his business. The guy was a real estate developer, and when he died, he was working on a project called EFH. That stands for Environmentally Friendly Homes. Anyway, I think the information is in here in the files and on the laptop." I placed the suitcase on the kitchen counter and opened it. I set the two packages of cookies and the Hersey bars on the counter, then stacked the files on top of the laptop and set them all on a table next to one of the large computer screens. I noticed the bag of Snickers candy bars with only two left. I grabbed the cookies and the Hersey bars and set them on top of the files.

"Oh, thanks, I was about to run out. You on any kind of timeframe with this stuff?"

"Timeframe? Not specifically, you know the usual, the sooner, the better. How does forty-eight hours sound, Mr. Intergalactic Grand Master Champion?"

He smiled and said, "That sounds like it will work. I've been gaming for almost seventy-two hours straight. Thank God for Red Bull and Snickers, but I'm going to need some shuteye pretty quick."

"Well then, I'll let you get to it. You want me to toss some of those pizza boxes in the trash?" I said, nodding at the four or five dozen large pizza boxes stacked up on a table behind him.

"Thanks, but not to worry. I order one or two just about every day, and when they deliver, I can always ask them to take a stack."

"Looks like you haven't asked in about a month."

"Hey, I've been busy. That's how I became the Intergalactic Grand Master Champion."

"Okay, if you say so. I'll see you in forty-eight hours. Get some sleep and call me if you have any questions. Don't know if I'll be able to answer them, but we can always try."

"Thanks, Dev. Much appreciated," he said, opening the package of Hersey bars and unwrapping one.

I gave a wave and headed back down the hall and out the door. Once outside, I took a couple of deep breaths to clear my lungs and then smelled my shirt to see if it had picked up any of the stench from Preston's abode. It hadn't seemed to, thankfully. I walked along the side of the house. Preston's mother was still reading, clearly deep into the book, and she didn't hear me coming. I glanced at the title, <u>Fifty Shades of Grey</u>. I walked past her, down the steps to my car, and she never even noticed.

Forty-one

I was halfway home when my phone rang. We have a law in Minnesota that makes it illegal to text or talk on a cellphone while driving. I pulled over to the curb and answered without looking at the screen. "Haskell investigations.

"Yeah, Dev. Aaron LaZelle, returning your call. What's up?"

"Thanks for calling back, Aaron."

"You know I can't give you anything on the Seymour Smeelie murder. The case is still under investigation and unless I hear from Miss Di Salvo's attorney—"

"Louie Laufen."

"Yeah, unless I hear from him, I can't discuss the case with you."

"Not a problem, Aaron, relax. I wanted some information on the purse snatching last night, where the dogs chased the guy off. Who has been handling those cases? I may have some information for them."

"Any information would be welcome. There've been close to forty of the damn incidents. From what we can piece together, it appears to be the same two or three idiots. The problem is they're so random, all across town. Any time, day or night and at gunpoint, we're lucky someone hasn't been shot. Would you happen to have a name?"

"I wish I did, but sadly no. This is kind of a back-door bit of information. I may have a line on the pack of dogs that chased the guy off."

"Really?"

"Yeah, they've been around the neighborhood, I think. A pack of four strays befriended Morton, and they're kind of staying at my place. I've been feeding them the last couple of days, letting them inside at night in bad weather. They're nice dogs." I waited for a response. "You still there?"

"What? Oh, sorry, I was taking some notes. Listen, the guy running that investigation is Billy Henden. Do you know him?"

"Name isn't ringing a bell, but maybe I'd recognize him."

"Would it be okay if I passed this along to him and gave him your name?"

"Yeah, I'd like to talk to him. Anything to get these dirt balls off the street."

"Preaching to the choir, Dev. I'll pass this on."

"Thanks, Aaron, much appreciated," I said and disconnected. I headed to the grocery store to pick up dog food, dog biscuits, and something for Taffy. I went home with two full grocery bags and another twenty-five-pound bag of dog food. I pulled into the driveway and parked behind Taffy's BMW. I carried everything up onto the front porch, then brought the bags inside and called, "Hi, Taffy, I'm home. Taffy? Oh, Taffy?"

No answer. I thought maybe she had gone for a walk, so I hauled everything into the kitchen, put the groceries away, dumped the dog biscuits into the cookie jar, and set the bag of dog food in the pantry closet. I was thinking about leaving a note and making a run over to Taffy's place to see if I had any luck catching that mouse when I heard the laughter from out in the backyard. I went out the backdoor and around the corner of the house, and there was Taffy, throwing the orange tennis ball to the dogs and watching them run around chasing one another.

"Are you making new friends?" I called.

"Oh, hi, Dev. We're just getting to know one another. They're all so wonderful. And this German Shepherd, it's like he's the general or something. What happened to his leg?"

"I have an idea. Based on his behavior, the way he watches everything and is aware of every move I seem to make, I'm guessing he was service trained, in the Army or possibly the Marines. That prosthetic can't be inexpensive and then the rehab so he could learn to walk again. Nothing short of amazing, and you're right; he definitely seems to be in command all the time."

She picked up the ball and tossed it in the direction of the fuzzy little white dog. He snatched the ball on the first bounce, stealing it from the Border Collie, and took off to the far end of the yard.

Taffy headed toward me and gave me a kiss. "The rest of your afternoon go okay?"

"Yeah, I guess I'll know in forty-eight hours. I dropped off a laptop with a guy to see if he can get some information from it. The thing belonged to that murder victim I told you about."

"Oh, so sad. How dark do things have to get that murder becomes the logical response?"

"Well, not to condone that action, but the guy had a long history of cheating people out of a lot of money. The list of people who are happy to see him dead is pretty long. The thing is, we've no idea who did it. The woman accused is innocent, I think. But enough of that, you interested in some dinner across the street?"

"Yeah, that sounds nice. Let me just slip into one of the negligees you packed for me, and I'll be ready to go."

"Oh, well, you see, I'm going to plead guilty as charged, and I'm not going to apologize. I can't help it if I think you're beautiful."

"Oh, you are one smooth talker when you want to be. Let me just change tops and fix my hair, and I'll be ready. Shouldn't take more than a minute or two," she said and headed into the house. A minute or two, yeah right.

I went inside and turned on my laptop. I went to the Pioneer Press site and found the contact link for Abigale Douglas, the reporter who wrote the article on the purse snatching and the dogs. I sent her an email, asking her to contact me and mentioning I might have information on the stray dogs. I sent a text message to Louie, telling him I had some general information and would touch base with him in the morning. I checked the forecast for the rest of the night, clear skies for the next five days, which meant everyone would be sleeping outside except Taffy and me. I checked the tweets on my Twitter site. I scanned today's edition of the Pioneer Press online. I checked my Facebook messages. Finally, against my better judgement, I checked the clock. That *shouldn't take more than a minute or two'* was approaching the forty-five-minute mark.

I turned off my computer and headed upstairs. Taffy was in the bathroom, doing makeup. "I'll just be a minute or two," she called.

I was tempted to say she said that forty-five minutes ago, but there was no point. I put on one of my less wrinkled shirts and said, "I'll be waiting downstairs by the front door."

She came down the stairs ten minutes later, looking like a million bucks. Amazing what an hour could do, but then I thought she looked great before she got all dolled up.

Forty-two

As the name suggests, LaGrolla is an Italian restaurant. The place was reasonably full, with a nice clientele, no loud shrieking, no booming music. Just good food and nice conversation with Taffy about everything and nothing. We'd finished our main course and ordered dessert. Taffy had added a glass of Prosecco.

"You mind if I ask you something, Dev?"

"I suppose it depends on what you ask."

"What's going to happen to those dogs?"

"I don't really know. Ideally, it would be great if they were all adopted by nice families. I mean, they really are nice, well-behaved, especially considering I've got five of them right now, including Morton. To be honest, I can't go on keeping them for very long. I think there's a city ordinance that says you can only have up to three dogs. I've got a call in to the police and another one into the woman at the newspaper who wrote a story about them. I was thinking, if we could get some good publicity that might get some folks interested in them and someone may want to take one of them home."

"I like that little guy," she said.

"Oh, yeah, he's a character. Apparently, he's the one who chomped onto the purse snatcher last night and wouldn't let go. Ultimately, they chased the guy away, but a big part of that was because the little guy bit him on the leg and hung on."

"Well, I think he's just darling. Would you mind if I got some folks involved? People who might be interested in adopting one of them and if they're not, they probably know someone who would be."

"I think that would be a wonderful idea. We need all the help we can get. I'm going to make some calls tomorrow on the Shepherd. I know a couple of veterinarians, and I'm also going to call the VA. I can't shake the thought that he was a trained military dog."

Our desserts and Taffy's Prosecco arrived. We finished up, I paid the bill, and we walked back across the street.

"How often do you eat there? It's really nice," Taffy asked.

"Not often enough, probably because it's too convenient. I'm going to get the coffee ready for the morning," I said and headed into the kitchen. Taffy followed me and then went out the backdoor. A moment later, she was back inside with Morton and all his pals.

"Oh, not to worry, I checked the weather. They'll be okay sleeping outside for the better part of the next week."

"Dev, you are not going to keep them outside overnight. I thought you told me they slept in the kitchen."

"Yeah, they did, the night it rained, well and maybe one other night," I said that second part almost in a whisper to myself.

"All right, so no big deal. They're already in here, so they can just stay." The Shepherd settled onto the floor in a corner, and Morton stretched out not far from him. I'd already lost the battle before it even began.

"Yeah, okay. Listen, you want to go upstairs or into the sitting room and watch some tv? I'm going to finish up in here and then close the door, so they're not wandering around during the night. How many cups of coffee do you want in the morning?"

"Two or three will do, and are you making breakfast?"

"Apparently."

"See you upstairs." She turned to face everyone stretched out on the floor. "See you all in the morning. Behave," she said and headed upstairs. I got the coffee pot ready for the morning. Set out two plates, silverware, and little bowls for the yogurt I'd bought and followed her upstairs.

I waited, sitting on the bed for the better part of twenty minutes, until she was finished doing whatever she was doing in the bathroom. "My turn?" I asked when she came into the bedroom.

"Yeah, it's all yours."

I went into the bathroom and tried to find my toothbrush among all the makeup, creams, the blow dryer, hairbrushes, eye shadow, and God only knew what else.

I checked three times and couldn't find it then opened one of the drawers and there it was.

Taffy was in bed under the covers when I stepped back into the bedroom. She watched as I undressed for bed and said, "That bruise on your butt is looking a little better. Does it still hurt?"

"Not as much as yesterday. Your tender loving care is much appreciated," I said and made a mental note to figure out a way to get even with Bumpy. "Are you going to check out your place tomorrow morning?"

She shook her head and said, "No way. Not until you get that mouse. Oh," she said and seemed to shiver, "it's just awful."

"Okay, I'll go over in the morning and check it out," I said as I climbed into bed.

Taffy gave me a kiss and then rolled over onto her side with her back to me. "Good night," she said, sending the message nothing else was on the agenda.

Forty-three

I was up at six the following morning. I slipped into my jeans and t-shirt as quietly as possible and headed downstairs. Almost everyone was still asleep. The German Shepherd only half-raised his head. Once he saw it was me, he immediately went back to sleep. I turned on the coffee and fired up my laptop. I had an email from Abigale Douglas, the reporter from the Pioneer Press. The message was sent just a few minutes after midnight, which suggested she either worked the night shift or she was just coming in from a night out.

'*Would be interested in chatting with you. Please give me a call on my private number tomorrow.*' The phone number followed. I added her phone number to my contact list. I let Morton and his pals out around half-past seven. I filled the two saucepans with food and put out a fresh pan of water. Maybe an hour later, I heard Taffy turn on the shower upstairs, so I mixed up a bowl of pancake batter and added fresh blueberries. I placed a bottle of real maple syrup on the counter next to the plates. I went out into the backyard and headed for the far corner. Everyone's head was up, watching me, but none of them made a move to leave.

A few daisies were hanging through the pickets in the far corner, and I cut four of them off and went back inside. I placed the flowers in a small bud vase someone had given me a few years ago and set the vase on the counter. I had the pan warming on the stove, and when I heard Taffy walking toward the stairs, I poured the batter into the pan.

She stepped into the kitchen and set her suitcase down at the door. "Mmm-mmm, it smells wonderful. Aren't you just the great cook. Oh, thank you," she said as I handed her a mug of coffee, and she took a sip. She settled in at the counter. "Nice flowers," she said and took another sip. She studied me for a long moment. "Saint Paul Saints t-shirt? Please tell me that's not the same t-shirt you were wearing yesterday."

"It is, but I'm a guy. Believe me. No one cares what I'm wearing. What's with the suitcase? Are you going back to your place?"

"Absolutely not. But I did make up a little list for you," she said, reaching into a pocket and unfolding a piece of paper. She handed me a list of items, more underwear, jeans, socks, tennis shoes - pink ones, a brown belt, a black belt, the list went on for another dozen items and at the bottom she'd written, NO NEGLIGEES.

"I'll head over there after breakfast. You sure you don't want to come with?"

"Thanks, but very sure. Besides someone has to stay here and watch our guests. I'll start getting in touch with people. Before I forget, can you add my laptop to your list?"

"I'm not sure there's any room on the list."

We had a nice breakfast. Taffy insisted on clearing the dishes and washing up. I headed out the door with her empty suitcase and drove over to her place. I packed her suitcase, remembered to add the laptop, and then checked all the adhesive traps. Nothing beneath her bed, in her closet, under the living room couch or beneath the stove. The last place I checked was her pantry closet.

There he was, all two inches of him, face down and looking awfully dead. I dropped the adhesive trap into a plastic bag, tied a knot around it, then walked down the hall to the trash chute and sent him on his way. I went back to her pantry and grabbed one of the nutrition bars. I broke off little pieces and placed them in the middle of all the adhesive traps, then closed the suitcase and drove back home.

Taffy was in the now spotless kitchen on the phone. As I set the suitcase down, she grinned and gave me a wave. A minute or two later, she finished with, "Thanks so much Gail. I'll send you the pictures in just a minute. Yeah, you too. Talk later," she said and disconnected.

"Good news?"

"Yes, very. That was Gail on the phone. She's got someone interested in the Lab. She volunteers at a rescue shelter, and she's going to check into some things. I took a bunch of pictures, and I'll send them out to friends. Did you find anything?" she asked, suddenly sounding very concerned.

"As a matter of fact, I did, a very dead intruder. He's wrapped up and in the trash. I think we'll leave those traps around for another day or two just to be sure."

She exhaled and closed her eyes. I could literally see the relief flooding over her.

"Oh, thank God. You can't believe the pressure I was under. I don't know how to thank you, Dev."

"I can think of a couple of ways."

"Of course you can."

"I'd better head down to the office. You okay to stay here alone?"

"First of all, I'm not alone, I've got my admirers out there. I might run an errand or two. Do you have a spare key so in case I go I can lock up?"

I pulled out a spare key from a kitchen drawer and handed it to her. "If you go anywhere, leave the dogs in the backyard. I'm curious to see if they stay put. I better get going," I said and gave her a peck on the cheek.

Forty-four

I headed down to the office. Louie was at his picnic table desk, with a number of files still scattered around. "Everything okay?" he asked as I stepped in the door.

"Yeah, fine. I've got Taffy staying with me until we get rid of her mouse problem."

"How is that working out?"

"Pretty good. It might take a day or two to get used to the makeup and hair stuff scattered around the bathroom, but I can deal with that, I think. I was over at her place this morning and found a dead mouse. We're gonna keep the traps out for a few more days just to be sure. I told you how wigged out she was over the thing."

"You mean when she told you there was an intruder and to bring your gun? Yeah, I did hear. Your message this morning suggested you may have found some information."

"I hope so." I went on to tell Louie about the files and the laptop I found hidden in the back of Seymour Smeelie's kitchen cabinet. "I took them over to Preston Leadbetter. He's going—"

"That computer whack job?"

"Yeah, that's him. Look, Louie, you think either one of us is going to be able to go through Smeelie's laptop effectively and get information? There's a good chance we'd end up erasing everything by pushing the wrong button. He'll go through all of Smeelie's emails and stuff. As far as the files go, they'll probably corroborate whatever is on the computer. It's just going to take a little time is all."

"You're sure he's going to go through everything instead of playing computer games?"

"Yeah, I don't expect that to be a problem," I said, thinking maybe now was not the best time to mention Preston had just won the title of Intergalactic Grand Master Champion. "Any word from Brianna? How are things shaping up on your end?"

"She seems sane, at least for the moment. She seems to have accepted the fact that her latest accessory is going to be that ankle bracelet."

"I'm more than a little surprised at that."

"Yeah, well, I haven't heard any complaints, so I'm keeping my mouth shut. The more I look at Smeelie's undertakings, the more convinced I get this is somehow related to his EFH project. He certainly screwed people in the past, but with the exception of a handful of lawsuits that ultimately were dismissed, no one did anything beyond complaining. No threats, no assaults, no one spray-painted his car."

"Thus far, all our circumstantial evidence points to Soapy McGriff," I said.

"Well, yes, but based on the evidence, especially the 'I'll Kill You!' notes, one could make the pretty strong case that it also points to Brianna. We need something more."

"I'm hoping that is exactly what Preston is going to find. Evidence that fingers Soapy McGriff and that thuggish idiot, Bumpy."

"Speaking of Bumpy, how's the butt?"

"Still in recovery mode but much better, thanks for your concern."

My phone suddenly rang. The screen listed Abigale Douglas, the newspaper reporter.

"I need to take this," I said. "Haskell investigation," I answered.

"I'd like to speak with Mr. Devlin Haskell, please."

"You got him. Is this Abigale Douglas?"

"It is, Mr. Haskell. Thank you for your messages. I'm sorry I'm so difficult to reach. I'm currently working four to midnight."

"Not a problem, and please, call me Dev. I read your article concerning the purse snatching the other night. Actually, it wasn't too far from my house. The description of the little white dog matches one of the dogs camping out at my place." I went on to describe the dogs. I mentioned Morton and the German Shepherd specifically and finished up with Taffy working to find homes for them.

"It certainly sounds like the same group. A little white dog was the one that thwarted the robbery. He bit this criminal in the leg and simply wouldn't let go. Not sure how much damage he did but certainly enough to chase the culprit away. The guy hopped into a black SUV and drove off, which matches the vehicle description in a handful of other cases. I do know the police were checking various hospitals for anyone coming in with a dog bite on the calf of their leg. It just makes you wonder."

"Would you be interested in stopping over some time and seeing the dogs?"

She paused for a moment before she said, "Yes, very much so. Would it be too much to ask if I could bring a photographer with me? My thought is I could do a story, add a photo, and it might help in finding families that would be willing to adopt."

"My girlfriend and I were thinking the exact same thing."

"Would later this afternoon work for you?" she asked.

"Yes, how about, say half-past four. You can photograph all you want."

"That would be excellent. What would you think if I could get the woman they saved to come with me?"

"Even better." We said our goodbyes, and I disconnected.

Forty-five

At about the same time, Loraine Willis parked her car in the Target parking lot. She was on her lunch break and hurrying in to get everything for her daughter's fifth birthday party on Saturday. The lot was full, especially considering it was a weekday, but then it was the lunch hour— no surprise she'd had to park in the far back end of the lot.

She was reviewing the list she'd written on the back of a card offering a cellphone discount for ninety days, half-planning which direction would be best for her to go once she entered the store. She wasn't really paying attention to anything around her.

"Just give me the purse bitch, and you won't get hurt," the deep voice suddenly growled in her ear and something jabbed her in the side.

Loraine's first reaction was to wrap both hands around her purse, turn around, and scream. "Just who in the hell—" she started but never finished. She saw the gun, large and black, just before he clubbed her across the forehead, twice.

"Are you okay?" a distant voice asked.

"Honey? Honey, you just stay still. We've called 911. The police are on the way. Did anyone see anything?"

"Is she going to be all right?"

Loraine opened her eyes for a moment, heard what was maybe a siren, distant, way too distant to worry about, and closed her eyes again.

Forty-six

I placed a call to a guy I know at the Veterans Administration. He's not employed by the VA, but he's a psychologist, and he does a lot of volunteer work over there. Everything from playing his guitar to psychological testing and helping vets with paperwork. He did two tours in Iraq and considers himself fortunate to be able to help.

"If you're calling me for money, I'm not giving you any," was how he answered his phone. "How you doing, Dev."

"Good, Randy, how about you?"

"Same day, different shit. Neither one of us has anything to bitch about."

"You got that right, not that it stops me from bitching."

"What's up?"

"I got a question for you." I explained about the dogs and mentioned their involvement in breaking up the purse snatching the other night. I went on to tell him about the German Shepherd and the prosthesis.

"That doesn't make sense," he said.

"What that the dog has a prosthesis? I'm telling you, man, he really does."

"No, I get that part. I mean, it doesn't sound right that he's a stray. Can you get close to him?"

"Let's just say he's allowing me to get closer. But if I peek in on them when they're all asleep, he's the one who immediately looks up. He seems to always be on guard. At least now, when he looks up and sees it's me, he puts his head down and goes back to sleep."

"Can you get close to him?"

"Yeah, pretty close. If my dog is lying next to him, and I'm scratching and rubbing my guy, the Shepherd's okay with that."

There should be a serial number on the prosthesis. If you could get me that number, I can do a quick search. You got any pictures of him?"

"My girlfriend does and—"

"Girlfriend? You mean some poor woman is patient enough to put up with you? Or did the court system assign her to keep an eye on you?"

"Yeah, well, she constantly tries to keep me on the straight and narrow."

"I'll have to talk to her professionally and attempt to help her out. You said she's got some photos of this dog?"

"Yeah, in fact, she just took them yesterday. We're trying to get them all adopted."

"Have her send me the images and maybe a closeup of the prosthesis. That might yank some memories somewhere. I'm just surprised if it's a military dog that there hasn't been an active search out there. Months of time and a lot of money are invested in training these animals. Not to mention the medical costs involved if this guy was fitted with a prosthesis. Have her send those images to my cellphone."

"Thanks, Randy, much appreciated."

"We'll get together soon, Dev. You keep me posted if you learn anything else about this dog."

"Will do, talk to you later," I said and disconnected.

I called Taffy and asked her to send the photos she had. I gave her his phone number, and she promised to send them as soon as we disconnected.

"Sounded like it went well," Louie said. "I'm thinking about grabbing some lunch. You feel like joining me up at Skinner's?"

Skinner's was a pub with great food just up the street. "Yeah, that sounds like the perfect—" My phone rang, an incoming call from an unknown number. "Haskell Investigations," I answered.

"Mr. Haskell, please." The female voice maybe sounded familiar, but I couldn't quite place it.

"This is Dev Haskell."

"Oh, hi, Dev. Melinda Jenson, did I catch you at a bad time?" It took me a second, Melinda Jenson, Soapy McGriff's niece and receptionist.

"No, not at all, Melinda. How are things on your end?"

"Mmm, interesting. I'm wondering if we can meet. Some stuff is going on around here and I'm not liking it."

"Yeah, sure, absolutely we can meet." I signaled Louie with a thumbs-up. "Are you still at work?"

"No, I couldn't wait to get out of there today."

"You got time for lunch?"

"I've got a statistics class at one, but lunch with you sounds a lot better. Where do you want to meet?"

"You know where Shamrock's is?"

"That place down on West Seventh?"

"That's the place. I could meet you there in thirty minutes, right around half-past eleven. I'll buy."

"I'll be there," she said and hung up.

"Good news?" Louie asked.

"Soapy McGriff's niece and receptionist. She said things are going crazy at the office, and she wanted to meet. You heard, Shamrock's in thirty minutes."

"Oh, pray that there's something happening on that end. We could sure use a break."

"Keep your fingers crossed, Louie. I'm going to head over there now and grab a quiet table in a corner. I'll call you with an update as soon as we're finished."

Forty-seven

I parked on a side street and entered through the backdoor at Shamrock's. The place is a highly popular bar and restaurant and seems to add another room every five or six years. Right now, there are four rooms. I left my name at the front desk and grabbed a booth in the next room over. I was the only one in the room. The server set down two menus, and when I asked if it was a problem I was sitting back here, she just shrugged and shook her head no. I ordered a decaf coffee and waited for Melinda Jensen to show. As it turned out, I didn't need to hurry over. Eleven-thirty came and went. Right around a quarter to twelve, the server topped up my decaf for the third time.

"You want to think about ordering?" she asked.

"That's probably better than thinking about strangling the person I'm waiting for. Give me a couple more minutes. If she doesn't show, I'll order. Thanks for being so patient," I said.

"No big deal," she said and left.

As she exited the room, Melinda suddenly appeared around the corner. "Oh Dev, there you are. I've been waiting at the bar for the last twenty minutes, and then it dawned on me you might be back here. Is this room even open?" she said, looking around.

"Yeah, we got a nice patient server. I'm sorry. I left my name at the front desk but no big deal. Sit down and check out the menu. Remember I'm buying."

"I already know what I'm getting. I studied it while I was sitting at the bar. Then a couple of guys were making eyes, and that's when it dawned on me you might be back here. How's your butt, by the way?"

"Fortunately not a problem. But I'll always have a special place in my heart for Bumpy."

"I can only imagine. He just gives me the creeps. Apparently, he lives at my uncle's house, but I've never actually been there, so I can't be sure."

"Never been there?" I said, conjuring up images of the library office, the dining room with the massive table, and the three bottles of rum in the front room cabinet.

"My mom was ready to strangle me when I took the part-time receptionist job at the start of the last semester. She would literally strangle me if she found out I ever went to his house."

Our server wandered back in and took our order. Once she left, I said, "So, you said things were kind of crazy today. Everything all right?"

"I'm not sure, maybe. I was just glad to get out of there today. My uncle was yelling at Bumpy. I mean, really, really yelling. Even with his office door closed, I could hear him. He just went on and on, literally ranting.

Every time Bumpy started to say something, my uncle would cut him off and yell some more. I almost felt sorry for Bumpy, except that he's such a creep."

"Any idea what he was yelling about?"

"Something about a bunch of files on some project and how they'd been blindsided. I'm just glad he doesn't allow me to touch any of his files. It's tough enough just sitting there all morning, every morning. He gets about three phone calls a day, maybe. Usually, at least one of them is some recording about car insurance or cellphone service. I'm just there as window dressing to help him look legit. It's a really rare occasion when someone comes in for a meeting with him. He and Bumpy go somewhere almost every morning, and—"

"Are they always going to the same place?"

"I don't think so, but I honestly don't know. They seem to have a lot of meetings with people working for the city and the state, but then given the nature of the business, building things, that doesn't seem so strange, does it?"

"No, in fact, it sounds entirely normal. But it was different this morning, with the yelling and everything?"

"Yeah, he was yelling at Bumpy and telling him he had better find the files if he knew what was good for him 'cause if he didn't, they were going to be out of business. The funny thing is, I always had the impression my uncle was the only one who ever handled the files. Bumpy's too stupid to read what's in them. Not that he ever would anyway. And my uncle is such a control freak, neither Bumpy or I have ever been allowed to even touch them, ever."

"Did you hear what files were missing, who the client or project was?"

"Yeah, a couple of letters, EHF, or something like that."

"How about EFH? That stands for Environmentally Friendly Homes. It's a project your uncle was involved in along with a guy named Seymour Smeelie."

"Isn't that the guy that was murdered?"

"Yes, he was poisoned, actually. His body was found in his office."

"Yeah, I think they were going to go see him the other day, but I never heard anything else about it. No real surprise, everything there is always one great big giant secret."

Our server came around the corner carrying two plates. I'd ordered the bourbon bacon chicken sandwich, and Melinda was eating some vegan thing I couldn't remember. She set the plates down in front of us, placed a tea in front of Melinda, and asked if there was anything else we needed. When we both shook our head, she left.

"Did you ever meet Seymour Smeelie?"

Melinda took a bite and shook her head no. When she finished chewing, she said, "I know they went down to see him in Florida last spring, but they were back the next day. I can't say if it was business or pleasure, but then I can never really see my uncle doing anything that would be fun."

"So, why are you telling me about all this?" I asked.

She set her sandwich down and looked at me. "Okay, so here's the deal. I'd be the first one to say my uncle is not a nice person. He cheats, he abuses, and he's basically just a very evil person. The money he pays me goes to my tuition, all of it, one hundred percent. I live with my folks. When I'm not sitting behind the receptionist desk studying or writing a paper, my life is focused on school, doing the best I can, and graduating early. I'll be graduating this December, and when I do, I can get a real job and get away from my uncle and that creepy Bumpy. Until that time, there is a very big part of me that feels like I'm just as guilty as those two because, even though I just sit there every morning at the receptionist desk, in a way, I'm contributing to their cause. And I don't like that."

Forty-eight

When I got back to the office. Louie asked "How did it go?"

"Interesting. No earth-shaking revelation. She didn't turn over bank records or anything. She basically said she's more or less stuck there until December when she graduates, and then she's going to be looking for a real job and getting as far away from her uncle as possible."

"Didn't she allude to some problem she wanted to tell you about."

"She did, and maybe that's the good news."

"I'm not following."

"She said Soapy was yelling at Bumpy. Telling him to find the EFH files. I think he was probably talking about the files I found hidden in the kitchen cabinet yesterday."

"What would be in those files that he wouldn't know about?"

"No idea. I'm guessing it's probably something that Smeelie kept from him. Some sort of game-changer that's in the files. Hopefully, Preston Leadbetter will uncover whatever it is, and we'll know tomorrow."

"I wonder if you shouldn't call him today? I could go over there and—"

I shook my head. "I told him he'd have two days, and I'd like to keep it that way. When's your next court appearance scheduled?"

"Three weeks and a day," Louie said, glancing at his calendar.

"With any luck, we'll have Brianna off the hook by then, and the authorities can give their undivided attention to Soapy McGriff."

"The sooner, the better," Louie said.

I hung around the office for another half-hour and then said good-bye and headed home. Taffy was out in the backyard, watching the dogs chase one another around.

"How's it going?" I called to her. The dogs immediately stopped for a moment at the sound of my voice, and then once they saw it was me, they started up again chasing one another around the yard.

"You're home early. Is everything okay?"

"Oh yeah, I contacted that reporter who wrote the article on the purse snatching the dogs stopped. She's coming over in about a half-hour and was going to try and get the woman who was attacked to come over too. She was thinking she would write an article about the dogs, have a photographer take some pictures. You know, get some publicity out there. I mentioned you were contacting friends. Any luck, by the way?"

"Some people are interested. Gail's going to get back to me later today or tomorrow. She's the one who volunteers at the rescue shelter. I'll see what she found out. Why don't I put some coffee on for when this reporter arrives?"

"Yeah, good idea. Let me ask you something. How close can you get to that Shepherd?"

Oh, the commander in chief? Pretty close, he let me scratch him behind the ears earlier. I can certainly pet him. Why? What are you thinking?"

"I told you I spoke to Randy. He's the psychologist, and he does a lot of volunteer work at the VA. He wanted some close-up photos of the prosthesis and hopefully the serial number on the thing. Once he has that, it might narrow down the search and speed up finding out what the story is on that guy."

"Maybe go get me a biscuit; in fact, why don't you get one for everyone? So no one feels jealous."

"Back in a minute," I said. I pulled five biscuits from the cookie jar and then pulled my phone out. I sent Abigale Douglas, the reporter, a text message telling her we were all out in the backyard. Everyone paid attention to me when I came back out with a fist full of dog biscuits. Morton and the other three stopped chasing one another around and hurried over. The Shepherd had been stretched out in the sun watching all the activity, and he suddenly sat up.

Taffy pulled her cellphone from her pocket and took a biscuit from me. I handed one to Morton and the other three as Taffy walked over to the Shepherd. She placed the biscuit in the palm of her hand and slowly moved her hand toward his mouth. He gobbled up the biscuit in two quick bites. Once he was finished, she scratched him behind his ears and was able to take a number of photos of the prosthesis and of him.

"Any luck on a serial number?" I asked as she strolled over.

"Yeah, I think so. Let me bring them up here and see if you can read the number. It was six or seven digits." She brought the image up on the screen and quickly shook her head, "Nope." Same thing with the next one, and the one after that.

When the fourth image came up on her screen, she stared for a moment then grinned and handed me her cell. There it was, a legible six-digit number. "Perfect. Great job. Send that to me, and I'll text it over to Randy."

The image came over thirty seconds later, and I sent it on to Randy. A few minutes after that, I heard a couple of car doors slam and looked around the corner of the house and down the driveway. A blonde woman with glasses waved. She was followed by a woman with salt and pepper hair and a big guy with glasses and a camera.

"Dev Haskell?" the blonde called.

I nodded as they approached. "Nice to meet you, Abigale. This is my friend Taffy."

Taffy smiled and nodded.

"Please call me Abby. Abigale was my grandmother's name. This is Janice Sterling. She was involved in the incident the other night not far from here, and Vincent Tocci, our photographer. And these must be the heroes of the hour," she said, looking over at the dogs, who had all stopped and were now watching warily.

"Yes, the Golden Retriever belongs to us. His name is Morton, and he somehow made friends with all these guys."

"We brought some treats for them," Abby said. "Would it be all right to pass them out?"

"Certainly, maybe just move slowly, until they get used to you, it's really only been Taffy and me around them. Well, except for when they've snuck out on the street."

"Janice, what do you think? Do they look familiar?"

"Oh," the woman said, "yes, yes, it's them. I recognize the little guy. He's the one who bit that bastard. And the big one," she said, pointing to the German Shepherd. "He seemed to bark the loudest, but they all played a part in chasing off those two. May I?" she said, pointing to a bag of little dog treats, Canine Carry Out Sausage Links. Abby handed her the bag.

The Border Collie stepped forward, apparently familiar with the treat. She tossed one to each dog and then repeated the process two more times.

"Oh," she said, looking at Taffy. "I can't thank them enough. If it weren't for them, well, I don't know what would have happened." The Border Collie stepped closer, and she petted him and then scratched him behind the ears. I heard Vincent on the camera clicking away.

The lab stepped up and got the same scratches behind the ears. She reached into the bag and handed out another round of sausage links.

"And this one fellow has a prosthesis?" Abby said.

"Yeah, we're thinking he was trained in the military, very observant. Obviously, that prosthesis wouldn't be inexpensive. I'm not sure where he's from or what his history is. Taffy took some photos of the prosthesis, and we sent one that shows the serial number to a friend involved in the VA. Hopefully, we can find out more about him and possibly even reunite him with someone."

"And you mentioned you're taking them to a rescue shelter?"

"No, I didn't say that. Taffy—"

"I'm talking to a number of friends who have expressed an interest in them," Taffy said. "One of my friends volunteers at a rescue shelter, and she's helping me. Morton, the Golden Retriever, stays here. The little white one is already spoken for," she said and flashed me a look.

"Oh, I've just the home for that Border Collie. Has anyone expressed an interest in him?"

"Not exactly," Taffy said, "but there are a lot of people looking, and we're hoping once this article gets published, they'll all be scooped up."

"Put me down for the Border Collie. I've the perfect home for the little dear. I just have to talk to my husband first."

"Really, you'll take him?" Taffy asked and gave Janice a big hug.

"Yes, absolutely, I just have to let my husband know first. Believe me, after the other night, there will be no argument."

"Would you mind telling me about the incident, Janice?" I asked.

"There really isn't much to tell. I parked my car and was walking to a friend's condo building. Suddenly, this person just appeared between two parked cars, grabbed my purse, and said, 'Give it to me or you're dead.' Not exactly the nicest introduction. Then out of nowhere, that little white guy latched onto the calf of his leg and wouldn't let go. He threatened to shoot him, but the others were suddenly barking and growling. I was on the ground and the Border Collie was standing over me, literally protecting me. That awful person shook the little one off, hobbled into the street, and hopped into a black SUV. But he never got my purse, and he didn't hurt me, other than a couple of bruises. And it's all because of these brave dogs. They're lifesavers," Janice said and reached into the bag and handed another sausage link to each one.

"How long have you been following this series of robberies?" I asked Abby.

"Almost since the start. The poor police are just stymied. Janice, how long from start to finish did your incident last?"

"You know I'm not really sure. Certainly no more than a minute, maybe just thirty seconds. It wasn't the middle of the day, but it wasn't quite dark either. Just after sunset. There were people driving past without their lights on."

"And that's a big part of the problem. It's all random, the time, the place, the victim. Whoever it is, they spot a likely victim on the street, a woman, and they attack. It's happened all over the city. It happens so fast the descriptions of these guys are just vague. A male, and in Janice's case, a male who was limping back to the black SUV. No one has been seriously injured yet, but it's only a matter of time. One has to wonder what's happening to our city."

Forty-nine

I was up early the next morning and put the coffee on. I had to tiptoe around, so I didn't wake up all the guests sleeping in the kitchen. This morning the Shepherd didn't raise his head when I walked into the room. I turned on my computer and brought up a copy of the Pioneer Press. There was Abby's article in the lower righthand corner of the front page, with a photo of all five dogs gathered around Janice. The headline read, 'Woman Meets Rescuers.'

My guests began to wake up, and after a few minutes, I let them out the backdoor and set out their food and water. I wrote a note to Taffy, telling her I was out to buy a newspaper, and then headed out the front door. I walked two blocks to the newspaper box stand. The thing was steel, blue, and stood next to the bus stop. I put three dollars in quarters in the coin slot, opened the box, and grabbed three newspapers. When I returned home, Taffy was in the kitchen pouring a cup of coffee.

"Oh, you're already up," I said.

"I got an early morning text message from Janice. I was half-awake anyway. They're going to take the Border Collie. She just wants to get some things set up for him before they come and get him."

"Oh, that's great. He'll go to a good home with plenty of loving attention. Check this out," I said, handing her a newspaper.

She opened the paper and then squealed, "Oh my God. That is so perfect with Janice and all of them on the front page." She sat down, read the article, and then glanced up. "I also had a message from Gail. She has friends with a farm out north of Stillwater. They've got two little girls, and they would love to take the Lab."

"Great, that just leaves the Shepherd and that fuzzy little white guy," I said.

"I'm taking him, Dev. He's the smallest and the toughest one of the bunch."

"Well, then that just leaves the Shepherd. I'll check with Randy later today and see if he's found out anything with that serial number. With any luck, I'm going to be going over a bunch of files this afternoon. Do you want to drive over to your place with me this morning and see if the coast is clear?"

"Are you kicking me out?" she asked but then smiled.

"God, no. You're welcome to stay as long as you want, but I figured you'd want to check your mail, maybe look around the place. I'll be with you, ready to defend you against any and all intruders."

She nodded and said, "Probably a good idea. Let me shower, get cleaned up, and then we can go."

"I was going to make breakfast. You up for some more blueberry pancakes?"

"Oh, I'd love them, but they'll go right to my waist. Maybe just a piece of toast for me."

I knew better than to argue. She seemed to be able to know when she added so much as an ounce of weight. I just nodded and plugged in the toaster. While she was in the shower, I mixed up the pancake batter, added the last of the fresh blueberries, fried up three gorgeous pancakes, and sat down to eat. I finished breakfast, loaded the dishwasher, washed the pan, put everything away, and was on my computer when she came back downstairs.

"Oh, that's so sweet. You didn't have to wait for breakfast with me."

"Happy to do it. In fact, I think just toast is a good idea. Can I make you some?"

She nodded as she filled her coffee mug then sat down and reread the newspaper article.

I put four pieces of bread in the toaster. When they popped up, I placed a couple pieces on each plate and then put the butter along with jelly and jam on the counter in front of her.

"Do you have any honey?"

"I do," I said and pulled a container out of the cabinet.

She put no more than a drop of honey on the toast, no butter, and then scraped her knife across the top. I loaded about a half-inch of raspberry jam on my piece of toast and carefully spread it to the edge on all four sides.

Taffy stared with her mouth half-open. "You sure you have enough on there? Did you even notice how little honey I used?"

"Yeah, I did, just enough to give you a hint about how good it would taste if you used the proper amount. I'm just having toast. The least I can do is enjoy the jam. Besides, it's raspberries, so it's really just fruit."

She shook her head. After the toast, we checked on the dogs in the backyard, then hopped in my car and drove over to her condo. She seemed okay until she took out her key to unlock her door.

"Maybe you should go in first and make sure it's safe before I come in," she said as she shoved her key into the lock.

"It'll be ok. If you see anything, just leave, and I'll deal with it."

"What if they follow me?"

"Taffy, if there is one, he's not going to follow you. Come in with me, so you can start to get over this fear thing."

"I don't know."

"Well, I know." I reached over and turned the key in the lock. "Come on. You can follow me." She hesitated for a moment then cautiously followed me in. Once inside, she stomped her pink tennis shoes a couple of times. "You just stand here, and I'll check the glue traps beneath the couch. Fortunately, they were clean. I went through the bedroom and all the closets, not so much as the hint of a mouse anywhere.

"Looks like you're good to go— no sign of any intruders. Let's just keep the traps in place, but I doubt there'll be another one," I said, crossing my fingers.

She closed her eyes for a couple of seconds and seemed to relax. "Thanks, Dev. I really mean it. I was ready to sell the place."

"Was that going to be before or after you burned it?"

Fifty

I was sitting at my desk talking to Louie on the phone. He was meeting with Brianna over at her house. "Dev, we need to know what was so important in those files that Seymour Smeelie kept them hidden. It would seem to me there's about a ninety percent chance whatever is in there is what had Soapy McGriff raving yesterday when his niece contacted you."

"I hope you're right, Louie, but let's not get ahead of ourselves. God forbid, but what if it turns out to be just pornographic pictures or something that he wanted to keep hidden?"

"I know for a fact it won't be pornographic photos, Dev, because if it was, you would have kept them all and never mentioned the files."

"Yeah, maybe, but you get what I'm saying. If it'll make you feel any better, I'll give Preston a call once we hang up and see if he's found anything. Any other area you'd like me to start looking?"

"No, just hoping for the best, meaning the worst, with this computer and the files."

"Soon as I hear something, I'll let you know," I said and hung up. My phone rang a couple of minutes later. I was in the process of watching two young women in shorts push strollers down the street. They turned the corner just as I answered, hoping it was Preston Leadbetter.

"Hi Dev, you free to talk?"

"Yeah, Randy, you bet. Were you able to check out those photos Taffy sent you yesterday?"

"Yeah, I did. In fact, that's the reason I'm calling. Turns out that German Shepherd is quite the guy. Let me summarize what I learned from his semi-official biography. His name is Oscar, by the way. He lost part of his leg in Afghanistan during an attack in 2017. His handler, Staff Sergeant Tommy Robbins, was wounded in the same attack and lost both legs. Both of them were sent back to Fort Bragg, North Carolina. Staff Sergeant Robbins, originally from this area, died from his wounds in 2018, leaving a wife and three small children. Oscar was awarded, and that word is in quotation marks, a Commemorative Purple Heart that had been donated for the purpose. Robbins is buried in Oakland cemetery, here in town. His wife's name is Patti, and I have a phone number here if you want it, but I don't know how current the number is."

"Yeah, give it to me, Randy. I'll maybe give her a call." As he gave me the number, I wrote it down. "Thanks for the number. Man, a widow with three small kids, I don't know if she'll be happy to hear from me or not."

"Well, if for some reason she doesn't want to talk, or take Oscar, let me know. After that article I saw in the paper this morning, there'll be a long line of folks wanting to give him a home."

"Thanks, I'll keep you posted." When I hung up, I sat and thought for a while. Would I be bothering Patti Robbins? It sounded like she had more than enough to worry about without some guy calling her about a dog. I decided to wait a bit before I made the call. I basically did nothing for the next hour and a half then finally got tired of waiting and placed a call to Preston Leadbetter.

He answered on the third ring, "Dude."

"Hi Preston, wondered if you were able to go through those files and the laptop I dropped off the other day." I could hear what sounded like explosions and fireworks in the background, which was not an encouraging thought.

"Yeah, I went through most of it. Whoever Three-fifty-eight-boy-toy is, he's one unhappy dude."

"I'm not quite following. I— Say, Preston, do you think you could pause that game I'm hearing in the background? It's hard to concentrate on what you're telling me."

Thankfully, the background noise suddenly stopped. "How's that?"

"Much better, thank you. Who was this person? Boy toy?"

"Yeah, Three-fifty-eight-boy-toy, that's his email address. A bunch of back and forth emails with the guy and your pal Seymour. Maybe a week ago. This Boy-toy person was clearly getting madder with every exchange. He finally says, let me bring it up here. Yeah, here we go. Dig this, *'I think you're trying to pull a fast one, and I won't have it. I'll be there in one hour. I'll expect to learn how you intend to straighten things out, or you're done. You had better be there when we arrive. '*"

"He doesn't sound like a very happy individual."

"Gee, you think? It's interesting, Seymour's got a number of emails from local and state agencies regarding property referred to as the Cummins site and the EFH site. From what I could determine, given the legal descriptions attached, they're the same place."

"So, what's with the emails?"

"Well, both emails and a number of registered letters threaten lawsuits, big lawsuits. Apparently, the area is very polluted, and they want him to clean it up. Let me rephrase that; they expect him to clean it up, sooner rather than later. We're talking millions."

"Explain what they mean by polluted?"

"From what I could determine, it's something called polyfluoroalkyl substances, PFAS for short. It's apparently contaminating drinking water."

"Does he say he'll do that? Clean the stuff up?"

"Absolutely not. A lot of dodging back and forth. State estimates were between six hundred and eight-hundred million bucks for the cleanup. From what I could see, he didn't mention this to anyone in any of the emails, but there was a one-way ticket to Venezuela in one of the files. He was set to fly down there two days before you dropped off all these files. Looks to me like he was probably planning to flee the country."

"Only someone got to him first. Interesting. Can you write me a quick summation on what you found? I'll be over shortly to take everything off your hands. What kind of pizza do you like?"

"Extra-large with everything would do me just fine."

"Coming your way in about an hour, Preston," I said and hung up. I phoned Louie but ended up leaving a message. "Louie, I'll be in the office for another thirty minutes. Call me when you get this."

While trying to get my head around eight hundred million, I went back to thinking about Patti Robbins and her three little kids for a bit. Suddenly, my life was looking pretty damn simple. I picked up the phone and ordered an extra-large pizza with everything on it. As I hung up the phone, I glanced out the window just in time to see Louie oozing out of his Geo Metro. He pulled a briefcase from the backseat and waited for a car to pass before he quickly waddled across the street. I heard the staircase groaning under his weight a moment later.

Fifty-one

ouie entered the office red-faced and breathing heavily.

"Nice going, you made it up the stairs," I said by way of a greeting.

He nodded, set his briefcase on the picnic table, and collapsed in his chair. "Oh, man. That is one hell of a long way up."

"How'd things go with Brianna?"

"They're coming along. She literally has a grocery bag full of Florida receipts, not that it matters. Right now, our best defense is shaping up to be she wouldn't get paid if she killed him. You're looking like the cat that swallowed the canary. You learn something?"

"I think so. I'm about to head over to Preston's. I got off the phone with him maybe twenty minutes ago."

Louie looked at me for a long moment, waiting, then finally said, "And?"

"Two things, first, emails back and forth with someone using the ID Three-fifty-eight-boy-toy."

"Who the hell is that nutcase?"

"I'm not sure, but I've got an idea. Perhaps more importantly, there are registered letters from local and state authorities regarding a polluted site. Specifically, the Cummins industrial site, the future home of the EFH project. Apparently, the powers that be would like to know when the cleanup of the site will begin. They're estimating a pollution cleanup cost of around eight-hundred-million. From what Preston could determine, Smeelie kept it secret. But there were a lot of vicious emails back and forth, and get this, a one-way ticket for Smeelie to Venezuela."

"What was he going to do down there?"

"Preston thinks he was going to flee the country, and I'm inclined to agree."

"Oh, this is fantastic. If there's enough fire in those emails, it may be enough to clear Brianna. If only there was some way to tie all this to Soapy McGriff," Louie said.

"I'm going to head out in a minute to pick up everything from Preston. You can start going through the files as soon as I get back."

"I'll be waiting for you," Louie said.

I drove over to Summit Ave, passed by Soapy's place, then swung over to the Pizza Shack and picked up the extra-large pizza with everything. Once I had the pizza secure on the floor of the passenger seat, I headed over to Preston's. His mother wasn't sitting on the front porch, so either she had finished reading <u>Fifty Shades of Grey</u>, or she was reading it in her bedroom. The coal cellar door was open, and I hurried into Preston's lair with the pizza.

I could hear explosions from a computer game before I saw him. Once I stepped around the life-sized Darth Vader cutout, I spotted him sitting behind his three computer screens. Fortunately, he was dressed today in a t-shirt and jeans. He wore a baseball cap wrapped in tinfoil on his head.

"Hi Preston, lunch is served," I called and took the pizza over to the kitchen counter. The suitcase I'd grabbed from Seymour's place rested on the counter exactly where I'd left it, only now the laptop and all the files were piled on top of it.

"Be with you in just a bit," he said, and he wasn't kidding. Less than a minute later, he paused the game he was on and groaned as he climbed out of his desk chair.

"Mmm-mmm smells delicious," he said, waddling toward me. His upper body jiggled with every step. He rubbed his hands together and licked his lips in anticipation of the pizza and reached for a piece. "I've been working up an appetite."

I was going to ask how you worked up an appetite sitting in a chair all day long but quickly thought that wouldn't be the best direction to take. Instead, I complimented him on his t-shirt. No doubt an extra, extra, extra-large black t-shirt with red and blue glittery fireworks and the gold banner that said, 'Intergalactic Grand Master Champion.'

"Congratulations on the t-shirt. Well done, Preston. That's pretty cool."

"Mmm-mmm, thanks, Dev," he said through a mouthful of pizza. "They over-nighted this to me. You can't buy these anywhere. They're only issued to the Champion."

"Well-deserved. How long do you get to hold onto that title?"

He stuffed an entire piece of pizza into his mouth and then said, "It's mine for thirty days, and then there's another competition, but I'll win that too."

"Is that hat keeping you warm?" I asked, nodding toward the baseball cap covered with tinfoil.

"Just a safety precaution. Someone might be able to scan my brainwaves and get a jump on whatever my next move is going to be."

He didn't seem to be kidding, and I nodded like that made perfect sense. "Can you give me a quick overview on what you learned from this stuff?" I asked, indicating the stack of Seymour's files and his laptop.

Preston shoveled the better part of a fresh slice of pizza into his mouth, tossed the crust back in the box, wiped his hands on his new t-shirt and said, "Umm, I did up a summation and put it in there along with all the emails I printed off." He pointed to a manila folder filled with pages. "Mind if I give you a little advice, Dev?"

"No, not at all, go ahead."

"Whoever this Three-fifty-eight-boy-toy is, be careful. He's doesn't seem like a very nice guy."

"Thanks, I'll keep an eye out," I nodded. We chatted a little more. Clearly, Preston was anxious not to have to share his pizza, and as Master of the Universe or whatever he was, he wanted to get back to his games. I thanked him, told him to send me a bill, and hurried out the door.

When I pulled to the curb across the street from the office, Louie was standing at the window watching me. I pulled the suitcase out of the backseat, gave him a thumbs-up, and hurried into the building. He opened the office door when I was halfway up the stairs.

"Please tell me you got something," he said.

"I'm pretty sure I do, and I have an idea."

"An idea?"

"Relax, it's pretty simple."

"Oh?"

"Yeah, you make a copy of everything in this file, and then I take it down to Aaron LaZelle in homicide. It looks like there's enough in this file and on the computer to take the heat off of Brianna and direct it toward this Three-fifty-eight-boy-toy person."

"But do you know who the hell that is?"

"I have a pretty good idea. It just so happens that three-fifty-eight is Soapy McGriff's address."

"No kidding? Oh, thank God."

"Yeah, and it looks like Seymour was about to flee the country after getting pressured from authorities about the pollution cleanup at the Cummins site. From what Preston could determine, it doesn't appear he ever told Soapy about it, and probably for good reason. The estimate to clean up the site is eight-hundred-million. I just want to get this stuff down to Aaron and let them move forward with it."

Louie seemed to think about that for a half-second and then nodded. "Yeah, let me start making copies."

"Make two copies of everything, and Preston has a separate file in there with a summation of everything and copies of the emails. Maybe keep that with us." Louie nodded as he turned on the copy machine and loaded it up with fresh paper.

Fifty-two

I phoned Aaron LaZelle and ended up leaving a message. Fortunately, he phoned back maybe ten minutes later. "Yeah, Dev, you called." I could tell from the sound of his voice he was busy.

"Yeah, Aaron, I've come into possession of some items that appear to be relevant to the Seymour Smeelie murder, and I would like to turn them over to you."

"What kind of items?" he said, sounding like I suddenly had his full attention.

"A number of letters from city and state authorities addressed to Smeelie concerning a pollution problem at the Cummins site, along with his laptop computer and a one-way ticket made out to Smeelie for a flight to Venezuela, which would seem to suggest he was fleeing the country."

"And you came into possession of these items, how, exactly?"

"I'm not at liberty to say, but they're authentic. I just think you guys should have them."

"And you have them now?"

"I do, and I could turn them over to you in the next hour or so."

"All right, bring them down. I'll alert Detectives Bennett and Schaffer. They're the team working that case."

"Okay, but I'm going to ask for you when I get down there."

"I'll let them know you're coming. Anything else?" Aaron said.

"No, that should do it. See you in about an hour," I said and hung up.

"He okay with that?" Louie asked and placed another sheet on the copier.

"He didn't sound all that thrilled, but I think once he takes a look at all this stuff, he'll hopefully be a little more positive."

It took Louie a little over an hour to make all the copies. Then we went through them one by one just to make sure we hadn't missed anything. Louie typed out the password for Smeelie's computer, placed it on the keyboard, and then closed the laptop. It was closer to two hours before I pulled into the parking lot and hurried into the station carrying Seymour Smeelie's suitcase with the files and the laptop. Gary was seated at the front desk, and he smiled at me as I walked through the door.

"About time. I've had two calls looking for you in the last half-hour. A number of people are wondering where in the hell you were."

"I'm guessing Lieutenant LaZelle."

"He was the second call. Detective Schaffer was the first. Apparently, you're in pretty high demand. Everything all right?"

"I think it's going to be just fine."

"Have a seat, Dev, and I'll let them know you've arrived. Shouldn't be more than a couple of minutes."

It seemed more like ninety seconds. Both Bennett and Schaffer hurried across the lobby before I'd barely gotten out of my chair. "You got something for us?" Schaffer said. They were both in shirts with the sleeves rolled up to their elbows, their ties were loosened, and the top buttons on their shirts were undone.

"It's all in here," I said and handed him the suitcase.

"Come on up with us," Bennett said as Schaffer led the way, and Bennett stepped in behind me. They effectively sandwiched me in between the two of them, pretty much eliminating any chances of my running out the door, not that I had been planning to do that.

They led me up to an interview room on the third floor. Not the carpeted room with the cushioned chairs Brianna had initially been in. This was a cinderblock room with a metal-topped table, uncomfortable plastic chairs, and a lingering scent of sweat and maybe fear. I'd been in there more than once over the years. As we walked in, I gave a little wave toward the two-way mirror on the wall just in case Aaron was in the viewing room watching.

"Take a seat," Schaffer said as he set the suitcase on the table. He pulled a pair of blue latex gloves from his pocket, slipped them on, then glanced at me before he popped the locks on the suitcase. The files were all stacked on top of the laptop.

They looked at one another, and Bennett said, "How did you come into possession of this?"

I shrugged and said, "Just lucky, I guess. That's Seymour Smeelie's laptop, and the files contain documentation regarding his project to redevelop the Cummins factory site. There's also a one-way ticket for Smeelie to fly down to Caracas, Venezuela. The flight was scheduled for two days after he was poisoned. I don't know this, but it looks like he might have been planning to flee the country."

Schaffer looked at me for a long moment then told Bennett to call forensics. They didn't really interview me. They asked some general questions, and we chatted back and forth for maybe fifteen minutes before a woman in a white lab coat pushed a cart into the room. Schaffer closed the suitcase, placed it on the cart, and told her he'd be down shortly. We had two more minutes of conversation once she left, and then they escorted me down to the lobby. Surprisingly, they thanked me and sent me on my way.

I drove back to the office. Louie was at his desk, working his way through the stack of copies. "Well, at least they didn't lock you up. How did it go?" he asked.

"Pretty well. They asked how I got the stuff, and I just dodged. Everything is down in forensics right now. I'm sure they're going through that laptop as we speak.

With any luck, it should quickly become apparent that Brianna is in the clear, and they should direct their attention toward Soapy McGriff."

"Let's hope so," Louie said. "Buy you a round at The Spot?"

"I'd love it, but I'd better head home and check on Taffy. Can I take a rain check?"

"Yeah, some other time."

As I climbed into my car, I was thinking of picking up a frozen pizza or something. My phone rang, and I checked the screen, Taffy. "How's it going? I'm just about to head home. You up for a frozen pizza?"

"Not really. I'm making dinner, and if you stopped and picked up a bottle of red wine on the way, that would be perfect."

"What are you making?" I asked.

"Dinner," she replied.

Fifty-three

Taffy had made a delicious chili with Italian sausage, fresh ciabatta rolls, and a little salad on the side. I sat at the kitchen counter, eating crackers with hummus as an hors d'oeuvre while she finished making the salad. She had the radio dialed into a classic rock station.

"So I get back from the grocery store, and they're all gone. The backyard is empty. I didn't know if I should call you, drive around looking for them, or start making dinner," she said and took a sip of wine.

"When did they get back?" I asked, glancing out the window at Morton and his pals all lounging in the backyard. I spread garlic hummus over a cracker and shoved the entire thing into my mouth.

Taffy shot me a quick look but didn't comment then said, "I'm not sure when they got back. All of a sudden, I looked out, and there they were. So I went out, gave everyone a dog biscuit, and they haven't left. We need to have them sleep in the kitchen tonight. That Janice and her husband will be here tomorrow afternoon to take the Border Collie home, and the farm family with the little girls will be picking up the Lab. Did you ever call that woman about the Shepherd?”

You mean Patti Robbins? Actually, I’ve had so much going on, it just slipped my mind. I’m a little worried about causing her more stress. I mean it’s bad enough she lost her husband, and she’s got these three little boys. Do you think she’s going to want a dog to take care of, too?”

“Maybe she could decide that for herself, Dev.”

“Yeah, I suppose. I just don’t know.” I reached for my wine, but Taffy grabbed my glass and slid it just out of my reach. “Call her now. And whatever she says, you can celebrate the fact that you made the offer. Just get it out of the way. I can tell it’s bugging you.”

I sat there for a long moment then took a deep breath, pulled out my phone, and made the call.

A woman answered on the fourth ring. I could hear kids making noise in the background. “Hello.”

“Hi, I’m trying to reach Patti Robbins.”

“Speaking.”

“Hi, Patti. My name is Dev Haskell. I live in town. I’m a private investigator, and—”

“A private investigator, what’s this about?”

“No problem, don’t worry. Actually, I’ve had a stray German Shepherd with a prosthesis staying at my house for maybe the past week.”

“A prosthesis? Is it Tommy’s dog, Oscar?”

I heard a kids voice in the background say, “Oscar? Did someone find him?”

"Yes, it is." I went on to explain about the picture of the prosthesis, Randy checking the serial number, and the confirmation.

"Oh, my God." She suddenly sounded like she was about to cry. She sniffled into the phone and said, "We moved about three months ago, and I know it sounds crazy, but we lost him during the move. Everything was so nuts. We posted pictures all over the neighborhood, and the Wounded Warriors even went door-knocking maybe six weeks ago, but we never heard a thing. Oh my God. Where do you live?"

I told her and based on her description of their new place out in a distant suburb, I guessed they were a good thirty miles away.

"Oh, I can't get in there tonight, but we'll be in the city tomorrow, Saturday. I could get over there in the early afternoon, maybe a little after the noon hour. Oh, my God, I can't believe it. You've answered our prayers. What did you say your name was?"

"Haskell, Dev Haskell. Listen, Patti, if it would help, I would gladly meet you somewhere. I can hear little voices in the background there, and I'm guessing every day is pretty busy for you."

She seemed to think about that for a moment and then said, "Yeah, actually, that might just work out really well." She told me where they'd be, and I agreed to meet them tomorrow at noon. I mentioned the newspaper article with a photo of the dogs and told her we'd send the photos Taffy took as soon as I hung up.

"Oh, you are so wonderful. I can't thank you enough," Patti said.

"Yeah, glad we were able to talk. Looking forward to seeing you tomorrow," I said and hung up.

"Sounded like that went pretty well," Patti said and slid my glass of wine back in front of me. "Aren't you glad you— Dev, honey, are you crying. What's wrong?"

"Nothing, it, it worked out great, really well. Better than I, than we could have hoped. Taffy, here's her number. Would you send her those photos you took, please? I'm going to get everyone inside, so they don't run off tonight, and then I want to dig into that chili."

I grabbed a handful of dog biscuits and hurried outside. I wiped the tears from my face and then walked towards Morton and his pals, all the while waving the biscuits. Everyone was up on their feet in an instant, even Oscar, the Shepherd.

"Come on inside, guys. Biscuits, biscuits." That was all the encouragement they needed, and they followed me back into the kitchen. Taffy got off her stool and closed the door leading to the rest of the house. She watched me as I handed out the biscuits but didn't comment. When I finished, she said, "You okay? Ready for some dinner?"

"Yeah, I'm doing great and I'm starving for some of that delicious chili."

Fifty-four

I slept fitfully that night and dreamt about a pal named Jimmy Delaney we'd lost in a firefight. I'd helped load him onto the Black Hawk MEDEVAC. The last thing I told him was to take care and to mention my name to the nurses. He'd nodded, smiled, and died in flight. I was up at four Saturday morning and downstairs checking to see if Oscar was okay. I know it was crazy, but with all the memories, I shoved the sticky holster with the nine-millimeter into my belt to feel a little safer. I went through YouTube for the next few hours listening to old rock music from my high school days.

I let the dogs out around half-past seven. Taffy strolled into the kitchen wearing my Minnesota Wild jersey, maybe forty-five minutes later. "How long have you been up?" she asked as she poured herself a coffee. "You were twisting and turning all night long."

"Oh, sorry. Must have been that second bowl of chili I had. It was really good."

She smiled at that and said, "Well, don't say I didn't warn you." She took a sip from her mug. "I'm thinking I might go up the street to the bakery later this morning and get some cupcakes or something. We've got people coming to get the dogs this afternoon. You're taking the Shepherd to Patti. Maybe invite them back, and we can have one big going away party. What do you think?"

"I think that's a good idea. After breakfast, I'll go out and umm, clean up the backyard. Unless you want to?"

"Clean up the backyard? Oh yeah, no thanks. I'm sure you'd do a better job at it than me, so don't let me interrupt."

I made pancakes for breakfast, wishing I'd taken the time to get more blueberries. I placed two pancakes on Taffy's plate and five on mine. She watched me as I spread butter over every pancake then poured syrup over the stack until she said, "Stop, Dev, that's enough. God, maybe you should just put a straw in the bottle of syrup, and that way, you won't waste any."

"I could do that."

"I don't doubt it." She poured maybe a spoonful of syrup on her pancakes, raised her eyebrows at me as if to say, 'See.'

I finished my stack just in time for her to push her plate away with the two pancakes only half-finished.

"What? You didn't like them?"

"No, they were delicious, but I'm just full. I don't know how you can eat all those."

"I guess I worked up an appetite."

"Yeah, all that tossing and turning last night." I shrugged, pulled her plate in front of me, and cleaned it. "Why am I not surprised?" she said. "I'm going to jump in the shower and then head up to the bakery. Do you want to come with? I'll have some boxes to carry."

"Yeah, sure, I can do that. I'll clean up in here and then get going on the backyard."

There was a lot to clean up in the yard, an awful lot with five dogs. When I finally finished and went inside, Taffy was walking into the kitchen, looking like a million bucks. "You going to take a shower before we head up to the bakery?" She asked the question in a way that suggested it was more of an order.

"I wasn't planning on it."

"Plan on it. You've been walking around in dog poop for the last forty-five minutes."

"I only stepped in it a couple of times," I joked.

Clearly, she didn't see the humor, so I decided to play it smart and headed upstairs to shower. When I came back downstairs, my shoes were sitting outside on the porch steps. Taffy looked at the cowboy boots I was wearing but didn't say anything.

"You set to head to the bakery?" I asked.

"Yeah, you want to tuck in that t-shirt and maybe bring the dogs inside?"

"I'll check on them, but it's going to be their last day together. Maybe we'll just let them stay outside."

"Okay, as long as you're sure they won't wander off."

I went out to the backyard and checked to make sure they had enough food and water. I'd enjoyed having them here, but it was time for the next step, placing them with families. That was going to begin at noon when I took Oscar, the Shepherd, back to Patti Robbins and her kids. I tucked my t-shirt in over the sticky holster and hurried back in the house. Taffy was sitting on a kitchen stool with her purse draped over her shoulder.

"All set?" I said.

"Yeah, I want to stop in that little shop next to the bakery, too. They've got all sorts of cute things in the window."

"I thought we were just going to the bakery. Is this going to turn into one of your shopping adventures?"

"Oh, relax. Believe me, you do not have to accompany me into the shop. Tell you what. We'll walk up together, and you can get a dozen, no, better make it two dozen cupcakes. I'll run into that little shop, and we'll walk home together, both of us very happy that you didn't have to check the place out with me. Fair enough?"

"That sounds like an excellent plan. Thank you."

"Believe me, it's for my own peace of mind," she said under her breath.

We headed out the door and up the block.

Fifty-five

It was a gorgeous day, and we enjoyed the pleasant morning sunshine as we headed to the bakery. Taffy paused in front of the flower shop and stared in the window at the buckets of cut flowers.

"Do you think we should get a bouquet to put in a vase for this afternoon?"

"Taffy, they're coming to pick up a dog. They're not going to be looking at a vase of flowers inside. Besides, we'll have cupcakes."

She gave me a look but didn't respond. We walked past the little restaurant. It looked full inside, and all four tables on the sidewalk had couples sitting at them drinking coffee and, in one case, eating French toast. Next to the little restaurant was the shop she wanted to check out.

"I'll just be five minutes or so."

"Take your time. But keep an eye peeled for me. I'll be standing outside with the cupcakes."

"Okay, crabby," she said, gave me a kiss, and hurried inside.

I stepped into the bakery and stood at the back of the line. It was Saturday, so the line made sense, maybe. I sent Taffy a text message, *'I'm waiting in line. Take your time.'*

It never ceases to amaze me when waiting in a line in a shop that the people ahead of me never seem to know what they want when they finally get up to the front. What have they been thinking of for the past ten minutes? The guy currently at the counter was asking all sorts of questions: Did they know the calorie count on the caramel rolls? Did they use butter or margarine in the recipe? Was the apple filling in the strudel fresh or canned? The girl behind the counter kept smiling, but I had the sense she was just as frustrated as the rest of us. The next guy picked up a large order. A woman ordered an anniversary cake and left a photo of people to be copied in frosting on the cake. The next woman couldn't decide on rye or whole wheat bread. Finally, the guy in front of me ordered one glazed doughnut, and then I stepped to the counter.

I glanced over my shoulder, and Taffy was out on the sidewalk, with her purse draped over her shoulder, a pink paper bag in her hand, and a smile on her face.

"I'll take two dozen of the red velvet cupcakes with the cream frosting," I said, pointing to the tray of cupcakes, each with an inch high swirl of frosting.

The girl behind the counter smiled, two guys in a row who knew exactly what they wanted. Will wonders never cease? She pulled two knocked down white cardboard boxes from a stack, quickly assembled them, and began placing the cupcakes, one by one, in the first box.

She filled the box, closed the top, taped it shut, and set it on the counter. She picked up the second box, began to smile, and suddenly a look of complete horror washed over her face, and she screamed. She was looking over my shoulder out onto the sidewalk.

I turned just in time to see a guy knock Taffy to the ground and reach for her purse.

"Call the cops," I yelled and ran to the door.

As I opened the door, I heard him yell "Bitch," and suddenly, there was a pistol in his hand. I reached for my sticky holster to pull out my pistol, flubbed it, and it fell onto the sidewalk. Everything was suddenly in slow motion. He pulled on the purse, literally dragging Taffy along the sidewalk. I picked up my pistol and shouted, "Don't move, asshole."

He looked over and began to point his gun at me just as a little fuzzy white dog flew out of nowhere and clamped onto his crotch. He screamed and swung at the little dog who wouldn't let go. He pointed his pistol at the dog, and suddenly, there was Oscar barking, growling. He clamped onto the guy's wrist and began to chew his way up the guy's arm viciously. He dropped his gun. Blood was squirting all over, and suddenly, a second figure ran in between two parked cars raising a crowbar over his head and heading toward Oscar. I fired two rounds, and he dropped to the ground, just as the Lab and the Border Collie appeared on the scene. They stood over him growling as he rolled back and forth, clutching his knee. A black SUV suddenly took off down the street, skidded around the corner, and slammed into a phone pole.

Taffy was on her feet, clutching her purse and bleeding from her nose.

"Taffy, you okay? Taffy, look at me. Look at me. You're okay? You're okay, honey."

She nodded but didn't say anything. I looked over at the tables in front of the little restaurant. Everyone who had been seated there was standing further back with shocked looks on their faces. Morton had just finished cleaning the two plates with French toast. I led Taffy over to a chair and sat her down. "Morton, watch her," I said, and he straightened up. Oscar was standing over the guy with the bloody arm, growling and snapping at his face. Using my boot, I slid his gun across the sidewalk then slammed the heel of my cowboy boot on top of his good hand and ground it into the sidewalk. There was a crunching sound, he screamed, and I grabbed him by the hair. "You so much as move and I'm going to tell that dog to finish you off, you piece of shit."

I heard a siren in the distance, and a moment later, another one coming from the opposite direction. I kept my pistol on the two jerks on the sidewalk as the squad cars pulled up. The officers came out with guns drawn, and I raised my hands then slowly set my pistol on the ground. "I'm licensed to carry. This punk was going to shoot my girlfriend," I said.

"Bastard sicced his dogs on me," the jerk I shot shouted.

"He was going to shoot that poor girl and steal her purse," a woman shouted. People started coming out of the bakery and moving in closer on the sidewalk. Everyone was shouting at the two purse snatchers lying on the sidewalk. An older woman with a cane walked over and spit on one of them.

"That's his gun over there," I said and pointed to the revolver I'd moved with my boot. "There's a third one. He was driving that SUV down at the corner and hit that phone pole. I think he might still be in the car."

Two of the cops hurried across the street. Another cop stepped off to the side and got on the radio, calling for more officers and ambulances.

I walked over to Taffy. She was still sitting in the chair with her head tilted back. Two women were tending to her. They'd cleaned the blood from her face, and just now, she was pressing a paper napkin up against her nose.

"How are you doing?"

"As soon as I stop this bleeding, I want to borrow your gun and shoot those two bastards."

"That tells me you're going to be okay."

More squad cars and two paramedic vehicles arrived. I suddenly noticed that the dogs had disappeared. I was seated next to Taffy at the table on the sidewalk for twenty minutes while the police were busy taking statements. The two purse snatchers had been hauled away to the hospital, handcuffed to their gurneys. Another paramedic vehicle was down at the corner. The crew was in the process of wheeling the gurney, with someone on it, into the back of the ambulance.

Taffy was sitting upright now. She had just removed the napkin from her nose when a guy in shirtsleeves walked over. He was wearing a lanyard around his neck with a police picture ID hanging from it. A pistol and a badge hung on his belt.

"How are you two doing?" he asked.

"You're Billy Henden, the guy in charge of trying to nail these pricks."

He smiled and said, "And you're Dev Haskell. Aaron LaZelle warned me about you. Ma'am, Billy Hendon. How are you feeling?"

"Fine, a little banged up, but fortunately nothing broken. I just wish we had the death penalty in this state."

"Not to worry, with the list of assaults on these idiots, they'll be going away for a long time. A very long time."

"Not long enough," Taffy said.

"You've given your statement to the officers?"

"Yeah, the Sergeant took both our statements."

"What about the dogs? Where did they come from?"

"They were involved in stopping a purse snatching just a couple of blocks from here the other night," I said. "They've been staying at my place just down the street for maybe a week. Actually, they're strays, and we've arranged for them to go to homes. In fact, they're getting picked up this afternoon. We were just getting some cupcakes at the bakery when all this happened. One of the dogs belongs to me."

"And I have another one. That little white dog that first attacked that guy with the gun," Taffy said.

"They should all get a medal," Henden said. "Okay, we'll be in touch. We've got to do a ballistics test on your weapon, Mr. Haskell. You should have it back within a week or two. We've got your information, and you'll receive an email and a letter. You're okay to head home?"

"Yeah, I just need to get my cupcakes."

"I won't keep you then. You two stay safe."

"We will, detective. Say hi to Aaron for me."

"He's tied up at the moment, but as soon as I see him, I'll tell him. Thanks again, glad you're all right, ma'am," he said and walked over to two of the officers.

"Mind if I get those cupcakes and we head home?" I said.

"I'll be waiting right here," Taffy said.

I stepped back into the bakery. There was a short line, just three people long. As soon as the girl saw me, she stopped what she was doing, picked up the two boxes of cupcakes, walked around the counter, and handed them to me.

"Thank you," I said. "What do I owe you?"

"Nothing, they're on the house. Are you okay?"

"I will be as soon as I have one of these cupcakes."

She smiled at that and said, "Thank you."

As we walked down the street, a tow truck was in the process of hooking up to the SUV that had run into the phone pole. A blood-stained, deflated airbag rested on the driver's seat.

When we got home, Taffy headed up to the bathroom. A few minutes later, I heard the shower turn on. I went outside, and there was Morton and company, lounging around on the grass as if nothing had happened. "Come on inside, guys, treat, treat. Oscar, come on inside, treat."

That seemed to get their attention, and they followed me inside. I gave each of them two biscuits and emptied the cookie jar.

Fifty-Six

We coaxed Oscar into the backseat of my car just before noon and headed over to meet Patti Robbins and her kids. "You're awfully quiet, Dev. Thinking about this morning?"

"No, not really. I'm just glad you're all right."

"I'm just glad that creep didn't break my nose. My elbows are skinned, but they'll heal in a couple of days. I still wish you would have let me shoot those two."

"That's the problem with witnesses. You can't always do what you'd like to do."

"Mmm, where are we going anyway?" she said then glanced at Oscar in the backseat. He was busy looking out the window. She reached back and scratched him behind the ears. "You are such a good boy, Oscar. You saved me. Saved both of us."

"Yeah, well, him and your little guy. You think of a name yet?"

"You know, I haven't given it much thought. Maybe something like Super Man or Captain America."

"Or crotch."

"No, Dev, that will not be his name." I put the blinker on and slowed to make the turn. "What are you doing? Where are you taking us?"

"This is where we're meeting Patti Robbins," I said as I turned into Oakland Cemetery. Oscar was suddenly standing in the backseat, and he whined as we drove along the winding road past gravestones, some over a hundred and fifty years old. I stopped halfway up the hill, next to a large granite cross with the name Förster engraved in a banner and the date 1865.

"We're meeting them here?" Taffy asked, looking around at all the graves.

"She was bringing the boys in to visit their dad's grave. I guess they do it a couple of times a year. Oscar's been here before." Oscar was now pacing back and forth, anxious to get out of the car.

We climbed out, and I went to open the backdoor. Oscar barked a couple of times. "Okay, now calm down, Oscar, just calm down," I said, trying to slow him down as he got out of the car. He dodged me and headed up the hill. "Oh shit."

"Dev, catch him before he gets away."

I hurried after him, slowly gaining, and then he stopped and laid down in front of a granite tombstone. I slowed down, stopped, and then knelt next to Oscar. The tombstone was red granite with the name and dates.

Thomas Robbins
June 12, 1989 - August 11, 2018

Oscar gave a couple of little whines and then stretched out and laid his head on top of his paws.

Taffy came up alongside me, looked at the tears running down my cheeks, and put her hand along the side of my face and pressed my head against her thigh. "Oh, Dev, honey."

A minute later, we heard car doors slamming behind us, and I turned around as three little boys jumped out of a van and ran up the hill toward us. I wiped the tears off my face as a woman I figured must be Patti came around the car and waved. The kids were oblivious and charged up the hill, trying to trip one another. They came to a stop about twenty feet away, and then the oldest one looked and suddenly called, "Oscar?"

Oscar's head jerked around, and he was suddenly on his feet, limping toward them as fast as he could go.

"Oscar, Oscar," the kids screamed, running toward him. They surrounded him with hugs and kisses. Oscar's tail was going a mile a minute. Patti joined the boys, and they were all on their knees, hugging and petting Oscar.

"Oh my God," Taffy said and started crying.

I had a lump in my throat and wrapped my arm around her shoulder. I had to clear my throat a couple of times to get my voice back. "Let's go down and meet them," I said, and we headed down the hill. We both got a big hug from Patti. The kids were too busy with Oscar to say much more than, "Thank you," once their mother told them to. We chatted for a few minutes, and then it seemed like maybe they needed some private time. Taffy invited them over for cupcakes, and after giving Patti the address, we headed to my car, and they walked up the hill to Tommy's grave.

"You are really something," Taffy said and gave me a kiss once we were settled in the car.

"Just returning Oscar to those kids," I said.

She shook her head and gave me another kiss. "It was much more than that, my hero."

Janice and her husband Bob arrived at two. Fortunately, Janice brought a box of dog treats. Five minutes later, the Linder family showed up with their two girls to take the Labrador back to their farm. The Robbins family arrived with Oscar shortly after that. It was an enjoyable ninety minutes, and then one by one, everyone left to get settled in at home. I think each one of the kids had three cupcakes, which was just fine; otherwise, I'd eat them all later tonight.

We had leftover Chili for dinner. It was actually even more delicious on the second night. I cleaned up the kitchen while Taffy went upstairs. I had just poured the last two glasses of wine from the bottle when Taffy came back into the kitchen.

"Okay, all packed," she said.

"Packed? You're heading back to your place to-night?"

"Yeah, don't take it personal, but the sooner Muffin and I get settled in, the better it will be. Besides, the other dogs have gone, and you and Morton can get back to whatever passes for normal around here."

"Are you sure? I'd love it if you stayed the night."

"You know what, Dev? I would too, but I want to get him acclimated, and the sooner I begin, the better."

"And you're really going to call him Muffin?

"Why? What's wrong with that?" she said, cocking a hip and striking a defensive pose.

"Oh nothing, nothing, it sounds really nice. I just poured a glass of wine for us. How about we—"

"Thanks, but I probably shouldn't if I'm going to be driving."

"Okay, well, can I carry your suitcase out to the car?"

"Yeah, that would be great. I hope you don't mind, but I took one of your suitcases, too."

"Not a problem, I'll stop over later tomorrow and grab it."

"You're a sweetie," she said and gave me a kiss. "Okay, Muffin, come on. Let's go home." The little dog gave her a funny look. "Come on, Muffin. Come to Mommy."

"I'll put those suitcases in your car," I said. Poor Muffin didn't have a clue what he was in for. I waved good-bye as she backed out of the driveway, tooted the horn, and then drove down the street.

I walked back into the house. It suddenly seemed very quiet and empty. There was maybe half a bowl of chili left, and I ate it right out of the pan. No one was there to comment on my lack of manners, and it was delicious.

At a little after eight, my phone rang, Aaron LaZelle. "Hi Aaron, how's it going?"

"I should ask you the same thing. I heard you had a busy day."

"Oh, you mean this morning. Yeah, wrong place, wrong time. Fortunately, Taffy's okay. Some bumps and bruises but nothing broken. It could have been a lot worse."

"Well, it's going to be for those three. A list of priors on all three of them. They're going to get some serious time, and we've got a laundry list of people willing to testify."

"Where are they now?"

"The one you shot is in recovery. There's probably a good chance he'll be limping the rest of his life. He'll be transferred back to jail by the end of next week. The driver is locked up. The man the dogs went after is stitched up and is being transported as we speak. A hundred and nine stitches. The dogs did a pretty good job on him."

"Taffy said she wished she could have shot him."

"She's not alone in that. Like I said, they'll be doing some serious time. You ready for the other news?"

"Don't tell me my conceal and carry permit has expired."

"No, nothing like that. The files you delivered yesterday, they pointed a pretty serious finger at your close personal friend, Soapy McGriff."

"You guys going after him and his thug?"

"Already have, they're both under lock and key. I don't know if you knew this, but that email ID, three-fifty-eight-boy-toy, turned out to be Soapy's address. Forensics sent him an email, and when he read it, the two of them packed a bag and were headed to the airport. We had teams waiting at the front and back of the house. We got a warrant, and teams are going through his house as we speak."

"That's great news. You know, I wonder if he had something like a liquor cabinet in his front room. Maybe there's a bottle of the same kind of Cuban Rum that poisoned Smeelie." I waited for a long moment then said, "Hello, you still there?"

"I think I'll just suggest you have a pleasant evening. Glad you and the lady are okay after that incident this morning."

"Thanks for the call, Aaron. If I can be of any help, just let me know."

"I think if you just kept a low profile for the next few months, that would be the best thing for all of us. You've had a very busy day. Rest up."

I placed a call to Louie but ended up leaving a message.

Fifty-seven

I woke up Sunday morning with Morton stretched out in bed next to me. I got dressed and headed downstairs. Morton remained sleeping. I put the coffee on then turned on my laptop— nothing from Taffy. I sent Louie an email telling him I had some good news. I heard Morton stretching upstairs maybe a half-hour later, so I filled his food and water dish. I gave him his perfunctory scratch behind the ears when he came into the kitchen and let him out the backdoor. He hurried outside then stopped as he came around the corner of the house, expecting to see all his pals. I watched out the window as he looked back and forth at the empty yard. A while later, I let him back in the house. He had some water but ignored his food dish, which was unusual for him.

I went down to the basement and inserted the battery in my nail gun then went out the front door. I nailed the two loose pickets into place then checked the length of the fence to make sure there weren't any other loose ones. When I went back to the kitchen, Morton was eating his food. I ate the last two remaining cupcakes for breakfast and then phoned Louie.

"Yeah, Dev, what's wrong?" was how he answered.

"Actually, nothing. Don't know if you got my message. I wanted to let you know that Aaron LaZelle phoned me last night. They've arrested Soapy McGriff and Bumpy. They're charged with the murder of Seymour Smeelie. When we talked, they'd already gotten a warrant and were in the process of going through Soapy's place. I suggested they may want to check and see if a liquor cabinet might be in the front room with bottles of the Cuban rum that Seymour was poisoned with. I would guess they'll be going through his office as well. In fact, I should call Soapy's niece and give her a heads-up. You going to be in the office Monday morning?"

"Yes, absolutely," Louie said. "Listen, let me give Brianna a call right now. I'll talk with you later. This is great news. Thanks for the update."

I scrolled back through my list of calls until I found Melinda Jensen's number and phoned her. She answered on the fourth ring.

"Dev?"

"Hi Melinda, how are you doing?"

"Fine. To what do I owe the pleasure?"

"Just calling to give you a heads-up." I went on to tell her about her uncle's arrest. I didn't mention I heard the information from Aaron, and she didn't ask how I knew. "Oh God, I'll have to hang up and go tell my mom. She's no doubt going to forbid me from ever going back to his office."

"Well, not going back may not be the worst idea. From the information I have, if he's in any way legally involved in the EFH site, he's going to be broke. Even if he's not found guilty of this murder, he'll probably lose his license to practice law, and he'll still be broke. I'd say stay away from the place."

"Hmm, sounds like I'll have a lot more time to study for finals. Thanks for the call, I guess," she said and hung up.

I took Morton for a walk later in the day. His tail started wagging when we passed a German Shepherd and again when we passed a black Labrador, but that was short-lived when they both ignored him. He seemed to be down all day. We went to bed a little after ten.

When I let him out the following morning, he hurried out to the backyard then stopped and looked around again for his pals. I felt sorry for him, but there was really nothing I could do. We headed down to the office. Louie had a pot of fresh coffee on and was in the process of ending a phone call. Morton headed over to his bed in front of the file cabinet and curled up. He let off a big sigh as if to say, *'This sucks.'*

"Okay, well, thank you for checking. If anything changes, please let me know," Louie said and hung up.

"What's up?" I asked.

"Checking to see if the charges have been dropped against Brianna."

"Have they?"

"Not yet, but then it's only nine o'clock on Monday morning. Frankly, I would have been surprised if they were, but I thought I'd check anyway. I'm going to head over there and see if maybe I can speed things up. You going to be around?"

"I hope to have *the* most boring day. I should be here whenever you get back."

Louie picked up his briefcase and headed out the door. I opened the file with the copies of Seymour Smeelie's emails, registered letters, and general information and wasted the next ninety minutes going through things. I suddenly heard the stairs begin to creak heavily and thought if Louie was coming back already it must be good news. Wrong again.

The door opened, and Tubby Gustafson stepped in, red-faced and gasping for breath. Fat Freddy Zimmerman was right behind him, looking like he'd just run a marathon. Freddy pulled out a client chair for Tubby then collapsed into the chair next to him and groaned.

"Good morning, Mr. Gustafson. If I may say so, I think your nails look lovely today. To what do I owe the pleasure?"

Tubby gave a quick glance at his fingernails and then shook his head. "It's anything but a pleasure to be here, Haskell. Those stairs are going to give me a heart attack. Now, you've had more than enough damn time to get me a copy of that contract McGriff had Seymour Smeelie sign. I need that damn thing yesterday. Where in the hell is it?"

"Were you planning on trying to work your way into that EFH project?"

Tubby shot a quick look at Fat Freddy, who immediately shook his head and said, "I haven't said a word, sir."

"Just where in the world did you get that information?"

"Just a wild guess, sir. Actually, I decided that wouldn't turn out to be a very good investment for you."

"Wouldn't turn out— Take a look around, Haskell. You've barely two nickels to rub together, and you want to lecture me about investments? Damn it, I need that contract by the end of the day, or you are going to find yourself in—"

"I think I have something that may serve you a little better, sir."

He rolled his eyes and said, "One can only imagine. And what, in God's name, might that be?"

I opened the file in front of me and pulled out copies of the registered letters from the city and the state informing Seymour Smeelie of the polyfluoroalkyl substances on the Cummins factory site contaminating the local drinking water. "I think, under the circumstances and the estimated eight hundred million dollars to clean the site, this may be a project you want to stay away from, sir."

"Are these legitimate?"

"Very much, Sir, then to compound matters, I heard from a source that Soapy McGriff and his assistant, Mr. Bumpy, were arrested last night."

"Arrested? What for?"

"Apparently, the murder of Seymour Smeelie. I believe the police were going through his home and office. Lord only knows what they'll find. I hope I'm not out of line when I caution you to stay away from anything regarding Smeelie or McGriff."

Tubby looked over at Fat Freddy and glared. "Exactly what were you doing when someone as inept as Haskell was gathering this information?" Fat Freddy stared at the floor. "Well, speak. Do you mean to tell me that someone of Haskell's ilk learned of this before you knew? Wait for me out in the car. Please, get out of my sight, Frederick." Fat Freddy looked like he was about to say something, but Tubby cut him off. "Go, depart, exit stage left, get the hell out of my sight," Tubby shouted.

Fat Freddy shot me a quick look as he rose from his chair and hurried out of the office.

"And as for you, Haskell," Tubby slowly stood and glared at me. "Exactly when did you plan on informing me? You're just lucky I had the foresight to pay you a visit. No telling how long you would have sat on that information, oblivious as usual. Honest to God," he said, scooping up the Smeelie file from my desk and shaking his head. "Why do I even bother?"

I watched out the window as Tubby waddled across the street. He slapped Freddy across the arm with the

Smeelie file and shouted something. Fat Freddy opened the rear door of the black Cadillac Escalade and held it open while the vehicle rocked back and forth as Tubby oozed into the seat. Freddy closed the door then glanced up at me and gave me the finger before he climbed in behind the wheel. A moment later, he sped up the street, and they disappeared from sight.

Louie arrived a little before noon with the news that the charges against Brianna Di Salvo had been dropped. "She sends her thanks and said she'd love to show you her personal appreciation. You're supposed to give her a call," Louie said.

I picked up my phone and dialed a number. Taffy answered on the third ring. "Hi, Dev, I was just thinking about you."

"Hopefully, good thoughts. Would you and Muffin be interested in coming over for dinner tonight? Morton and I are missing both of you."

"We'll be there. I'll bring the wine."

"Great, we'll see you around five," I said and hung up.

"Smart guy," Louie said. "Maybe there is hope for you."

The End

Morton and I thank you for taking the time to read **<u>Bow-Wow Rescue</u>**. If you enjoyed the read please consider leaving a review, it really, really helps. Thanks in advance . . .

Don't miss the following sample of <u>Cold Case</u>, the next book in the Dev Haskell series.

Sneak Peek

Cold Case

Second Edition

MIKE FARICY

Prologue

He took the bottle from the ice bucket and deftly tore off the foil covering the cork and pointed the bottle toward the entrance to the kitchen. He edged the cork up until it exploded and shot into the kitchen. "No, Maddie, now not another word. I'm cooking dinner for you. It's the least I can do. You've been so kind. I've got a special family recipe in the oven. It will be ready in an hour. Until then, your job is to get comfy on the couch, tell me about your day, and try this champagne. I hope you like it,"

"Oh, wow, that was so cool, and you didn't spill a drop."

"Practice makes perfect, now not to worry, there's plenty more. I've got two more bottles in the refrigerator. I got these last month in Chateau Thierry," he lied. "A little town about sixty miles north of Paris. A lovely place. I took the train up there, spent the night in a seventeenth-century B&B. Then back to Paris the next day. I thought this would be the perfect night to open a bottle or two."

"It sounds wonderful. I want to hear all about your trip. I was so worried when I didn't hear from you. I thought maybe I said something, and you decided you weren't interested anymore."

"Last minute flight. I meant to call, but my phone wasn't working in Paris. Let me just fill our glasses. They're in the kitchen. I'll be right back." He hurried into the kitchen, glancing over his shoulder to make sure she hadn't followed. He tore the nine dollar price tag from Liquor City off the bottle, moved her champagne flute off to the right-hand side, and slowly filled it with champagne. He filled his flute, then took her's in his right hand, swirled the champagne for a moment, picked up his flute with his left, and hurried back into the living room.

"Here you go, darling. In the few weeks we've known one another, you've come to mean so much to me. Now, a toast to you. I, I love you," he said, holding his champagne flute out to toast her. He leaned down and kissed her on the forehead.

"Oh, wow," she said, as his beard lightly tickled her forehead. She clinked her crystal flute with his and took a sip. "This is just what… I mean, you've no idea. I've wanted to hear you say that from the moment we first laid eyes on one another. I adore you, and these last weeks have been so special. You've made me feel like a princess. You've been so kind, so gracious, so loving."

"Believe me, you're the one who's been so wonderful. Now," he said, extending his flute as they clinked crystal once more, "to both of us and for a wonderful future. Drink up now. As I said, I've got two more bottles and a delicious meal coming. Let's both relax and enjoy the evening."

"Oh, I will, and dinner smells delicious."

"An old family recipe. I know you're going to love it, and I'm quite sure you've never had anything like it."

"What is it?" she asked and took a large sip.

"Oh, no. You just wait. Finish that glass while I get the bottle," he said and hurried into the kitchen. He came back with the champagne bottle, topped up her glass, and placed the bottle in the ice bucket. "Another toast, this one to my princess," he said, extending his flute once again. She raised her flute a bit too fast, and champagne spilled over the side.

"Oh, shit, sorry about that." Her speech was beginning to slur, and she moved her head from side to side for a moment in an attempt to regain her balance.

"Not a problem. Finish that up, and I'll refill it for you."

Maddie attempted to gulp down the champagne, oblivious to it running down her chin. He took the champagne flute from her hand, refilled it, and set it on the coffee table. She seemed to be fighting to keep her head up as he walked into the kitchen. He pulled the garlic bread out of the oven, took the frozen pizza out of the freezer, placed it on a cookie sheet in the oven, then set the timer.

He'd been watching porn on the computer for twenty minutes before he checked on Maddie, now comatose on the couch. As he pulled her up onto her feet, she mumbled something incoherent. He draped her over his shoulder and carried her into the guest room. He laid her on the plastic-covered bed and attached her wrists and ankles to the leather restraints. He placed a length of duct tape over her mouth then headed back into the kitchen to turn off the timer and take the pizza out of the oven.

One

Taffy looked at me and said, "What's wrong with you, Dev? This is going to be fun. Besides, Allison has turned out to be a great new friend, and I want to give her support."

This was going to be complicated. I'd dated Allison Dankwell three times, right before I met Taffy. On top of being an absolute control freak, Allison is just plain nuts. About a week after I met Taffy, she suddenly became Taffy's Facebook friend. Maybe two weeks after that, they met for coffee. Whacko Allison has been in the picture ever since. Tonight was going to be the first time I'd actually seen Allison since I nicely told her it wasn't working out and then ran as fast as I could to my car and locked the doors.

I put the blinker on, turned into the parking ramp, and waited for the line to inch forward. "You know how I am about concerts, Taffy. The tickets cost a big chunk of change. We have to pay for parking, and once we get inside, two things are going to happen. First, whoever is in front of me will stand for the entire concert. Second, there'll be some drunk next to me who'll sing along off-key to every song."

"God, Mr. Crabby, sorry if I ruined the night you had planned with all those classy guys at The Spot bar. Maybe just let me out here, and I'll find a ride home afterwards. Look at all the people here for the concert, Dev. The place is jammed. Hello, get with the program. You're always listening to music from thirty years ago. The stuff you like is almost older than me."

I looked around as we inched our way into the parking ramp. There was a line of cars on either side and a long line of cars behind us. I was boxed in and couldn't leave even if I wanted to. I saw no point in telling her, ninety-nine percent of the traffic was people coming to watch the first preseason hockey game. "I didn't mean it like that, Taffy. I'm here with you. I'll be nice. It's just not my thing to do is all."

"Mmm, well, maybe I'll just remember that next time I don't want to do *something*," she said, emphasizing that last word and sending a very clear message.

"Okay, okay. I'm looking forward to it," I lied, hoping there weren't any sharp objects in the place that Allison could use to stab me. "I'll be Mr. Positive."

"Oh, really," Taffy said then folded her arms over her chest and stared ahead.

We parked up on the fourth level. At least half the people getting out of their cars were wearing Minnesota Wild jerseys or hats.

"Oh my God, this is so wonderful. All these people coming to hear Allison."

There was no point in telling her most of these people would run the other way once they heard Allison sing. I wasn't sure how she got the gig with a pickup band in the River-View room, but I had my suspicions. We took the elevator down to the second floor and then walked through the concourse over Kellogg Boulevard one-story below. The line of traffic going into the parking ramp was three times longer than just fifteen minutes ago.

"Oh, I'm so excited for Allison," Taffy squealed. "This is going to be the start of a great career. Finally, the break she's worked so hard to get."

That didn't quite match up with the history I knew. Allison had started a restaurant, actually her version of a food truck. She put on a bikini and sold hotdogs from a Styrofoam cooler she had in her car for two or three days before the city confiscated the cooler and fined her. She had a lap dance business for maybe a week. Somehow, she had found her way into a vacant apartment and advertised on the internet until the neighbors got together and physically threw her out. The painting business lasted, I think, just a day before her first customer, her sister, fired her. After school daycare was a disaster, teaching kindergarteners how to mix martinis. The dog care business tanked when her dog impregnated the two dogs she was supposed to be watching. Now, she somehow talked four guys into forming a pickup band so she could sing. God only knew what it would be like.

We came to a side door along the concourse with a handwritten sign on a piece of paper torn from a spiral notebook. The sign was taped to the door with two pieces of blue masking tape.

ALLISON DANKWELL
RIVER-VIEW ROOM

"I guess we go in here," Taffy said and gave a questioning look at all the people walking past, headed for the hockey game.

"Maybe we just have special upfront seating," I said and opened the door. We walked down two flights of stairs to a basement room. A woman was seated at a card table in front of the door. A gray metal cash box sat on the table with a sign that read, '**$10.**'

"Is this where Allison Dankwell is singing?" Taffy asked.

The woman sipped from a glass of dark liquid I doubted was tea and said, "It is. Just ten dollars each, please."

Yeah, I'd need a drink too, just to build up enough courage to tell people they had to pay to hear Allison. I pulled out my wallet and handed her a twenty.

"Just through that door," she indicated with her head. "They'll start in about thirty minutes."

"Thanks," I said and held the door open for Taffy.

We walked into the River-View Room, and the first thing I noticed was there weren't any windows, as in no actual view of the river. All sorts of tables and chairs were scattered around, looking like a hodgepodge of furniture donated for people in need. At the far end of the room sat a small portable bar on wheels with maybe a dozen people standing around it.

Taffy looked stunned as we headed toward the bar. I heard her mumble under her breath, "Oh, my God. This is not good."

"Oh, Taffy, so nice you came. Allison will be so pleased," an older woman said. I recognized her as Allison's battle-ax mother, although I'd only met her once.

"Oh, hi, Mrs. Dankwell. How nice to see you. How are you?" Taffy said.

"Just fine, dear, just fine. And this is?" she said, giving me a quick once over and frowning. From the unimpressed look she gave me, it was suddenly obvious where Allison got her personality.

"This is a friend of mine, Dev Haskell. Dev, this is Allison's mom."

I smiled, hoping she didn't pick up on my name. "It's very nice to meet you, Mrs. Dankwell."

"Yeah, that's what everybody says," she said, not joking. I was introduced to Allison's two sisters, an aunt, Mrs. Dankwell's neighbor, who had a walker and couldn't escape, and some guy named Jasper. The six other people turned out to be three high school friends and their not too happy looking husbands. I got an overpriced glass of wine for Taffy, a beer for me, and drifted toward the three husbands complaining to one another over in a corner.

It was closer to forty-five minutes and two beers before Allison and her band appeared. There wasn't a stage. A set of drums and a piano were arranged in a corner, and four guys took up positions. Two guitar players, a five-string and bass, plugged into two small amplifiers. One of the amps gave off a high-pitched squeaking sound that got everyone cringing. Once that was turned down, Allison stepped up to the microphone.

"I'd just like to thank everyone for coming tonight," Allison said and flashed a half-second glare in my direction. "Thank you all and just screw everyone else." She turned toward the band and slowly counted, "One, two, three, four," before she burst into a dreadful, off-key rendition of 'Do you Believe in Magic.' It was a good thing there weren't any sharp objects around, or I might have slit my wrists. I noticed the woman with the walker rubbing her ears until it dawned on me, she was really turning off her hearing aids. Even the pickup band shot one another looks that said, "What the hell?"

Things went downhill from there. I don't think I've ever heard so many wonderful songs absolutely abused and destroyed, but Allison just kept on singing. There were always at least two people at the bar getting refills just to ease the pain. I stopped at three beers, only because I was driving.

It felt like a long week had passed before Allison finished up abusing Linda Ronstadt's 'Long Long Time.'

The musicians fled the scene out a side door as Allison took a bow. Everyone clapped, but I think only because they were thankful she was finally finished. The three girlfriends smiled, waved, and caught up with their husbands already storming out the door.

Taffy took a deep breath, smiled, and said, "Oh, Allison. I just don't know what to say."

"So, what did you think?" Allison said, looking at me again with the glare.

"You've certainly got your own unique sound."

She eyed me, but clearly wasn't sure how to respond.

"Wonderful, darling, just wonderful," her mother said and turned to the woman with the walker. "What did you think, Marilyn?"

"I think you should take me home," Marilyn said.

God bless her, that brought things to a close.

"Dev, would you mind? I'm going to grab a ride with Allison."

Oh great, probably a 'tell-all' moment with Allison after which Taffy would dump me. "You sure? I mean I thought we might—"

"Dev, I'm going to grab a ride with Allison." She leaned toward me and whispered, "She needs some support right now."

She needed a dozen kicks in the ass, but I said, "Not a problem, I've got an early morning tomorrow. Mrs. Dankwell, nice to meet you. Allison, congratulations on your first show." They both gave me the evil eye. I leaned in to give Taffy a kiss. She turned her cheek at the last moment, which pretty much served as the icing on the cake for the night. I walked as fast as I could to my car, drove home, and then Morton and I watched a movie of no redeeming social value.

TWO

It was just a little after five the following afternoon. I was sitting on a stool at The Spot bar, chatting with my office mate Louie Laufen. Morton was stretched out at my feet, waiting for the next deep-fat-fried pork rind from Louie. He'd already eaten the better part of the bag. I was in the process of listening to Louie tell me about his latest DUI court case.

"So, they pull him over, and he gets out of the car, naked."

"The guy is naked?" I asked.

"Well, he had on tennis shoes and black socks."

"Where were his clothes?"

"In the back seat. In fact, that was exactly what he told the cops when they asked him the same thing. Then he went on to explain that it was his birthday, and he just assumed it would be okay to drive around in his birthday suit."

"You're making this up. You gotta be. Was there a girlfriend in the back seat?"

"If only, it probably would have helped my defense. He's going down on the DUI, unfortunately his second. I'm just hoping to get the Indecent Exposure charge dropped or maybe pled down to obscenity. I mean, he had no intention of getting out of the car except that the police pulled him over and then requested that he step outside his vehicle."

"And that's when they realized he was driving around naked?"

"Yeah," Louie said, nodding, maybe bouncing the theory off me to get my reaction before he presented it to a judge.

"Any chance of PTSD or some form of mental insta-bility?"

"So you're thinking my effort to plead down to ob-scenity isn't going to fly."

"I'm thinking it might just do more harm than good," depending on who the judge is.

"Unfortunately, I can't disagree," Louie said and took a sip from his glass.

"I think you're both full of shit," the guy on the stool next to me said.

I turned to face him, and he started to laugh. "Hi, Dev. Long time no see," he said and held out his hand. Ben Jackson, a retired homicide detective. I recognized the twinkling blue eyes and the scar through his bottom lip. Last time I saw him, he was a big muscular guy. Now he looked lean and almost frail.

"Ben Jackson. How have you been? I thought some-one told me you moved down to Florida."

We shook hands, and Ben said, "You heard right. We moved down to a little town called Venice. Finally had enough of the tax rates and the winters up here. We've been Florida residents for the last six years. We're just back in town for a niece's wedding tomorrow. Thought I might look you up."

"Amazing you found me here at The Spot."

"Not really," Ben said and didn't laugh.

"How have things been going? Oh, hey, this is a friend and my office mate, Louie Laufen. He practices law."

"Nice to meet you," Ben said and nodded. "Yeah, I recognize the name. You represent a lot of folks on DUI charges, don't you?"

Louie nodded.

"Listen, Dev. I was thinking of you the other day. I got into this mystery series and thought you might enjoy it. Wanted to give you this book." He opened a grocery bag and pulled out a paperback. The cover was solid black with the title, One After Midnight, in bold red letters.

My first thought was *'Why would I want to read this,'* but I smiled and said, "Oh, gee, Ben, you didn't have to do this. I have to tell you, I don't really read too many books, and I've got a lot on my plate right now."

"Yeah, Dev, sure you do. Come on. Don't kid a kidder," he said and waved Mike the bartender over with a nod of his head. "Let me buy a round for these two ne'er'-do-wells and better give them another bag of whatever they're feeding that poor dog on the floor."

"Pork rinds," Louie said.

"Obviously, a health food," Ben said, meaning anything but. He opened the book and placed a business card inside. "Listen, give me a call when you're finished with the book. I'd love to hear what you thought about it."

"Did you write this thing?" I asked as I took the book from him.

"Me? Hell no. I've neither the time nor the inclination. This one is actually the first in a series. I think you might find it interesting."

"Well, thanks for thinking of me, Ben. Much appreciated," I said and smiled.

Ben shook his head, tossed a ten on the bar, and looked at Louie. "You must be one hell of a patient guy to put up with all of Haskell's bullshit."

"Some days are easier than others," Louie said, and the two of them laughed.

Ben slid off his stool just as Mike delivered our drinks, then reached behind, pulled a bag of pork rinds from the rack, and dropped it in front of Louie. "Good seeing you, Dev. I'll be waiting for that phone call. Keep the change," he said to Mike and headed out the door.

Louie opened the bag of pork rinds and stuffed three or four into his mouth.

I looked at the book and shook my head. "What the hell am I going to do with this?"

"Maybe read it," Mike said. He picked up the ten-dollar bill and said, "I need another two bucks for the bag of pork rinds."

Louie quickly set down the open bag.

I dug into my wallet and pulled out a five-dollar bill, the only bill I had in my wallet. Mike took the five and slapped the edge of both bills on the bar, indicating 'thanks for the tip' then walked over to the cash register.

We chatted for another five minutes, and then I slid off my stool.

"You heading out?" Louie said and took a sip.

I drained my beer mug. "Yeah, Taffy's fixing dinner tonight for Morton and me. We have to be over there in an hour, and I'm thinking it just might be a good idea to take Morton on a little walk before we head over."

"See you in the morning?" Louie asked.

"Yeah, we should be in around nine. You have a good evening."

"I intend to," Louie said and raised his glass.

Three

We pulled up to Taffy's building right on time and headed inside. She buzzed us in, and we took the elevator up to the third floor. She and her dog, Muffin, opened the door to her condo as we were walking down the hall.

"Amazing," she said, shaking her head. "For all the goofy stuff you do, you're almost always on time."

"It's from all that military training I had."

"Hmm, too bad they didn't spend time in some other areas."

As we stepped inside, I handed her the bottle of wine I'd picked up. Morton and Muffin were already engaged in chasing one another with a chew toy. Muffin currently had the thing in his mouth and had just shot around the back of the couch. Morton was too large to fit behind, and he met Muffin coming out the other side.

"Come on out to the kitchen," Taffy said.

"The place smells wonderful. What are you making?" I asked. I noticed there were three places set on the kitchen counter.

"Chicken curry. I actually made it yesterday. I don't know what it is, but it just seems to taste better on day two. Open that wine, pour us each a glass, and we can sit out on the balcony. How was your day?"

"Wonderfully uneventful. How about you?" I noticed there were three wine glasses on the kitchen counter.

I was just about to ask who else would be joining us when Taffy said, "I got called into my boss's office this morning."

"Oh? Everything all right?"

"Even better than that. We have a team coming in to interview three candidates for a management position, and he wants me to be one of them."

"What? Oh, congratulations. That's fantastic news." I twisted the cap off the wine bottle and filled two glasses. I handed a glass to Taffy then raised mine in a toast. "Here's to your success. When does this happen?"

"Interviews are two days from now."

"Do you know who you're up against?"

"No. It's all hush-hush. As part of the interview process, you're sworn to secrecy. I called my folks, and I've told you, but that's all."

"Oh, Taffy, that's really great news. I know, if they have any brains at all, you're going to be the person they choose. Congratulations! Well done, you."

The intercom suddenly signaled someone down at the security entrance. "I'll get that. Why don't you head out to the balcony? I'll join you in a minute."

"Who's coming?"

"Dev, the balcony," she said and pointed to the double doors leading outside.

"Okay, okay, I'm going."

I was thinking it was Taffy's mother who would be joining us. A nice enough woman who had told Taffy more than once she could do better than me. Unfortunately, I was wrong. About three minutes after Taffy buzzed in whoever was in the lobby. I heard the squeals and shrieks at the door. Taffy and Allison. I was going to need something stronger than wine.

"Oh… you," Allison said a few minutes later as she stepped out onto the balcony. She sounded more than a little disappointed and made a face like someone had just farted in church. As the three of us sat out on the balcony in the setting sun, Taffy told Allison what she was going to wear to her interview. She told her about the hair appointment and pedicure she was going to get tomorrow evening, the night before the interview. She went on and on, and I smiled, nodded, and watched the occasional person walking past on the street below. It was more of the same over dinner. Taffy limited herself to one glass of wine for the entire evening. Allison had pulled the wine bottle closer to her and had talked nonstop for the past half-hour. I cleared the table, loaded the dishwasher, and washed the curry pan. Once I finished cleaning the kitchen, I thought I might encourage Allison to hit the road.

"Congratulations on your performance last night, Allison, very umm, unique. Hope you enjoy the rest of the evening. It was nice to see you again."

"Yeah, that's what everybody tells me," shades of her mother I thought.

"Allison, pour yourself another glass of wine and join me in the living room," Taffy said. Then she pasted a smile on and said, "Thanks for joining us, Dev." With that she shooed Morton and me out the door.

So much for a romantic evening, but then I couldn't blame her. The interview was a really big deal, and she'd worked hard to get this far. It was obvious a kiss wasn't in the cards, so I wished her luck, and we drove home. We settled in front of the tv, and after twenty minutes of going through all the series and movies I had no desire to watch, I turned off the tv and, against my better judgment, opened <u>One After Midnight</u>.

I put some coffee on a little after ten and kept reading. It was an interesting story, not the least of which because it was set in my town, Saint Paul. I recognized the streets, the church where the wedding was, the descriptions of buildings, even the seasonal weather. It was just like being there, although since it had been published in 2006, a few things were different. Someone used a payphone. There was no mention of the internet. At one point, the victim was trying to make a decision in a Blockbuster Video store. Yeah, it was dated, but it was still interesting. Eventually, I was nodding off, with less than sixty pages left to read. I plowed through and then was left hanging when the perpetrator, the man who stalked and then murdered the young woman, got away with the crime. To say I was disappointed was an understatement. I went up to bed, and I think I was asleep before my head hit the pillow.

I was in the midst of a dream. The victim in the book was in Blockbuster Video, and I spotted her as I stepped in the door. I tried to warn her, but she kept moving to a different aisle, and I couldn't get close enough to talk to her. I was about to climb over a rack of videos when my alarm went off.

Morton slipped his head beneath the pillow as I crawled out of bed and headed for the shower. He came downstairs an hour later. I gave him his perfunctory scratch behind the ears then let him out the kitchen door. I fooled around on the internet for a bit, sent Taffy an email thanking her for dinner, and let Morton back in. I grabbed the book I read last night, and we headed down to the office. I was putting the coffee on just as I heard Louie making his way up the stairs.

He opened the door a moment later, red-faced and gasping for air. He made his way around his picnic table desk and more or less collapsed in his office chair. I took his coffee mug, dumped the remnants in the sink, refilled it with fresh coffee, and set it in front of him. He nodded thanks and took a couple of sips before he was able to talk.

"You going to give me the details of last night's adventure?"

"You mean with Taffy?"

"You've got more than one?"

"Nothing to tell, Louie. She's got an interview to-morrow morning for a promotion, and it was pretty much the only thing on her mind. Not that I can blame her. But she was completely focused on that. She already had the outfit picked out she was going to wear. She's getting her hair done and a pedicure tonight. She'll probably sleep about fifteen minutes the entire night, not all at once, and then breeze through the interview. I've seen her like this before. It would drive me crazy, but it's just the way she operates, and she's nothing if not success-ful."

"What are you going to do with the book that retired detective gave you?"

"Maybe give it back to him. I finished it last night around two this morning."

"You actually read the thing?" Louie asked.

"Yeah, to tell you the truth, I was more or less hooked. The story takes place in town here, and there were all sorts of places I recognized. The thing was a little dated. I mean, it was written about fifteen years ago, but I still enjoyed it."

"Dev, up late and finishing a book. Who knew?"

"Well, between Allison's horrible singing and Taffy focused on her job interview, I've got the time. Matter of fact, let me give Ben a call right now. I want to tell him I finished the book. I know he gave it to me thinking I'd never open the thing." I opened the book on my desk, took out Ben Jackson's card, and dialed the number.

Ben answered on the third ring. "Jackson."

"Hi, Ben. Dev here. Just wanted to say it was nice to see you last night, and I wanted to thank you again for the book."

"Dev, You have to read it. I'm telling you, it—"

"I finished it last night, Ben."

"Finished it?"

"Yeah. I enjoyed the hell out it. A great read. It might just get me back into the reading mode."

"Seriously?"

"Yeah, I'm not kidding you. I put the coffee on and finished it a little after two this morning. It was a really good read."

"Tell you what, Dev. I want you to do me a favor when you get home tonight."

"What's that?"

"Check your mailbox."

"What?"

"Something wrong with your hearing? I said check your mailbox. I'm leaving a little something for you."

"Oh, you don't have to do—"

"At my age, Dev, I don't have to do anything I don't want to do. You just check your mailbox. Anything else?"

"No, sir, I guess not."

"You got time for coffee tomorrow?"

"Always for you, Ben."

"Good. Call me in the morning, and we'll get together. Talk to you then."

I worked through the day checking job applications and verifying employment records. Louie suggested we head over to The Spot around half-past-four, but I was anxious to get home and check the mailbox, so I begged off.

I parked in the driveway, let Morton in the front door, then checked my mailbox. There were two credit card offers, the power bill, and another book, this one entitled, <u>Two After Midnight</u>. The cover on the book was essentially the same, the title in bold red letters with a solid black background. I closed the door behind me and headed into the kitchen. I let Morton out into the back and tossed the mail on the kitchen counter. I debated opening a beer, decided it might make me sleepy, and grabbed a water instead. I sat down on a kitchen stool and started to read the first page.

Four

I heard Morton scratching at the back door and glanced at the clock on the stove. It was after eight. I glanced out the window, and it was almost dark. Morton had been in the backyard for the better part of three hours, and I'd been engrossed in <u>Two After Midnight</u>.

Morton gave me a look then stepped inside and stood in front of the kitchen counter looking at the cookie jar where I kept the dog biscuits. I couldn't blame him. I'd completely lost track of time. I tossed him a biscuit, placed the Lean Cuisine Taffy got me in the microwave and got lost again in the book.

It was similar to the first story. The chief protagonist was the same guy, seemingly a nice, social kind of guy, who met young women and courted them, apparently with the idea that he would eventually murder them. Once again, the tale was set in Saint Paul, and the descriptions of street corners, bars, and restaurants matched my experience.

The microwave started beeping, and I pulled out the Lean Cuisine. Morton waited around for a taste. Eventually, I heard him give a loud sigh, and he made his way into the living room, climbed onto the couch, and stared out the window. I continued to read.

In the book, the couple were attending a Saturday wedding. The protagonist begged off alcohol because he was driving while, at the same time, making sure his date's glass was never empty. Prosecco seemed to be her drink of choice, and there was plenty of it. She was dancing on a table toward the end of the reception, and he carried her out over his shoulder to all sorts of cheers from her friends and headed out the door. They drove back to her home, where he placed her in bed, basically unconscious from Prosecco. He proceeded to spend the next few hours going through her computer, her files, desk drawers, bank statements. You name it. He photographed a number of documents and copied her computer password. He took her house keys to a twenty-four-hour shop and had copies made. He left a nice note next to a glass of water and a bottle of aspirin on her bedside table and went home around four in the morning.

He phoned her at eleven that morning, offering to take her out to breakfast. He guessed she was still in bed, maybe with a cold compress over her eyes. She answered her phone with a groaning voice. She begged off from his offer for breakfast, apologized for her behavior the previous night, and disconnected. He called his mother and offered to bring dinner over, ever the perfect son.

I realized my dinner had been sitting on the counter for at least a couple of hours. It wasn't even warm, it was cold. I nibbled away at it while reading. After a couple of yawns, I put the coffee on, had a candy bar, and continued reading. The book ended basically the same way as the one the night before. The guy murdered the woman and was never caught. I finished a little earlier than last night and headed up to bed at half-past-one. Morton was stretched out on the bed and didn't so much as move when I climbed in.

My alarm went off at seven. I stumbled into the shower, where I remained for a good twenty minutes. I dressed and headed downstairs, leaving Morton in bed with his head shoved under the pillow. I made a fresh pot of coffee, ate two pieces of cold pizza for breakfast and sent Taffy a text message, *'Wishing you all the best in your interview this morning.'*

I heard Morton jump off the bed a half-hour later. He made his way into the kitchen, stretched, then strolled over to me for his perfunctory morning head scratch before I let him out the back door.

I received a short text back from Taffy, *'Thx'*. I Googled the author of the Midnight series, a guy named Virgil Tueur. Based on his picture, I placed him at maybe forty. Dark, curly hair combed back with a full beard. Google had a list of his books, there were six, and a very short biography. It turns out he was from Saint Paul, which explained the excellent job on his descriptions of places. The biography described him as 'extremely private.'

I let Morton in, fed him and after thirty minutes, we headed down to the office. We arrived before Louie, who had once again neglected to turn off the coffee maker. I dumped the scorched remnants into the sink and made a fresh pot. I was on my second cup when I heard Louie coming up the stairs.

He entered red-faced, set his briefcase on his picnic table desk, and collapsed into his desk chair, gasping for air. I got up and poured some fresh coffee into his mug. He pulled the mug toward him, took a sip, grimaced, and said, "Not bad."

"How late were you at The Spot last night?" I asked.

He took another sip of coffee and said, "I was there until close, whenever that was. You meet up with Taffy?"

"No, she's focused on that job interview today. She was getting her hair done and a pedicure or something last night. Probably tried on a dozen or so outfits this morning and I bet she left her place dressed in the one she originally chose. I stayed home last night reading."

"Sounds like Ben Jackson all of a sudden turned you into an egghead," Louie said and slurped more coffee.

"Mmm, thanks for reminding me. I'm supposed to call him this morning for coffee." I checked the time on my phone, it was nine-fifteen, and I called Ben.

To be continued...

Taffy? Allison? And hang on but after reading the books, Dev is about to be looking into a number of unsolved murders committed over the past years? Better grab a copy of **Cold Case** and find out what happens…

Books by Mike Faricy
Crime Fiction Firsts

A boxset of the first four books in four crime fiction series:

Russian Roulette; Dev Haskell series
Welcome; Jack Dillon Dublin Tales series
Corridor Man; Corridor Man series
Reduced Ransom! Hot Shot series

The following titles comprise the Dev Haskell series:

Russian Roulette: Case 1
Mr. Swirlee: Case 2
Bite Me: Case 3
Bombshell: Case 4
Tutti Frutti: Case 5
Last Shot: Case 6
Ting-A-Ling: Case 7
Crickett: Case 8
Bulldog: Case 9
Double Trouble: Case 10
Yellow Ribbon: Case 11
Dog Gone: Case 12
Scam Man: Case 13
Foiled: Case 14
What Happens in Vegas… Case 15
Art Hound: Case 16
The Office: Case 17

Star Struck: Case 18
International Incident: Case 19
Guest From Hell: Case 20
Art Attack: Case 21
Mystery Man: Case 22
Bow-Wow Rescue: Case 23
Cold Case: Case 24
Cash Up Front: Case 25
Dream House: Case 26
Alley Katz: Case 27
The Big Gamble: Case 28
Bad to the Bone: Case 29
Silencio!: Case 30
Surprise, Surprise: Case 31
Hit & Run: Case 32
Suspect Santa: Case 33
P.I. Apprentice: Case 34
Rebel Without a Clue: Case 35

The following titles are Dev Haskell novellas:
Dollhouse
The Dance
Pixie
Fore!
Twinkle Toes
(*a Dev Haskell short story*)

The following are Dev Haskell Boxsets:
Dev Haskell Boxset 1-3
Dev Haskell Boxset 4-6
Dev Haskell Boxset 7-9
Dev Haskell Boxset 10-12
Dev Haskell Boxset 13-15
Dev Haskell Boxset 16-18
Dev Haskell Boxset 19-21
Dev Haskell Boxset 22-24
Dev Haskell Boxset 25-27
Dev Haskell Boxset 28-30
Dev Haskell Boxset 1-7
Dev Haskell Boxset 8-14
Dev Haskell Boxset 15-19
Dev Haskell Boxset 20-24
Dev Haskell Boxset 25-29

The following titles comprise the Jack Dillon Dublin Tales series:
Welcome
Jack Dillon Dublin Tale 1
Sweet Dreams
Jack Dillon Dublin Tale 2
Mirror Mirror
Jack Dillon Dublin Tale 3
Silver Bullet
Jack Dillon Dublin Tale 4
Fair City Blues
Jack Dillon Dublin Tale 5

Spade Work
Jack Dillon Dublin Tale 6
Madeline Missing
Jack Dillon Dublin Tale 7
Mistaken Identity
Jack Dillon Dublin Tale 8
Picture Perfect
Jack Dillon Dublin Tale 9
Dublin Moon
Jack Dillon Dublin Tale 10
Mystery Woman
Jack Dillon Dublin Tale 11
Second Chance
Jack Dillon Dublin Tale 12
Payback Brother
Jack Dillon Dublin Tale 13
The Heist
Jack Dillon Dublin Tale 14
Jewels To Kill For
Jack Dillon Dublin Tale 15
Retirement Scheme
Jack Dillon Dublin Tale 16
The Collector
Jack Dillon Dublin Tale 17

Jack Dillon Dublin Tales Boxsets:
Jack Dillon Dublin Tales 1-3
Jack Dillon Dublin Tales 4-6
Jack Dillon Dublin Tales 1-5

Jack Dillon Dublin Tales 1-7
Jack Dillon Dublin Tales 6-10

The following titles comprise the Hotshot series;
Reduced Ransom! Second Edition
Finders Keepers! Second Edition
Bankers Hours Second Edition
Chow Down Second Edition
Moonlight Dance Academy Second Edition
Irish Dukes (Fight Card Series)
written under the pseudonym Jack Tunney

The following titles comprise the Corridor Man series:
Corridor Man
Corridor Man 2: Opportunity knocks
Corridor Man 3: The Dungeon
Corridor Man 4: Dead End
Corridor Man 5: Finger
Corridor Man 6: Exit Strategy
Corridor Man 7: Trunk Music
Corridor Man 8: Birthday Boy
Corridor Man 9: Boss Man
Corridor Man 10: Bye Bye Bobby

Corridor Man novellas:
Corridor Man: Valentine
Corridor Man: Auditor
Corridor Man: Howling

Corridor Man: Spa Day

The following are Corridor Man Boxsets:
Corridor Man Boxset 1-3
Corridor Man Boxset 1-5
Corridor Man Boxset 6-9

All books are available on Amazon.com
Thank you!

Contact the author:
- Email: mikefaricyauthor@gmail.com
- Twitter: @Mikefaricybooks
- Facebook: Mike Faricy Author
- Website: http://Www.mikefaricybooks.com

Published by

MJF Publishing

www.ingramcontent.com/pod-product-compliance
Lightning Source LLC
Chambersburg PA
CBHW071404200726
48294CB00002B/291